PRAISE FOR THE NOVELS
OF EMMA WILDES

"A luxurious and sensual read. Both deliciously wicked and tenderly romantic.... I didn't want it to end!"
—*New York Times* bestselling author Celeste Bradley

"This wickedly exciting romance will draw you in and take hold of your heart."
—*USA Today* bestselling author Elizabeth Boyle

"A stylish blend of dangerous intrigue and scorching desire that is bound to captivate fans of Amanda Quick and Nicole Jordan."
—*Booklist*

"Regency fans will thrill to this superbly sensual tale of an icy widow and two decadent rakes.... Balancing deliciously erotic encounters with compelling romantic tension and populating a convincing historical setting with a strong cast of well-developed characters, prolific romance author Wildes provides a spectacular and skillfully handled story that stands head and shoulders above the average historical romance."
—*Publishers Weekly* (starred review)

"Wickedly delicious and daring, Wildes's tale tantalizes with an erotic fantasy that is also a well-crafted Regency romance. She delivers a page-turner that captures the era, the mores, and the scandalous behavior that lurks beneath the surface."
—*Romantic Times* (4½ stars, top pick)

continued ...

TWICE FALLEN

LADIES IN WAITING

Emma Wildes

WITHDRAWN

A SIGNET ECLIPSE BOOK

SIGNET ECLIPSE
Published by New American Library, a division of
Penguin Group (USA) Inc., 375 Hudson Street,
New York, New York 10014, USA
Penguin Group (Canada), 90 Eglinton Avenue East, Suite 700, Toronto,
Ontario M4P 2Y3, Canada (a division of Pearson Penguin Canada Inc.)
Penguin Books Ltd., 80 Strand, London WC2R 0RL, England
Penguin Ireland, 25 St. Stephen's Green, Dublin 2,
Ireland (a division of Penguin Books Ltd.)
Penguin Group (Australia), 250 Camberwell Road, Camberwell, Victoria 3124,
Australia (a division of Pearson Australia Group Pty. Ltd.)
Penguin Books India Pvt. Ltd., 11 Community Centre, Panchsheel Park,
New Delhi - 110 017, India
Penguin Group (NZ), 67 Apollo Drive, Rosedale, Auckland 0632,
New Zealand (a division of Pearson New Zealand Ltd.)
Penguin Books (South Africa) (Pty.) Ltd., 24 Sturdee Avenue,
Rosebank, Johannesburg 2196, South Africa

Penguin Books Ltd., Registered Offices:
80 Strand, London WC2R 0RL, England

First published by Signet Eclipse, an imprint of New American Library,
a division of Penguin Group (USA) Inc.

First Printing, January 2012
10 9 8 7 6 5 4 3 2 1

Copyright © Katherine Smith, 2012
All rights reserved

SIGNET ECLIPSE and logo are trademarks of Penguin Group (USA) Inc.

Printed in the United States of America

PUBLISHER'S NOTE
This is a work of fiction. Names, characters, places, and incidents either are the
product of the author's imagination or are used fictitiously, and any resemblance
to actual persons, living or dead, business establishments, events, or locales is
entirely coincidental.
    The publisher does not have any control over and does not assume any respon-
sibility for author or third-party Web sites or their content.

This is for the readers who fell in love with Damien Northfield. I have to admit I wondered myself how the younger brother of the Duke of Rolthven would fare when he met just the right woman.

ACKNOWLEDGMENTS

My heartfelt gratitude to Kerry Donovan for how she edits with a hint of humor and a great deal of wisdom. As always, a salute to Barbara Poelle, who could not be a better agent.

Chapter 1

London, 1816

A library, she'd discovered, was a delightful place to sit during a formal ball.

First of all, it was quiet, Lady Lillian Bourne thought blissfully, settling back against the comfortable cushions. True, she probably had only twenty minutes at the most—if she was particularly daring—but the respite was needed, and though the orchestra was faintly audible in the background, she was at least not assaulted by conversation and music from all sides. It wasn't that she disliked socializing completely; it was more that she preferred peace and quiet....

Even as she reflected on how she despised the press of so much noise and too many people, the library suddenly lost its status as a solitary refuge.

The door opened, it closed, and then it opened again almost at once.

Lily could have sworn she heard a muttered curse in a deep male voice that contained an intriguing word she didn't recognize.

"*This* is where you were going, my lord?"

The second speaker was a woman and the question

held a sultry female intonation. Propped carelessly on the velvet-covered settee in an unladylike pose with her ankles crossed, Lily had to resist the urge to sit up and see who had entered the room, but she wasn't all that anxious to be discovered herself, so she stayed still.

"Yes, for just a few minutes of *solitude*."

The weighted emphasis on that last word was lost on his companion. The woman's laugh was musical and light. "You are always so droll."

"Am I?" Lord Whoever's voice was dry but not in an offensive way, just offhand. "I wasn't aware. Can I help you, Lady Piedmont?"

Lady Piedmont? As in the wife of the man some speculated might become the next prime minister? That was interesting. Lily didn't just follow the society papers; she also was careful to pay attention to the political machinations of the English system of government and she knew the name well.

"I think you know full well why I followed you."

She might not be as sophisticated as rumor had it, but that murmured sultry inflection was hard to miss. Low, with a heated note that told her she definitely did not now want to make her presence known, and the lack of a response indicated that some sort of physical contact might just be occurring.

How the devil *did* she get herself into these situations? Lily wondered with a mixture of irritation and chagrin. All she'd wanted was a few minutes of peace and quiet before having to face all of society gawping at her and not succeeding in concealing their avid interest in her every move, lest she stumble again.

Falling from grace once had been entirely too much.

"Miriam," the unknown man said, his voice a notch deeper, "don't. I refuse to cooperate."

"Ah, but there is evidence to the contrary. Your cock is getting hard, darling."

"A beautiful woman is endeavoring to unbutton my breeches. I think with most males there would be a predictable physical reaction, but that does not mean I want this to go any further."

"No. Rumor has it you are remarkably well endowed. I am rather anxious to verify that for myself." The words were said in a low, persuasive purr.

"Good Lord, don't you females have anything better to discuss? I'm sorry, but I am uninterested in assuaging your curiosity."

Lady Piedmont was undeterred. She said quite breathlessly, "Kiss me again."

"I didn't kiss you the first time," he argued. "*You* kissed *me*. It's quite different, my dear."

Lily could no longer contain the impulse, easing up to take a quick glimpse over the top of the settee. It was a large, long room, and she was in the shadows at the far end. The beleaguered but as of yet unidentified lord was no doubt busy enough fending off his determined seductress and certainly Lady Piedmont's attention was focused on her quarry, so she doubted they would see her.

Sure enough there was the very lovely Lady Piedmont, who might not be in the first bloom of youth but could still put most ingenues to shame with her flame-red hair and generous figure, and a well-dressed man whose hands at the moment shackled her wrists, obviously to keep her from her pursuit to unfasten his clothing. The lady in question was still pressed up suggestively against him, his back to one of the bookcases. Were it a reluctant young lady being accosted by a male, Lily would have grabbed a handy weapon such as the heavy Chinese vase sitting on the table to her right and come to her rescue, but from what she could see, the object of Lady Piedmont's desire was tall and wide-shouldered and looked entirely capable of taking care of himself.

"I'm flattered," he said with a hint of humor, "at your interest, but our mutual absence from the ballroom will be noted. I think it is more than prudent for you to return as soon as possible."

"Prudence has never been my main virtue."

Lily could believe that, especially the way the woman was plastered up against him. Virtue didn't apply. The word *shameless* came to mind.

"Do you really want to become the target for a barrage of backhanded whispers?"

No, Lily thought from firsthand experience, *trust me, you don't.*

"Can we discuss this . . . later, then? Some place more discreet?"

"No."

"Darling, I—"

"No." His tone was gentle, maybe even indulgent, but there was an undercurrent that implacably supported his denial.

"Why not?" There was a definite pout in the question, but at least it indicated she finally understood he meant his refusal.

"For myriad reasons."

Then and there Lily felt a flicker of admiration. After all, it wasn't as if most men in society didn't indulge themselves in casual affairs, but his rejection wasn't tempered with a variety of explanations. He didn't bother to offer his reasons. No was no.

Good for him.

Then he dropped Lady Piedmont's wrists and instead scooped her up bodily despite her outraged gasp, somehow deftly opened the door and deposited her outside, before stepping back inside, closing it quickly, and turning the key in the lock.

Lily ducked back down before he turned, hearing him mutter, "By the devil, there had better be brandy in here somewhere."

There was. The tray with the decanter and glasses was on a small polished desk very close to where she sat wondering how fate could be so wily as to contrive to conjure a scenario in which she, who meticulously strived to avoid any situation that might be even mildly indiscreet, suddenly found herself locked in a room with a strange gentleman.

Her reputation could not survive another scandal.

If there had been a way to decamp out the window, or maybe scamper under a convenient chair, she would have taken it, but he moved purposefully in her direction and her breath caught in her throat.

Damnation, as her older brother, Jonathan, might say. This was awkward.

Then again, it wasn't like she'd done anything wrong except exactly what her unwanted companion claimed to do—seek a bit of a reprieve from the ball. It was not *her* fault he'd attracted the importunate Lady Piedmont.

There was nothing to do but brazen it out.

* * *

The faint elusive hint of violets when he'd first entered had been the initial clue someone else was in the room. The sweet scent was more subtle than the overwhelming gardenia perfume Lady Piedmont wore, but definitely there, and in a library full of the smell of dusty leather and gently decaying paper, out of place.

Then had come the subtle rustle of silk as she moved, giving away her location, which happened to be a settee in a small grouping by the tall windows at the back of the room, where he imagined if one sat in the daylight for a quiet afternoon read, they would have a lovely view of the garden.

Just the spot he would have chosen. Already, Lord Damien Northfield thought, he was intrigued by the mysterious lady he imagined was in a slight state of panic over her inevitable discovery. That he could tell also, for while the sound of the orchestra in the ballroom still came faintly, her quickened breathing was audible to someone who had spent a great deal of the Peninsular War using all five of his senses to keep himself alive.

Smell and sound were all well and good, but sight, touch, and taste were usually the most interesting. This beginning held promise....

He could understand why she might not have announced her presence when he arrived with the rabid Lady Piedmont on his heels, but the real question was why was she hiding in the library in the first place?

As he needed that brandy, and he was interested in the answer to that question, he limped down the length of the room, his damned leg aching every step of the way. The wound was healed, but the physicians had been very frank about his injury, and they had been absolutely correct. He was never going to walk normally again. It was, in short, a damned nuisance. Damien said in a neutral voice, without even glancing at the settee, "Good evening."

There was a short silence, punctuated only by the clink as he removed the top of the decanter, and then the splash as he poured some of the liquor into a small crystal snifter.

"You knew I was here?"

Add her soft voice to his impressions. Damien liked the lilt and cadence of her question. The mysterious lady spoke in a lovely contralto, carefully modulated, and though it was tempting to turn around and see what she looked like, he denied himself, taking a sip from his glass. The brandy, he was happy to discover, was the best France had to offer and very smooth. "Yes."

She sat up. He knew it because of the sound of her feet touching the floor and the slight—almost inaudible—creak of the springs of the settee. "Why didn't you say anything?"

"Why didn't *you*?" The brandy was heady and he swirled the liquid once before taking a second sip and slowly turning around.

His first impression was that his quiet spy was striking. No, not beautiful, at least not like Lady Piedmont with her generous breasts and flaming hair, but ... different. Pretty. Memorable even. Her hair was a rich color that in the insufficient light looked light brown with a few golden glints, and her figure was slender, not overly voluptuous, which was pleasing enough, and her skin pale and smooth. Her gown wasn't beribboned and festooned with lace, but instead simple and yet fashionable, the neckline emphasizing the gentle curves of her breasts, the rose color offsetting the creaminess of her complexion.

She had a very defiant tilt to her shapely chin.

It must be a personal flaw in his intellectual composition, but he found that militant air fascinating.

"I was here first."

It was a valid argument, so he shrugged, but he was *watching* her. Would he ever shed the habit? God, he hoped so. He was always watching. It was not an option in the existence he'd just left and he was uneasily settling into this new one. But he didn't wish to go through his entire life vigilant and on guard.

Actually, he was lucky to even *be* alive.

"Yes, you were." Damien took another drink. He'd done countless interrogations, and word had it he was very, very good at it. In fact, he knew he was. "Since there is no one to introduce us, and you just witnessed a rather personal scene, I think informality is in order." He bowed slightly. "Lord Damien Northfield, at your service."

There was a perceptible hesitation, and then she said in a cool tone, "Lady Lillian Bourne."

He hadn't been back in society long enough to really know any of the current gossip, not that he cared all that much about the generally superficial sins of the aristocracy anyway after so many bloody years in Portugal and Spain, but there was something in her voice that told him she thought the name might mean something to him.

It did actually. It belonged to her. Lillian. He liked it. It was elegant, and yet not too prim.

"May I offer my apologies for what you overheard?"

It was the least he could do, for if she was an unmarried young lady—and he would stake his life on it—that hadn't been the most appropriate of dialogue.

"It seems to me you were not the one being improper, my lord."

Lovely *and* intelligent. The dry note in her observation was duly noted. "I was doing my best to dissuade her," he agreed with a slight, hopefully disarming smile.

"She's very beautiful."

He was a little surprised at the directness. "Yes." He swirled the liquid in the glass again, took a sip, and then expounded, "But unabashed pursuit is not appealing to me. I've been hunted enough."

The lighting was dim, but he caught the flicker of surprise in her eyes. She said, "That is an interesting statement. Are we still discussing eager women throwing themselves into your arms?"

"No."

"I thought not."

Anyone else might simply inquire as to why she wasn't in the ballroom dancing her dainty feet off, but he rarely took a straightforward path to directly gain information. His methods were much more subtle. "Though I confess I am no longer accustomed to the workings of the *ton*."

Lady Lillian, he discovered then, was not predictable. He anticipated she'd either comment she'd heard of him, or ask him why he'd been absent from the exalted circle he mentioned, but she did neither. Instead she rose in a flurry of rose silk and violet perfume.

"I need to get back to the ball and cannot be seen leaving the same room as you. As unlikely as it would be that anyone would be observing the library, will you still please do me the favor of waiting a decent interval before rejoining the party?"

And here the evening had just taken on a warm new glow and she wished to leave.

Fortunately he was a master at negotiation.

His smile was affable. "Of course." He paused. "If you will tell me why you prefer this dark library to the festivities."

"You set *conditions* on being a gentleman?"

Damien didn't blink an eye. "Absolutely. I think you will find I set conditions on everything."

Strategy was a simple matter usually. *Judge your opponent and react accordingly.*

"I will find?" she repeated delicately, and truthfully, he found the phrasing odd himself.

Damien Northfield, who once might have been more important to the campaign on the Iberian Peninsula than even the Duke of Wellington, was not sure how to respond.

"Should we meet again," he equivocated and watched her give a nod and move gracefully toward the door.

He liked the sway of her hips.

He also admired the curve of her spine, and the soft color of her hair in the lamplight.

Oh, yes, he vowed silently, *we will meet again*.

For she had not answered his question.

Chapter 2

She may never have risen at dawn and gone to the field in an early London mist, but Lily recognized a duel when one took place. It was clear enough as she walked the length of the library with as much dignity as possible to make her way back toward the ballroom, that Damien Northfield—*Lord* Damien Northfield—had just challenged her.

And she had no idea how to feel about it.

Even as she reached for the ornate key left in the lock, she tried to recall what she knew of him. It wasn't much actually, she realized. His brother was the Duke of Rolthven, but other than knowing he'd been in the war to the bitter end and wounded in the last battle, hence his pronounced limp, she couldn't really say she'd heard much about him.

That alone was interesting.

Lord Damien was a stranger.

Tall, his chestnut hair thick and just slightly wavy from what she could see without adequate lamplight, his mouth curved in a faintly sardonic smile. His features were classically modeled in angles, the line of his nose straight, his mouth sensual, and while he was undeniably handsome, oddly enough that was not what first struck her. It was more the intensity of his dark eyes.

And here she'd thought she had met every eligible bachelor in society, thanks to the formidable—some would say terrifying—Dowager Duchess of Eddington. In retrospect, it was one matter to fall under the surveillance of her discerning eye, and quite another to become her special project. Her older brother, Jonathan, was entirely to blame for that, as he'd married the dowager's granddaughter and brought Lillian's notoriety and unwed state into focus. Now she was left to suffer with having one very determined aristocratic matron trying to repair her damaged reputation and marry her off. She wished the duchess luck. It wasn't going to be an easy task and certainly wouldn't be helped by her prolonged absence this evening.

The lock was stiff and ruined her grand departure as she struggled to turn the key.

Then disaster struck.

Not a small disaster either, a *large* one.

The key broke off in her hand. It was big, ornate, and obviously antique, and even as she held up the handle and gazed in dismay at the twisted metal, she realized that no doubt hundreds of years of use had compromised the shaft to the point where right now, at this point in all those centuries, it chose *this moment* to snap off in the lock.

Slowly, she turned around—saying an inner curse no lady would utter aloud—and instead spoke as calmly as possible. "I think we are locked in."

"Oh?" At the distant end of the room, still standing there, negligently sipping his brandy, Lord Damien's expression was too shadowed for her to interpret. "That's inconvenient."

Inconvenient? Maybe only inconvenient to him, but she really could not afford to be found in a barred room with an unattached male—and how the devil would they explain *why* the door was locked without mentioning Lady Piedmont's advances anyway? *Or* their presence together in the private library of their host for that matter.

"The key broke."

"Yes, I heard the snap. It causes a bit of a problem. I can easily pick a lock. But one cannot make the tumblers cooperate with a bit of metal lodged in them."

The calm tone of his voice caused her to think about lifting up the heavy volume of sonnets sitting on a nearby table and hurling it at his head. Instead she quelled the surge of panic and asked with admirable composure, "How are we supposed to get out of this room?"

"A good question. The windows, I suppose, though I must say it appears to have started to rain."

What?

Sure enough, when Lily dashed forward and flung back the draperies, the leaden skies from earlier in the evening had decided to pelt down an early-fall deluge, water sluicing down the glass.

Her inarticulate sound of dismay was both loud and heartfelt. Even without the barrier of a thorny row of roses under the window, she could hardly jump out and return to the ball soaking wet. Especially if anyone had observed her leaving in the first place; her murmured excuse for her departure a need for the ladies' retiring room.

Taking in a steadying breath, she turned, her hands clenching into fists in her skirts. "We need to do something."

"I find it curious you phrase it that way." Damien Northfield still stood by the drinks table, his pose nonchalant. The dark elegance of his clothing suited him, for he was every inch the refined English gentleman.

Except for those eyes. There was a certain watchful intelligence there that gave her pause. Perhaps even a hint of danger. She asked, "What way?"

"We." His smile was slight, just a glimmer of amusement. "You did not demand to know what *I* was going to do to solve our little dilemma. Most women would."

"I am not most women."

"Yes, I am getting that impression."

Was that derision or humor in his tone? She'd have to think about it later. Lily did not relish explaining to him why it would be so very unfortunate if they were caught together. "Lord Damien, I truly must get back."

"Let me take a look at the door." He set aside his snifter—after draining it—and walked toward the other end of the room, taking a long tin instrument out of some sort of sheath in his boot in a deft motion. Then he knelt and in one motion slid it inside the mechanism. When after a few minutes he shook his head, she believed him, for he seemed entirely too proficient in what he was attempting to do to fail if it was possible to get the door open.

"Maybe the rain is letting up," she suggested, a little desperate, but the steady sound of the water lashing at the window indicated just the opposite.

The duchess was going to have her head on a platter.

"I am not sure I agree." His tone was dry. "The window I do believe I can manage whenever you wish to exit, but right now seems a poor time. Give it a few minutes for the deluge to lessen."

A few minutes? She did not have a few minutes. Before long she would be missed, if she wasn't already. She could claim a sudden illness. Lily detested lying, but there was also the issue of disappointing the duchess, so how to handle this was a delicate matter.

"Here."

She glanced up to find that Lord Damien was offering her a small glass of a substance that looked exactly like what he was drinking. He arched a brow. "Brandy is an acquired taste, but I highly recommend it for stressful situations such as being locked in a library with a man you do not know. There is no sherry, I'm afraid."

The evening was deteriorating at a rapid pace already and she doubted it was going to get better soon. She took the glass. God knew she'd done more reckless things in her lifetime. The first sip made her cough and it burned every inch the way down. Lily sank back onto the settee she'd reclined on earlier and thought she saw a flicker of relief cross her companion's face as he selected a nearby chair. It hadn't occurred to her that his leg might pain him so much politely standing before she was seated was tasking, but maybe it was. His limp was certainly quite pronounced.

How did a person make small talk in such a situation? She had no idea. Of course he didn't comprehend her dilemma, and she wasn't going to enlighten him. Instead she blurted out, "How were you wounded?"

*　　*　　*

Damien leaned back negligently, his legs crossed at the ankle, a replenished drink in his hand, which helped his aching thigh. He liked an ordered world, which might account for why he was such a valuable spy.

No, *had* been a valuable spy. It was time to adjust to the change. Now he was just Lord Damien Northfield, formerly the heir apparent to the impressive title of Duke of Rolthven, but since the birth of his nephew not nearly as prestigious in society. Not that he cared; he preferred it this way, but at the moment, what puzzled him was the open panic in the very blue and *very* lovely eyes of the young lady sitting across from him, clutching her brandy.

And puzzles were, after all, his specialty.

"I'm not quite sure," he said, doing his best to seem nonchalant. He'd almost lost the leg . . . dear God, it had been close, and if he hadn't struggled to consciousness just in time to stop them, the surgeons would have taken it off. "To the best of my knowledge, the French were on the run by the time it happened, but quite frankly, in the melee, for all I know an Englishman wounded me. Battles are confusing sometimes. The bullet hit an artery. I knew I was wounded but not how badly until I fell."

And the blood, the air acrid with smoke, men yelling, and the wounded moaning on the field, horses down . . .

Not quite the thing to mention to a well-bred young lady.

Lillian Bourne glanced at the window again. Nothing had changed. It was still raining quite hard. She lifted the glass in her hand to her mouth in a graceful movement, and grimaced as she swallowed. Her voice was slightly hoarse. "I suppose in an abstract way we who have not experienced it glamorize war when the reality is quite different."

Very insightful. He murmured, "Take my word for it; it is anything but glamorous."

She turned to look directly at him. "You answered my question and I should extend you the same courtesy. I'm in the library for the same reason you gave Lady Piedmont. I wanted some solitude."

Damien studied his glass for a moment. "Why? I admit I am out of touch, but I thought most young ladies like to dance and enjoy the social aspects of this kind of affair."

"I am not that young."

There was that lift of her chin again. He didn't know why he found it so charming. No, he thought, taking his time—her comment invited it—looking her over, she wasn't a simpering young lady fresh from the schoolroom. Yet she was hardly on the shelf either, no more than two and twenty if he ventured a guess. Luscious breasts under the bodice of her fashionable gown, that shining rich hair, those fine-boned features, not to mention her beautiful eyes . . .

"Why haven't you married?"

Reposed against the velvet of the settee, a vision of feminine elegance in rose silk, she smiled, but it was a cynical curve of her soft lips. "Are you always so forthright, Lord Damien?"

That was an interesting question. It halted him in the act of taking a drink of the brandy in his glass. He admitted softly, "Actually, I am never forthright. My talents lie in other disciplines and few of them involve full disclosure."

"I have heard you were a spy for Wellington."

He just took another sip. The war was over. "What does it matter what I've done in the service of our country?"

There was a slight adversarial edge to her regard. "I didn't realize the comment would offend you."

"Neither did I," he replied honestly.

She seemed to reconsider the conversation. "Can I rephrase?"

"Feel free."

"With your superior skills in evading potential disaster, how will we get out of this less than perfect situation?"

Her beauty aside, he might actually like this straightforward young woman. "I can see any number of solutions."

"Oh? As far as I can tell it is still pouring rain outside. And might I mention I need to return to the ball as quickly as possible—without anyone realizing I've been here alone with you—before the dowager duchess realizes I have been gone too long?"

That statement clarified her anxiety a bit. "The dowager duchess?"

"Of Eddington."

His brother, Colton, was a duke, and truly there were not so many peers in the exalted circles of British society that Damien didn't recognize the name easily. "I take it she's sponsoring you?"

"My brother married her granddaughter. If there are a number of solutions to get us out of this, tell me what they are."

It wasn't as if her blunt approach put him off; he was

just not used to it. Lady Lillian, it seemed, did not allow much latitude for doubt over her position. She wanted a viable answer to their dilemma.

Damien gently cleared his throat. "You can go out the window and reenter the ballroom soaking wet."

"That option has occurred to me, thank you, but seems a choice only if there is no other way. Can you not come up with another idea?"

"I can go out that window and be the one to ruin my evening kit. I can then summon help to dismantle the lock and open the door. I am more than willing, but the trouble is, you will still have to come up with a plausible explanation for why you are locked in here and how I knew it."

"Once again, that's obvious enough."

"Or we can use the secret passage."

Finally he got a glimmer of respect. The lovely Lillian sat up straighter. "What? Where?"

"By the fireplace." He idly pointed. "They were often put in libraries in houses built during the period this one was constructed because it was a logical place to store important documents. I suppose I was just being a bit dramatic. If you closely examine the paneling you can see it well enough, but at first glance it isn't obvious. There have been times in English history, I am afraid, when if your political views were unpopular enough a person might want to have a quick way to gather any books or papers that might be considered inflammatory and exit the house as quickly as possible, but not neces- sarily through the front door."

"How do you know this house has one?"

He was sorely tempted to act as if it was through his

superior powers of deduction, but after a moment he shrugged. "Pondsworth is a friend of mine. He showed it to me once. It is part of the reason I chose this spot to hide from Lady Piedmont. Unfortunately, she is a bit more fleet of foot than I anticipated."

For the first time, his companion actually laughed, though the moment passed quickly.

Lady Lillian was very pretty when she smiled. Actually, she was very pretty when she frowned also.

"Where does the passage go?" Clearly she was intrigued.

"Unfortunately, to the cellars. And if I recall, it is extremely dusty and narrow. Your lovely gown would not escape the journey unscathed."

"Oh." His companion looked disillusioned. "Not much of a solution, then, is it? And I have to say I am not at all fond of dark, closed spaces."

"I didn't say any of the options were ideal, just that they existed."

She seemed to remember her drink and tried it again, very cautiously, making a slight grimace and coughing lightly. "What would you do if you were in my predicament? At the least I am going to get caught out in a lie because where I said I was going is quite the opposite direction from here, and at the worst, I will be discovered locked in with you."

Obviously she had no idea how quickly he could disappear if need be. It had saved his life more than once or twice.

But this wasn't war, he reminded himself. This was just a frivolous social gathering. Neutrally, he said, "I don't think anyone else besides ourselves will seek the library this evening, but should they, I will gladly take the cobwebs and the cellars, so you needn't worry we'll be discovered together." Damien considered a moment. "I'd settle for the drenching if I were you. Perhaps intimate that you stepped outside for a bit of fresh air and were caught in the downpour. We've never even been introduced, so our mutual disappearance from the gathering won't be connected, and quite frankly, I am not anxious to see Lady Piedmont again this evening. I believe I will just summon my carriage and return home. No one will see us together and it will all appear very innocent."

And it was. More was the pity, for Damien wouldn't mind a very *less than innocent* interlude with the appealing Lady Lillian.

It startled him, for he was usually quite careful in his relationships with the fairer sex. Not that he didn't enjoy women—he certainly did—but he had taken care never to become involved on an emotional level, for in his particular profession, it simply wasn't wise. Marriageable ingenues normally did not interest him.

"Innocent?" She stood and decisively set aside her glass on a nearby table. "That is the problem, my lord. I am no longer considered innocent in any situation. Now, will you help me out the window?"

Chapter 3

Eugenia Francis, the Dowager Duchess of Eddington, studied the dance floor. The ladies were elegant in their brilliant gowns, bedecked by gleaming jewels, the gentlemen a contrast in most cases in their dark evening wear, though there were always a few peacocks wearing waistcoats in hues of brilliant aquamarine, or worse, purple. She could not abide a man who thought he should wear such a color, much less a froth of lace and diamond shoe buckles and other frippery.

For Lady Lillian, she wanted a suitor who would complement her independent personality, not a foppish fool.

It wasn't going to be simple. She had no illusions there, especially if the girl kept disappearing. Though she'd come to admire the young woman's individual spirit, Eugenia found it a blasted nuisance when it came to trying to marry her off.

For instance, where was she now? Not among the whirling dancers. Lily was noticeable enough, especially this evening in her rose gown that, if she did think so in a rather smug way, Eugenia was quite willing to take the credit for as she'd selected both the color and style. The material was the perfect foil for Lily's pale skin and gleaming brown hair, and as her charge was not exactly right out of the schoolroom, the neckline was just a subtle bit more daring than Eugenia would normally have chosen, but it was a calculated maneuver.

That had *worked*. Many a gentleman had noticed Lily as they'd arrived and been announced, which made her sudden absence all the more alarming.

As of right now, her charge's alluring appearance and significant dowry were making the venture of possibly gaining her an aristocratic husband a success, but another scandalous lapse would hardly be helpful. Lillian's favorite friend was the extraordinarily unfashionable Miss Vivian Lacrosse. Maybe she would know where the girl had gone off to this time. Eugenia had not said anything about Lily's choice in friends, for truly, she did realize that a good friendship was important, and though it was entirely *outré* for any female to dabble in botany of all things as Vivian did, she supposed there could be worse choices. Dirt, plants . . . Eugenia had no taste for it, but certainly most of the beau monde indulged in much less wholesome activities than growing a flower or two. Still, the unusual hobby had not done the girl any favors socially.

Drawing herself up to her full height, conscious that if at the moment she seemed unsettled others might take notice of her distress and wonder why, Eugenia made her way over to where Vivian sat with a small group of other young women. Lady Juliet Stather, she noted, was among them, a blond beauty who could be the reigning belle of London society but tended to seclude herself with the least popular set.

Do these young ladies not realize the advantages of a fashionable marriage?

"Miss Lacrosse?"

"Your Grace." Vivian jumped to her feet and made a not-so-graceful curtsy. Apparently plants were much more her forte than the social graces. Still, Eugenia noted, she was attractive in an understated way, with her dark hair and green eyes.

Perhaps a later project . . . She had to be at least as old as Lillian. . . . What a challenge to find a man who wanted a spinster interested in reseeding gardens or whatever it might be. . . .

But for now, Lily. *Right.* She needed to find out where she'd gone. One challenge at a time.

"When did you last see Lady Lillian?" Eugenia's voice was low and crisp and her spine was ramrod straight. That demeanor had a predictable effect on people.

"Oh." Miss Lacrosse prevaricated, and not very successfully, as she'd taken on a bright color over being confronted. She and Lady Juliet exchanged a quick glance. "I'm . . . not sure."

Her dress too, is frumpish, though really, with a real maid to do her hair she could be a beauty. . . . Look at those remarkable eyes, green and gold. . . .

Eugenia said more sharply than she intended, "All you need tell me, child, is when she left the ballroom."

"I'm not really a child any longer," Miss Lacrosse muttered. "Ask anyone."

"She isn't," Lady Juliet added helpfully. "We are the same age."

Why on earth isn't the beauteous Juliet married? . . . Oh, never mind, that is hardly the issue. . . .

"You are trying to distract me with details." The observation was curt and straightforward. Eugenia asked succinctly, "Where did Lillian go?"

"She didn't say," Vivian offered, her voice hushed.

"Ah, so now we are getting somewhere. You *did* see her leave."

"Your Grace, she just excused herself. I did not inquire where she was going."

"However, if you had to guess as to what is keeping her for so long?"

In the face of a very direct, stern stare, Miss Lacrosse's resolve to keep her friend's secret crumpled. "The library."

"That would be my guess also," Lady Juliet murmured.

Fate was truly conspiring against her.

In the end, the window did not prove an option. The frame was either swollen from the moisture, or the lock on it rusted shut, but it would not budge. Lord Damien did his best, but it was clear that it was as immovable as the broken lock.

"Your friend needs to maintain his home a bit better," she muttered, the case clock in the corner making an ominous tick as the minutes went by.

"I could break the glass." Damien Northfield sounded unruffled by their predicament. "But that solution is a bit noisy, I'm afraid. It could be no one would hear it, but it could also cause a passing servant or guest to raise an alarm, thereby not helping our desire for discretion. The way it is raining, it would also no doubt cause some damage to the contents of the room."

He was irritatingly right. And he didn't need to point

out that a connection might easily be made between the broken window and her sodden reappearance at the ball. Her story of needing a breath of fresh air and getting caught in the rain would become suspect at once.

"Of course, we have our other choice."

The secret passage. So now she was reduced to scrambling about in dank, hidden hallways? She wasn't at all sure she could. When she'd told him she disliked dark enclosed places, she had been hedging. They *terrified* her for some inexplicable reason. When she'd accidentally gotten locked in an armoire during a game of hide-and-seek as a child, her screams had brought the entire household running.

Lord Damien waited, his expression inscrutable, but then again, she thought crossly, the man had not denied being a spy. Finally, she nodded. "I suppose we have to get out somehow. The most important thing is that I am not discovered locked in here with you."

His smile was ironic. "How flattering."

"I didn't intend to give offense." Her voice was stiff. She couldn't help it. "It isn't personal. I would not want to be discovered locked in with any gentleman."

His gaze was searching. "So I gather." Then he turned and limped over to the fireplace, running his hand over the wall.

To Lillian's amazement the panel of the hidden passage slid back without a sound under the pressure of Damien's long fingers, though the doorway it revealed was obviously old and the hinges creaked in a screech that made her jump when he pulled it open. Hopefully no one else heard it.

"My advice is to take off your dress."

She blinked at the ludicrous suggestion. "I beg your pardon?"

Is he completely mad?

He was already shrugging out of his jacket. "I can cover my shirt with my coat if it gets dusty, and let me assure you, it will. You could do the same. Carry your dress and put it back on when we get to the end. Your undergarments will suffer, and you might have to concoct a story for your maid, but otherwise no one will be able to tell."

It took a moment before she sputtered, "I . . . I cannot undress in front of you."

His smile was just a faint curve of his lips as he tugged at his perfectly tied cravat. "I assure you I will not be shocked, my lady."

Somehow she doubted anything shocked Damien Northfield. No doubt, with his good looks, he'd seen an undressed lady or two. She was not an ingenue any longer and understood that gentlemen were very rarely inexperienced by the time they were his age, but still, his suggestion was out of the question. "I am hardly concerned with your sensibilities. It just isn't . . . proper."

"I think you should choose between propriety and practicality at this point." He folded the length of his white cravat carefully inside his coat. "I can keep a secret. My Lord Wellington would attest to that. And though as lovely as you are, Lady Lillian, I promise I do not wish to ravish you among cobwebs and unlit, filthy corridors, but you are welcome to decide as you see fit. Stay here and risk discovery, or come along."

Did he have any idea that her gown was the least of her concerns at the moment? It was true, the door he'd opened was festooned with cobwebs, but mostly it was dark and there were stairs that led straight downward.

Into blackness.

Her chest tightened.

She was, in a word, *terrified*.

Had it not been for her tarnished past, she would have never considered it. She still wasn't sure she *was* considering it, but at that moment someone knocked smartly on the door.

Whatever happened, she did not want to be found locked in the library. If Lord Damien went down the passage alone, she'd still have to explain why she would ever lock the door in the first place, and though maybe later she could come up with something clever, at the moment she could think of nothing plausible. On the other hand, his solution *could* work.

There was a second knock, louder than the first, and the handle rattled.

"Quick," she whispered, whirling to present her back. "Help me."

She actually thought he might have let out a small muffled laugh, but with dexterous ease he undid her gown and she stepped out of it, wondering if she'd completely lost her senses. Clad only in her chemise, stockings, and slippers and gathering the material of her gown into a bundle, she was relieved to see he wasn't staring at her now half-clad body, but had taken the small lamp from the table, moving so silently despite his disability she suddenly believed all the stories about his service to the Crown.

To her surprise he extended his folded jacket and she

took it in a reflexive response and then he offered his hand.

There was no time for debate on the matter.

She placed her fingers in his and she could swear she caught the glimmer of a smile; then he led her into the passageway, pulled the panel closed, and eased the door shut with only the slightest groan of the hinges.

Well done.

Only it was worse than she'd imagined, the ceiling low, the walls smelling bitter with age, but at least the clasp of his hand was strong and warm and the light flickering as he held it in front of him was better than complete darkness. Lily took in a shuddering breath and contemplated closing her eyes, then decided it would not lessen the terror but increase it. Plus the narrow steps were treacherously steep, so she concentrated on his broad back and followed him down the stairs. He'd been right about the dirt and dust; it was everywhere. And she kept the fabric of her dress and his folded jacket clutched close to her body, for if she was willing to do this, she wanted it to be worth the effort.

Close walls, the musty odor, the darkness . . .

"It will take them a while to get into the library," Lord Damien commented, his voice echoing a little. "By then we will have rejoined the party."

"I'm still not sure how we'll explain the cobwebs in our hair," Lily said in a small voice, but hopefully he was right and as he was a good deal taller and in front, he was getting the worst of it anyway. She was reluctant to admit it, but he'd been right about removing her dress, for she could see even in the flickering light held in front of him as they descended that his white shirt was already smudged, his shoulders so wide they brushed the walls, though even with his pronounced limp he moved with what seemed like effortless ease.

He still held her hand and his fingers tightened a little. "Are you frightened?"

It wasn't precisely fright, more like panic, but oddly enough his presence seemed to quell her usual reaction when faced with an enclosed space. Maybe it was his air of quiet competence, as if no situation daunted him.

"I'm trying not to think about it, my lord."

"That usually works best. I tend to picture myself on our family estate in Essex when faced with an environment like this. Rolthven has a spacious park, and the river where I swam as a boy is wide and slow."

"It bothers you as well?" She couldn't hide the surprise in her voice.

"I've have myriad experiences with closed spaces and none of them were enjoyable." His tone held a sardonic edge that even in the distraction of her predicament and the close confines of the narrow way she registered.

"In the war?"

"My apologies, but I don't answer questions like that, Lady Lillian. The past does not matter."

It *did* matter, she almost pointed out in the most acerbic manner possible. If it didn't, she would not now be in this dank passage, winding down a dark stair to the cellars, only half-dressed and hand in hand with a man she'd just met. Male privilege might make it easier to ignore, but the past *mattered*, especially if it involved one very drastic mistake.

It was one devil of a standard that held women to a

different mode of conduct than men, but then again, supposed gentlemen had created the rules. Males wanted their wives chaste and their mistresses wicked. They controlled the world, but could not comfort a crying child. They often cared more for their precious horses than their loyal servants. . . .

In general, her opinion of them was not all that high.

Then again, she had adored her father. Her brother, Jonathan, the current Earl of Augustine, was also—while not conventional in any way—a good man and very much in love with his new wife.

But, his emancipated views on females aside, Jonathan would disapprove, Lily suspected, of her current whereabouts, because while her intentions had been to just snatch a moment or two of solitude, here she was in a very compromising situation.

Again.

There was a bend in the steps and for a moment Lord Damien faltered, obviously a bit off balance, his breath going in with an audible hiss. This time she was the one who tightened her grip, steadying him, but he recovered almost as soon as it happened, murmuring, "Thank you. We should be there soon. If I remember correctly, this comes out in what is now the wine cellar."

He was right, she discovered a few minutes later as he pushed open a door with a shriek of protesting hinges and the cool air washed over them, the lamp in his hand illuminating racks of dusty bottles, the light bouncing eerily off the shadowed corners.

It was odd, but when he let go of her hand, Lily experienced a small, unexpected sense of loss, and now that it was over, she began to shake.

He reached for his coat and cravat, plucking them from the bundle in her arms. "As escapes go, that one was not too taxing. I feel confident Pondsworth's butler locks the cellar, but that should not be a problem without a broken key jammed inside it. All we have to do now is make it upstairs undetected."

"Is *that* all?" Lily was so relieved to be out of the passageway her mortification over being in such a state of undress didn't even matter. Besides, it wasn't as if Lord Damien was even paying attention, which was actually a bit insulting. She'd never thought of herself as a raving beauty, but men did notice her, though apparently retired spies were immune. She slipped her gown on with a little difficulty as she was used to having help from her maid, and, as when she was taking it off, he came to her aid in a way that spoke of more than a scandalous passing experience with the process, swiftly buttoning up the back.

"My breeches and boots are a little dusty," he said as casually as if their recent escapade was an everyday occurrence, tying his cravat. "Otherwise, how did I fare?"

There was a cobweb or two in his thick, wavy hair and without thinking Lily reached up to brush them away. The strands were unexpectedly soft and silky in contrast to the masculine cast of his fine features and his lean, athletic build. The gesture was surprisingly intimate and the immediacy of it startled her.

"Quite presentable now, my lord," she managed to say, practically snatching her hand back.

"You have a smudge." He cupped her chin and rubbed the pad of his thumb lazily over the curve of her cheekbone. "There, that's done the trick."

"Thank you." An odd tingle went through her.

His brows snapped together. "Are you quite all right? You're trembling."

"I told you, I don't like enclosed spaces."

"Yes, you did tell me exactly that. You did very well, Lady Lillian."

For a split second they gazed at each other and there was a second treacherous inner quiver she had not felt since the debacle her first season and her bungled elopement. Then he smiled and dropped his hand. "Let's see how quickly I can confound Pondsworth's butler into thinking he left the door to the precious wine cellar unlocked, shall we?"

True to his word, Lord Damien was a wizard when not thwarted by errant weakened keys stuck in diabolical locks, and moments later they were climbing the steps to freedom. It wasn't too difficult to find her way back to the ballroom—the sound led her there even from the back corridor. Her companion in her little adventure went the opposite direction, and she assumed he was going to do as he declared earlier and quietly take his leave.

When Lily slipped back into the ballroom, she was triumphant for about five entire seconds until a restraining hand snagged her arm. "Do you mind telling me just where the devil you've been?"

She glanced up into the normally composed face of her cousin James, saw the concern in his blue eyes, and swallowed a sigh. She might have known that if the ever diligent duchess had noticed her gone, James would be even more likely to have noticed it. He was, after all, her official male chaperone for the evening.

"It is terribly crowded in here and I needed a moment to myself." That was true enough. Later she might tell him the entire story, for if she trusted anyone on this earth, it was James. But for now, she wanted to find a dance partner before the duchess returned. She surreptitiously checked to see if her gown was properly in place—it seemed to be—and lifted her chin. "I wasn't gone that long."

"Long enough," he disagreed grimly. "I don't care for a crush myself, but you have a habit of disappearing, and people are watching you."

"That's hardly a revelation," she said a little hoarsely, which actually wasn't surprising because her mouth was quite dry. He was right, of course. James was frequently right. Not self-righteous, thank goodness, because that she would not be able to take, but just logical in a level-headed way that made her wonder if he ever was impulsive and reckless.

"It shouldn't be," James agreed, sweeping his gaze out over the crowd, sophisticated and handsome in his evening wear, nonchalant on the surface, even though she knew he was truly worried about her. "You know how judgmental society is, Lily."

She collected her best serene smile. "There's nothing to judge. Now, if you'll excuse me, I am going to go find Vivian. I promised I would help her avoid Lord Gregory."

"Females," he muttered under his breath.

Lily gave him a considering look. "I would suggest you waltz with her instead, but you've been remarkably aloof when it comes to marriageable young ladies lately.

I have noticed you suddenly will only dance with the elderly matrons."

"I think," her cousin said with a bland smile, "I see Miss Lacrosse trying to blend into a potted plant in the north corner of the room. When you are ready to depart, I will be in the card room."

Thoughtfully, Lily watched him shoulder his way through the crowd, before she shook off any speculation over her cousin's unusual reticence and started to make her way toward Vivian.

Considering the narrowly avoided disaster of this evening so far, hiding in the corner seemed an excellent idea.

Chapter 4

The woman beneath him moaned. In response, James Bourne licked her lush lower lip and murmured, "You like that."

It wasn't precisely a statement, nor was it a question, because, quite frankly, he was never sure what to expect from Regina. Her beautiful eyes opened, and she arched beneath his naked body, her nails lightly raking up his back, his hand between her open legs. Her tumbled mane of glossy dark hair framed ivory shoulders and her skin had taken on a certain glow he recognized as sexual arousal. "Do it again," she ordered, her voice husky in the shrouded bedchamber.

He obliged, at the same time sliding two fingers deeply inside her vaginal passage and slowly circling his thumb between the satin-soft folds of her cleft. Her inner muscles clenched around the carnal invasion and she quivered in response to the intimate caress, her taut nipples tantalizingly brushing his chest.

Oh yes, she liked it. She was wet, hot, ready for him. . . .

It was his turn to let out a low groan as her hand slid between them and her slender fingers wrapped around his erect cock and squeezed. "Roll over on your back," she whispered. "Now let *me* pleasure *you.*"

The imperious tone of her voice wasn't exactly a surprise because he'd learned a month ago when their affair started she was a woman who liked to have equal control—if not *more* control—in bed. It was intriguing, but then again, Regina Daudet was intriguing in every way. Not just beautiful and sophisticated, she was an enigma with her artistic bent and determined independence.

Unlike any woman he'd ever met. Gifted, moody, tempestuous . . .

They were opposites in almost every aspect of their lives except she had an attachment to the aristocracy more tenuous than his. He might be first cousin to an earl, but that granted him no title, and as Jonathan's new wife was pregnant, he doubted he would remain heir apparent for long. Regina was the daughter of a viscount, but she was illegitimate and therefore not all that acceptable in the exalted circles of the *haut ton*.

It would be stupid not to oblige her and follow orders because he'd never had such an adventurous lover, and he had no doubt whatever happened next he would enjoy immensely. He lifted off of her luscious body and shifted so he lay on his back. Her bedroom was as eclectic as she was, with brilliant saffron bed hangings and an exotic print that was clearly Oriental in origin in the coverlet on the bed, the sheets a soft fabric he didn't recognize. On the walls was a bizarre mixture of art, some of it a bit terrifying, including a mask from Africa that showed a contorted human face. It hung right next to what he could swear was an original Gainsborough portrait of what appeared to be Regina herself as a child, even then scandalously dressed in breeches and a loose white shirt instead of the usual dainty, embroidered dress one might expect on the daughter of a viscount.

"Look at this." She lounged next to him, her lithe body propped on one elbow, one hand sensually traveling up the length of his rigid erection until a teasing fingertip wiped a bead of semen from the tip. Putting the finger to her mouth, she smiled and sucked the iridescent droplet away. "Can I have more?"

He might have answered if he was able, but at that moment she leaned forward and slowly licked the crest of his cock and the acute pleasure of it shuddered through him. "Regina . . ."

There was no answer, her mouth sliding downward, taking him as far as she could to the back of her throat, his body going taut with the bombarding rapture to every nerve ending. James ran his fingers through her hair, reveling in the softness, her scent, her unabashed sexuality, the sight of her long dark hair spilled over his thighs almost as erotic as what she was doing to him.

Sybaritic bliss.

Decadent heaven.

Splendor unsurpassed . . .

He might have been able to come up with other flowery descriptions of the sheer sensation of how she skillfully stroked his testicles and at the same time swirled her tongue in an intoxicating dance over the head of his cock, but he could hardly put two words together, much less three, and instead he lay there and did his best to keep his control.

It was a losing battle he decided moments later and he

tugged her head upward, with a murmured apology abruptly rolled her over, and spread her legs with his knees. The breath left his lungs as he slid inside her, impaling her fully. He was so close he almost ejaculated right then and there and he stilled, briefly closing his eyes.

"Yes . . . yes." She arched a little, taking him a fraction deeper.

James kissed her then, with ardent insistence because he'd learned already she preferred passion to tenderness, and her hands were frantic already at the small of his back, urging him to move, her pelvis lifting into his withdrawal and thrust in a perfect match to his carnal rhythm.

Just when he was sure the thread of his control had dwindled to the point where he couldn't hold on a second longer, he felt the first tremor of her climax. Perfectly in character, Regina was not shy about her enjoyment of sexual release. She gripped his buttocks and held him deep, and the way her inner muscles contracted was more than enough to send him into oblivion, the journey one of exquisite pleasure, as if he was being tossed past the stars and moon. Her cry mingled with his low groan.

They lay panting together in the aftermath, her slender legs still locked around his waist, her voluptuous breasts soft against his chest. It had been as dynamically charged as ever, and though he doubted she would appreciate the gesture, he lifted his head and gently kissed her eyelids until they fluttered open. He murmured, "I wouldn't mind staying in this position for . . . well, the rest of my life would do."

Wrong thing to say, you damn fool. . . .

If he could take it back, he would immediately. To a woman of Regina's stalwart self-reliance he should have known better than to mention any length of time in regard to their relationship, much less bungle so badly as to use the phrase *rest of my life*.

Luckily, and perhaps it was just in the aftermath of such explosive pleasure—or it had been for him at least—she was apparently in a forgiving mood, for she merely smiled with languorous charm. "I like the feel of you inside me, too."

A tricky moment successfully passed. The amount of relief he felt would need to be analyzed later because this was not the time or place, not while he was still in her arms, his weight braced above her, their bodies still intimately joined. "We are in accord, then." He grinned to make the statement sound light and careless, his emotions just the opposite.

"I think we are." Regina stretched her arms playfully over her head, pressing her breasts more firmly against him. The evocative scent of lovemaking mingled with the hint of some exotic flower he hadn't been able to place in her perfume. With one foot she lazily rubbed the back of his calf. "Hmm. I feel wonderful, Mr. Bourne."

"I couldn't agree more," James responded softly, his erection still rigid despite his recent release. His fingers feathered down the silken skin of her shoulder. "You do feel wonderful. I would be more than happy to demonstrate again the sincerity of my words if you will give me a few moments."

Her eyes were a mesmerizing gray color and those silver depths held a hint of amusement. "That sounds promising. In the meanwhile, we can bask in the glow of mutual appreciation, or we can share a glass of wine. Would you like to take a look at my new work?"

James was startled. She didn't offer that. Or at least she never had before. In his twenty-eight years he'd had his share of lovers, but none quite as private as Regina. He wasn't sure if that was why he was so drawn to her, but there was something intangible about her allure that really was not about her beauty or her glorious responsiveness in bed.

He greatly feared for the first time in his life, he was falling in love.

It was damned inconvenient it was with a woman seven years his senior who had no need of his money— she was far wealthier than he was due to an inheritance from her father—and who had made it plain from the fateful moment they'd met at a small dinner given by a mutual friend that she led her own life without apology. Somehow that evening he'd ended up with an invitation to accompany her home, and what had followed was one of the most memorable nights of his life.

That had been a month ago and he had joined her in the evenings every opportunity offered, slowly discovering the fascinating state of her individuality.

She didn't need a man to protect her—neither did she want one, and it seemed she had eschewed altogether the idea of being a dutiful wife and mother, and being typically Regina, had no regrets over it either.

One night, when in a more open mood than usual, she'd admitted frankly she was fond of her half brother, the current Viscount Altea, and also her half sister, Elizabeth, the legitimate children of her father, but their relationship seemed to be based very loosely on a family dynamic that did not involve any of the normal protocol of English society.

"I wasn't aware you'd finished the painting." He ran his fingers up her arm, marveling at the smoothness of her skin.

She was an extraordinary artist but did not discuss her work, much less ever offer to give him a private viewing before now.

"I haven't." Her tone was noncommittal. "It is still an unfinished piece."

"I would be honored," he told her quietly, hoping she saw the sincerity in his eyes, and then with some reluctance, he eased free of her body. "Shall I dress?"

With a musical laugh, Regina shook her head and slipped off the bed, a naked nymph—no, goddess might be more appropriate—with her tumbled long hair brushing her waist and her voluptuous curves. "There's no need. My staff is limited to a housekeeper and one maid. They are used to my eclectic habits. I think they are reluctant to venture out of their rooms in the middle of the night lest they see something scandalous."

A part of him wondered if that meant she occasionally had male visitors—a jealous part he wasn't aware he even possessed—and a more reasonable voice reminded him he didn't own her past. She was not a virginal miss. Far from it. Never had she made apologies or offered explanations, but certainly she was the most arousing lover he'd ever bedded. It wasn't her beauty alone either, but more the mysterious aura that surrounded her.

He wondered if he'd ever know her in any way except a carnal one.

And the challenge intrigued him.

*   *   *

What had possessed her?

Regina slipped on her dressing gown and turned to glance at the man who still reclined on the tangled sheets of her bed. James was magnetically attractive—that was undeniable—though she usually liked the dark brooding types, not blond males with sky-blue eyes who were undeniably even-tempered and might even be labeled as "conventional." He was lean, but athletically built, and his refined features had an almost boyish cast. But there was no doubt at all his quiet smile and reserved air of masculine confidence was what had caught her attention in the first place.

That boring dinner she hadn't wanted to attend had turned into an interesting evening when she was seated next to him, and an even more delightful night when she'd suggested he might escort her home. Since then he'd regularly shared her bed, but she'd done her best from the beginning to make it clear they were lovers and nothing more. The idea of a permanent relationship didn't appeal to her. It never had. Her art filled her life.

Besides, there was the difference in their ages. She was thirty-five and he was a good deal younger.

Oh, yes, she'd had a younger lover once. It hadn't been a wonderful experience because he'd been eager and fumbling and she'd decided then and there that older men undoubtedly had a bit more finesse.

Not that she'd tested that theory very often.

She was a bit of a sham.

Regina Daudet, the eccentric half sister of Viscount Altea, not precisely accepted in the most exalted social circles because of her birth, her scandalous hobby as an artist shunned, was actually not as unconventional as everyone assumed, but she didn't mind the notoriety. Her brother Luke had offered more than once to use his influence to gain her acceptance to even the most exclusive of London society's various entertainments, but she had always declined.

Her relationship with her father had been precious to her. Though he'd never married her mother, he had always treated her as his beloved eldest child and Luke's birth hadn't altered that between them. She and her father's wife had a cautious but conciliatory relationship, given that she was the product of an earlier liaison. Regina had decided early on she disdained the snobbish social aspect of aristocratic society. She controlled her inheritance so she didn't *have* to marry, and always, always, she kept her lovers—the few of them there had been—at arm's length, and she gloried in her freedom.

Never had she offered anyone a glimpse of her latest work.

Until James Bourne.

He rose from the bed in a lithe movement, the ripple of muscle impressive under his skin, and she offered him a dark blue robe she'd left draped over the chair. There was no problem interpreting the faint ironic twist of his mouth as he accepted it, and she didn't doubt he was wondering who might have left it behind.

One day she might tell him it had belonged to her father. She had bought it for his birthday but he'd suddenly become gravely ill and died, and she'd never been able to give it to him. For now, if James assumed it had belonged to one of her previous lovers, she was disinclined to explain.

She *never* explained or made excuses. Not even to her family. And even she was puzzled as to why she had gotten out the robe in the first place.

Because you don't want James to get dressed and leave.

Their association unsettled her life. She'd expected it to be like her past brief affairs, but she hadn't tired of him rapidly. If anything, she was more fascinated than before and maybe that was why she had just made the unprecedented offer of the robe and a viewing of her art.

"This way." She tied the sash of her dressing gown carelessly and preceded him out the door, not looking back. Her studio was downstairs in the back of the house, originally intended as the formal drawing room and had tall French doors that opened to the garden. When Luke inherited the title and the much grander family residence, he had given her the town house he'd purchased for himself in his bachelor days. She'd been delighted, not because the house was elegantly appointed and in a fashionable neighborhood—it was, but that hadn't really mattered much to her—but because the drawing room was situated so it received glorious natural light. To the horror of the housekeeper, she'd had all the beautiful furnishings sent to the attic and instead had easels, shelves for her paints, and some shabby chairs brought in, and she worked there every afternoon without fail unless the day was truly dismal. The largeness of the room and the sparse furnishings pleased her as there were few distractions and the bare floor was cool against her feet. Occasionally, when she was not certain how she would proceed, she went and sat, paint-stained smock and all, in one of the old wing chairs and stared out the window, just thinking.

It was serene, and though some might find the clutter of oils and brushes and rags and discarded palettes unappealing, she found it helped her focus on her creative purpose.

The painting she wanted to show James had needed no such contemplation. It had flowed easily, at first a trickle, but then a flood, from her mind to her hand. It wasn't quite done, but the main figure was clear enough, as was the ethereal background of mist and forest, and she was particularly pleased with the way a single ray of light pierced the clouds.

The earlier rain had departed and there was enough moonlight she could find her way to light a lamp, slow and deliberate, because she still wasn't quite sure of her motivation in inviting her lover to her sanctuary. The easel stood angled to the glass of the doors, the dried palette nearby. "This is it," she murmured, motioning with her hand. "What do you think?"

James picked up the lamp and moved closer, the illumination sliding over the canvas.

Does he realize how much this matters to me?

His expression was difficult to read, the dark color of the robe accenting the light gleam of his hair and the fine line of his handsome profile. "The work is superb. Can I venture a guess?"

"A guess?" Regina crossed her arms under her breasts and lifted a brow.

"As to what you want it to represent."

"What makes you think I want it to represent anything?"

"Why create something so beautiful to no purpose?"

Damn. She'd been afraid all along he might understand the underlying complex nature of not just the art itself, but maybe even the artist. Perhaps that was why she was so drawn to him. She said curiously, "If you want to guess, then, please do."

"Thank you." He took a moment, his brow faintly furrowed. "The setting is obviously something you've seen. The detail is so well done I can fairly hear the flutter of the leaves."

Regina didn't comment, just waiting.

"The allegorical figure in front is interesting." James lifted the lamp higher for better light. "He looks slightly weary. His crossbow is hanging low, but then again, his expression holds a certain unmistakable resolve. This is a man with no choice. We cannot see what he faces, but he does know it must be done. He isn't a martyr, but an ordinary man in extraordinary circumstances."

It took a moment—for her throat had tightened—but she said calmly, "Go on. I am always curious as to what people take away from my work."

"He doesn't want to do what he must do. His bow is in his hands, but his arrow pointed at the ground. The set of his shoulders shows tension, but the fear is not for himself. Am I correct?"

So very correct she could almost kiss him. Or melt into a puddle at his feet. Neither of which she'd done before. He'd kissed her as a prelude to lovemaking and she'd allowed it, but she'd never kissed *him*. And she'd never imagined melting for any man, but he seemed to be capable of surprising her. "Close enough."

"There's a story ... William Tell, the legendary Swiss hero who was just a common man." James glanced up at her. "It's an old tale, but if I recall, he has to shoot the apple off the head of his son with a crossbow. I've always thought it so compelling . . . the risk . . . awful but yet heroic. An ordinary man pushed beyond his limits."

She actually had to clear her throat because he was absolutely right. She'd always wanted to capture that instant when Tell's bow must have lifted and he'd notched the arrow . . . and then when the moment had come, instead she'd painted the hesitancy before that fateful decision. It was more the choice that interested her than the deed itself. How did he come to it? How *could* he?

And James had seen it so easily.

It unnerved her. "That story has always fascinated me," she admitted.

He glanced up. "I think you did it justice. Well done."

"I chose to not put his son in the picture." She walked toward the easel for the first time, ashamed her palms were damp just from letting anyone—him especially— look at an unfinished work. "It isn't about his son's possible death if he makes a mistake, but rather the dilemma of ever taking the shot. I wanted to capture the personal conflict of his confidence in his ability and the possibility of error we all face." She paused, studying with critical analysis the expression on the central figure's face. "His cost being the dearest possible if he chose wrongly."

"Oh, indeed." James pointed at an apple tree in the background of the painting, mingled with the other trees. "A rather nice comparison to Eden and the first human error. Was that your intention?"

She wasn't sure. Life was profound in many ways and shallow in others. . . . She often felt not so much like a participant as an observer.

James, on the other hand, was so at ease with himself.

Did he realize it? If there was any arrogance in his nature, she hadn't seen even a hint of it and maybe it was that air of quiet confidence she found so attractive. He was a talented and ardent lover, yes, but they seemed to share an intellectual bond as well. She'd never been close to any of the men in her life except her father and Luke.

He was still looking at her with an inquiring expression on his face and she shrugged, now wondering if it had been wise at all to bring him to her studio. If what she wanted was to detangle herself from this relationship, this wasn't how to do it.

It was time to send him on his way.

But she wasn't ready.

Regina sat down in one of the chairs and deliberately let her dressing gown drape open. "Do we really want to discuss biblical applications of artistic endeavors, or shall we explore yet again the more earthy aspect of the term *biblical*?"

He grinned. "I favor the latter."

Chapter 5

In the light of day, her little adventure of the evening before seemed fantastical, like a scene from a romantic novel, complete with a handsome prince, danger, secret passageways, and then the dramatic rescue.

Only in her case, Lily thought as she stirred her chocolate and took a small sip of the steaming beverage, Lord Damien was not precisely a prince but instead a somewhat cynical ex-spy with dubious skills such as wielding a picklock, the danger had been social rather than physical, and the secret passage about the least romantic dank staircase imaginable. Besides, she'd never read a story where the heroine—she was hardly qualified for that role—stripped off her gown before a man she didn't know. In retrospect, she couldn't believe she'd done it, but then again, maybe it was worth it.

There *was* a happy ending.

They'd managed it. After all the bad luck that had gotten her into the situation in the first place, a ray of light had glimmered. She'd slipped back into the crowd seamlessly enough even with James catching her out, and Lord Damien was nowhere to be seen the rest of the evening. Whether or not he'd left to avoid Lady Piedmont as he'd said he would or was in one of the card rooms, she had no idea, but the impression she had of him was that if he chose to remain out of sight, he could do so easily enough.

She had to admit, while most of the gentlemen she knew were rather dull, he'd at least been *interesting*.

The duchess had accepted the excuse that Lily had felt rather dizzy and had gone to lie down for a bit—not all of it was a lie, she wasn't a swooning kind of female but she'd definitely had a horrified moment when the key broke off in her hand—and since the library door had been locked when the duchess went looking for her, the explanation was plausible enough.

A knock interrupted the reverie. Reclined against the pillows, Lily called out, "Come in."

Her younger sister, Betsy, entered, attired in a day gown of striped lemon yellow and cream, her hair tied simply in a satin bow. Immediately her brows rose. "Still in bed? That isn't like you."

It didn't seem prudent to describe the harrowing experience when she'd brushed up against potential scandal, so Lily just maintained what she hoped was a neutral expression. "I was tired. Tell me, is Harold Dougherty calling again today?"

Betsy's blush well enough answered that question. Good, her sisters were both being courted by quite respectable gentlemen, for Carole also had Lord Davenport sending flowers and showing an avid interest and all Lily wanted was for them both to be happily married to men of their choosing.

"Jonathan quite likes him." Betsy settled into a chair, her bright skirts in a froth of muslin around her. "That is quite a coup. I think Mr. Dougherty was fairly terrified of him at first."

It was true. Their brother was only half English, and the other half was about as barbaric as possible in the eyes of most of society, being a mixture of French and an American Indian tribe. His unusual dark looks did lend him a dangerous air among the pale polish of the *ton*.

Amused, Lily murmured, "Yes, well, he might be an earl, and have recently married the daughter of a duke, but I still think the beau monde expects him to at least exhibit some sort of savage behavior or they will be sorely disappointed."

"You forbade him to act anything but the gentleman." Betsy's smile was mischievous. "I think he might be just a little afraid to disobey you, Lily."

To picture Jonathan, so tall and utterly capable of taking on any danger, afraid of anything brought a laugh. "I think he took my advice so he could impress the lovely Lady Cecily and win her as his wife. It is quite different. Now he is the besotted husband and sequestered in the country with his wife. Not exactly the savage, but remarkably like a refined English lord."

"Perhaps." Betsy paused. "What will you wear to the tea this afternoon?"

It was delicately asked and Lily had to stifle a groan. "I'd forgotten," she muttered, setting aside her chocolate. "I'd rather not attend at all, but—"

"But the duchess is doing it just for you and you beg off often enough as it is."

"I never asked to be thrown into her clutches," Lily pointed out acerbically, which was absolutely true. It was all Jonathan's doing, drat him.

Yet to her benefit, and that of her sisters, so how could she complain?

"She is a bit daunting," Betsy admitted, her fingers plucking at her skirt. "I swear if she looks at me I practically freeze into position like a garden statue. However do you stand it?"

"I look back," Lily said tartly. "Not that I don't appreciate the effort she is undertaking on my behalf, but it isn't for me precisely, but for the sheer sport of it, I imagine. She is much too well bred to admit she finds it a challenge to try to marry me off."

"Not such a challenge. You're lovely."

"You might be biased."

Betsy shook her head. "I'm simply telling the truth. Had it not been for Lord Sebring—"

"It wasn't entirely his fault," Lily interrupted, her tone quiet, not precisely defending the man who had destroyed her reputation but not willing to defame him either. "Let's all recall I agreed to the elopement. That makes me equally culpable in my downfall."

"You are too fair."

"I am realistic."

"You are stubbornly protecting a man who does not deserve it."

Well, there was a reason she loved her sisters after all. Loyalty was as precious as gold. Lily picked up a scone, took a quick bite, and chewed and swallowed, changing the subject. "So I take it Mr. Dougherty will be at the tea and that is why you are so concerned over my attendance."

"And Lord Davenport, so both Carole and I want you to not pull one of your infamous disappearing tricks."

The evening before, the "disappearing trick" had gone severely awry. Or almost so. Perhaps it was a sign she should conform better and not try to sneak off, even if it meant excruciating formal balls and boring teas with her sisters' suitors. "I will be there," she murmured and finished her chocolate.

The house was rather modest, the exterior weathered a bit, and if the servant that answered the door was any indication, the staff limited. Damien relinquished his cloak—the weather had done an abrupt turn from the lovely morning and the day was cool and rainy—to the stolid steward. He then allowed himself to be escorted into the presence of one of the most powerful men in the British Kingdom.

Naively, and he was so far past naive he could not believe it had happened, he'd thought his involvement with Charles Peyton was all over. His host glanced up, set down his pen, and gestured at a chair. "Northfield. Have a seat."

He sat, the antique chair creaking under his weight. It wasn't that he hadn't been in shabby houses before— this was luxurious compared to some of the places he'd stayed in his checkered career—but it was somewhat of a surprise, though he had to admit the view out the window of the Thames was quite spectacular. "Sir."

"I summoned you here for a purpose."

"You do nothing without a purpose, so I suppose that is not a difficult deduction."

The prime minister's most trusted adviser gave him an enigmatic smile. "I wouldn't dream of wasting your time, my lord."

That declaration made him wary indeed. Damien realized he was unconsciously rubbing his aching thigh and stilled his hand at once. His smile was wry. "What do you need, Charles?"

"It's a small matter, really."

No, he was sure it wasn't. Nothing that concerned Sir Charles Peyton was ever a small matter. "I see." Damien settled back, crossing his booted feet in seeming nonchalance. "Go on."

"A mere formality really."

"Ah, well then, I am sure you have any number of lackeys that can handle it for you."

Middle-aged, mild-mannered but sharp as a honed rapier, Charles chuckled, his pale blue eyes suddenly direct. "If so, I would not have sent for you."

"I believe I was relieved of duty when I was wounded and half-dead on the field as the war ended."

"Men like us never retire." Charles sighed and set aside his pen, looking out the window for a moment, his expression contemplative. Then he said, "I think we have a problem. I told Liverpool I would talk to you. His response to consulting you was very flattering, I assure you."

Whenever the prime minister's name came into play, it really was a problem. Damien deliberately looked blander than ever. "Was it?"

Charles was not easy to fool. "You're interested. Good."

"I'm not—"

"You *are*." Peyton leaned forward, picked up a pair of spectacles and put them on, his hand carelessly scooping up a piece of vellum from the cluttered table. "I saw it in your eyes. I assume you will be available if I need you, then."

"You aren't going to tell me exactly what you want me to do now?"

"Did Wellington?"

Ah, so what he remembered of Charles Peyton held true. Wily, evasive, and one of the best manipulators in the business. "Eventually," he commented, knowing a dismissal when he heard one. "Usually at the least opportune time," he added dryly.

"Is there ever an opportune time?"

"It depends on the task. We are no longer at war."

"Aren't we? And here I thought you were English. Surely you took history at Cambridge. We are always at war." Charles shook his head. "Don't be so ingenuous."

Damien was fairly sure he hadn't been called that since he was in knee britches. "Care to explain?"

"I don't often—you know that." Sir Charles stood then and inclined his head. "I'll be in touch."

Damien had to admit he was mystified when he rose and left the room. Even when he walked up the steps to his club nearly an hour later he was not quite sure what the purpose of the summons had been. The interior was familiar, the lighting subdued, the scent of brandy and tobacco in the air, and the sound of voices punctuated by the occasional laugh. The furniture was dark and heavy, the carpet thick, and there seemed to be a fair number of members having either an early dinner or a drink or two. He absently handed his cloak to the attendant and it was a pleasant distraction to be informed his oldest brother was present.

Not that Colton would approve of his recent visit to

Sir Charles, but because Damien occasionally needed a solid dose of stalwart common sense.

If the current Duke of Rolthven was anything, he was pragmatic and dutiful.

"Have a whiskey," his brother said as Damien approached, pushing a half-full glass across the table. "I'll get another."

Damien almost argued, but his leg *did* hurt and he sank down gratefully and picked up the tumbler. Very rarely was his older brother intuitive, so he must have been showing the strain. "Thank you."

"Not at all." Colton glanced at the waiter and the man hastened to bring another glass and the decanter. "You look a little pale. Is something amiss?"

Well, there were treacherous secret staircases and lovely maidens and cryptic spymasters such as Charles Peyton . . . but otherwise life was utterly calm. Damien smiled—he couldn't help it. Perhaps he was just destined to be in the midst of intrigue. "No. Not at all. I had a meeting. I didn't realize you were in town. How is Brianna?"

Colton's blue eyes narrowed as if he wasn't fooled at all, but he said readily, "Fine. The doctors assure me the pregnancy is healthy and normal."

"She looks quite as beautiful as ever to me."

"She has some moments when her stomach is unsettled, but if it is like it was with Frederick, it will pass soon. I make sure the basin is handy in the mornings."

The idea of the very austere Duke of Rolthven assisting someone as they tossed up their breakfast was comical enough Damien had to fight a grin. But the whiskey was smooth and of the best quality and he savored the next sip before he commented. "I'm not sure I am envious of that part of the process of fathering a child."

"Are you envious of any of it?" Colton asked bluntly, his mouth quirking. They resembled each other with the same chestnut hair and Northfield features, but his older brother was definitely more serious, though his marriage had wrought a miraculous change in many ways. He was devoted to his beautiful wife and adored his young son and he smiled now more often. His ducal duties were still important, but no longer the focus of his life.

The change was a welcome one, but Damien found his once self-absorbed brother's recent interest in *his* life and future an irritant. Why was it all married men found a sudden urge to spread the state of matrimony to all single males of their acquaintance like it was a contagious disease?

"I believe I'd enjoy the actual conception," he said dryly. "But I have no obligation as you did to marry and sire an heir for the sake of name and title. There are some advantages to being a younger son. If at some point I meet a woman who captures my interest and keeps it long enough for me to consider a permanent arrangement, *then* I will worry about the less-than-desirable scenario of having to keep a basin on hand for those tricky moments."

"Brianna has said to me more than once that it is far better to be the one holding it than the one using it." Colton refilled his glass, at ease in his chair, long legs extended.

"A valid point," Damien agreed with a laugh. Brianna was a refreshingly candid person. "There are some advantages to being a male."

"And some disadvantages also, such as the privilege of going to war. I'm assuming the drawn look is because of your leg."

He should have known Colton wouldn't let the subject go so easily.

"It hurts now and again." Damien affected a shrug. He was crippled to an extent, but the minor inconvenience and discomfort was a reminder he was lucky to be alive—lucky to still have his leg at all, and he refused to dwell on it other than as a symbol of triumph rather than misery. His family's concern was touching, but really, unnecessary. There was a far more intriguing topic than his leg. "I'm out of touch with society. Tell me, what do you know of the Bourne family?"

Colton was not exactly attuned to the latest gossip and he had never cared for it in the first place, but by necessity he spent a lot of time in London and men talked every bit as much as women. Though it did no young lady's reputation any favors to be found locked in a room with a gentleman who was not her husband, it seemed to Damien—and he'd been thinking about it quite a lot—that Lady Lillian's reaction to the situation had been a bit extreme. There was also the reference to society not considering her innocent. With her beauty she should have been married off several years ago, and he admitted to some curiosity over what had happened.

He was also having some difficulty putting out of his mind how she looked clad only in flimsy linen trimmed with lace, her slender arms bare, the top curves of her creamy breasts exposed, her dainty calves and ankles visible. . . . He'd done his best to conceal his purely male reaction and thought he'd succeeded, but that did not mean the image of her scantily dressed body wasn't all too memorable. She was definitely shaped to his tastes, graceful and feminine.

Even more entrancing than her undeniable physical appeal, she had two traits he very much admired. Courage—he'd felt the way she'd clung to his hand when they entered that extremely narrow dark passageway— and intelligence. Empty-headed females, no matter how beautiful, bored him.

"The Earl of Augustine's family?" Colton frowned. "The American? I only know him in passing, actually. He very recently married Eddington's daughter."

"So his sister mentioned."

"Which one? There are three of them, I believe."

"Lady Lillian." Damien did his best to sound neutral, and he did neutral very well. "We met last evening."

"Oh?" Colton lifted his brows a fraction.

"At Pondsworth's rather tedious rout. At least she could carry on a sensible conversation, but maybe that is just her age. A bit past it for a debutante, isn't she?"

His brother was silent for a moment. "I'm trying to remember. Something happened ... I recall only because she and Brianna made their bow at the same time. I believe Augustine's sister eloped with Viscount Sebring, and as it turned out, he didn't marry her after all. There was a scandal and she retired from society."

That certainly would account for her panic and willingness to resort to a drastic solution to avoid being caught in another very compromising position. "I know Sebring," Damien said slowly, thinking back. "That all seems rather unlike him unless he's changed considerably. We were at Cambridge together and good friends.

I've always thought him a decent sort. Because of the war I haven't seen him in years, but it still seems out of character for the man I once knew."

"I'm not privy to the details." Colton's gaze was speculative. "Shall I ask Brianna if she knows more? You seem quite interested."

Damien wasn't sure how to answer the question.

That of itself was interesting.

Chapter 6

A quiet evening at home was like a gift.

The clink of china came softly, the candles flickered in the candelabra, and they were already past the fish course. The paneled formal dining room was lit by a fire against the cool fall breeze, the flames warm and cozy, if cozy was possible in a room of its size. Once dinner was over, Lily had plans to escape to her room, where Miss Austen's latest work sat by her favorite chair, at this time only half-read. She couldn't wait to finish it.

"I understand you aren't accompanying us out tonight."

She glanced up as the plate of duck with roasted figs was slid in front of her by a footman. James sat across the table, the flickering light doing nice things to the planes of his face. "No," she informed him. "I'm staying in, and if you have plans to scold me for it, don't bother." Lily took a sliver of duck and put it in her mouth. It was delicious, succulent and savory, yet sweet from the figs. She chewed and swallowed it before she added, "It is like a rare glimpse of freedom when one finds herself under the hawklike supervision of the Dowager Duchess of Eddington to have a relaxing night free of societal interaction, and especially so after today's somewhat grueling tea."

"Lily, please," her younger sister Carole said in remonstrance. "I thought it was lovely."

"That is because you were not seated next to an aging baronet," she said, doing her best to adopt a teasing tone.

Lily *had* been seated next to Sir George Hardcourt, who was at least two decades her senior and was already twice widowed. Yes, he was by all accounts wealthy, not unattractive, and while a bit on the dull side, still considered a tolerably good catch, but it had been all she could do to make the requisite small talk, choke down a sweet biscuit, and swallow several cups of tea while glancing as covertly as possible every few minutes at the clock.

Surely the duchess didn't think that Sir George, no matter that he was quite openly in the market for a third wife, would make a suitable husband.

"No, I wasn't," Carole admitted, blushing. She'd sat next to her Lord Davenport, who was both young and attentive, and truly, Lily was delighted her sisters were enjoying such success this season.

"There, you see." Lily took a sip of wine, in her mind the argument settled. It was one matter to sit and flirtatiously enjoy the attentions of a man you liked, and another to suffer through an hour and a half of meaningless conversation with someone old enough to be her father who eyed her as if sizing up a prize mare.

She and Carole might have attended the same tea, but they hadn't quite had an identical experience.

"I understand," James said from across the table, his smile slight. "One traumatizing event a day is more than enough."

He *did* understand her and always had despite his admonishments at the ball, acknowledging that she needed time to herself. That was one lovely aspect to their relationship. He was six years older but they had still spent a great deal of time together as children, and now with Jonathan in the countryside with his new wife for the next few weeks, James had become responsible. Lily couldn't tell if he minded officially squiring them to functions or not, but surely it cut into his personal life—which she hadn't given much consideration to before their interesting exchange last evening. She'd just assumed her cousin followed the usual pursuits of young men from aristocratic families, and actually, though he'd always been discreet, she rather thought he had.

But now she had the impression he was being downright *secretive*.

Interesting.

"I agree." She took another bite of duck, which was actually all the more delicious now that she knew her family was not going to argue her absence from the evening's festivities.

After dinner was over, Lily started to rise and join her sisters as they went upstairs to change but she hesitated, reminding herself she was just going to put on her dressing gown and settle down with her book anyway, and waited as the decanter of port was brought to the table. When the footman exited the room, she cleared her throat. "Do you mind if I stay a moment?"

"Of course not." James sat back down, but there might have been just a slight glimmer of wariness in his eyes. "Would you like a glass?"

Ladies didn't usually join the gentlemen for their

after-dinner port, but then again, they didn't sip brandy while locked in libraries either. "I think I would. Yes, thank you."

Her cousin obligingly went to the sideboard and got a glass, pouring her a measure. Then James lifted his brows in polite inquiry, reclining in his chair, his posture relaxed. "I'm rather glad you decided to join me. Port after dinner is a lonely business when you are the only one present. What is it you wish to discuss with me?"

"Isn't this when you loudly debate politics and tell bawdy jokes?" She smiled back, not quite willing to be so direct, so quickly. "I've never been invited before, but that is what we ladies assume transpires."

"Ah, you see how very dull it would be for me to argue Liverpool's policies all alone, and bawdy jokes are much less amusing when told to oneself. I would much rather discuss what has you so preoccupied. You've been very quiet this evening. Is something amiss?"

"Other than the duchess's misguided matchmaking this afternoon? Sir George as a possible candidate? Truly?"

"In Her Grace's defense, he's a good sort, and considering he asked me about you the other day at Tattersall's, I suspect the seating arrangement was by his request. I believe he referred to you as the 'lovely Lady Lily.'"

It hadn't really occurred to her the duchess might just be obliging her guest. Grudgingly, she said, "I suppose then I can forgive her. I was afraid she was getting discouraged enough she was starting to think the best I could do was a man two decades my senior who would be willing to overlook my less-than-pristine reputation to obtain a young wife."

"I'm certain she thinks no such thing. It isn't your lack of prospects that bothers her, but rather the array of possibilities." James grimaced. "She gets a certain gleam in her eye when she accompanies you to social events, which I admit as a bachelor fills me with terror. Luckily, since I am your cousin, I am not the focus of her attention. I imagine her like a general, with chart and diagrams, and lists of bloodlines and bank accounts. You'll make a brilliant match. I've no doubt of it. She won't have it otherwise."

"I'm glad you find it all so amusing. I could delicately hint that you could use some help in selecting a wife," she said tartly.

"Lillian Bourne, don't you dare."

"Can you tell me what you know about Damien Northfield?"

That stopped him, the glass of port suspended in his fingers, his blue eyes registering surprise. She was a bit surprised too, for she hadn't meant to blurt it out that way. However, this was James. If she could ask anyone and be assured it would stay just between the two of them, he was the one.

The grandiose dining room was quiet, the footmen having departed with the dishes and salvers. James finally said slowly, "Northfield? Rolthven's younger brother? He's a few years older than I am. He left for Spain and he has only recently returned to England even though the war has been over for some time. He was severely wounded at Waterloo as I understand it."

Lord Damien's pronounced limp certainly indicated that was true. "I see," she murmured, remembering the faltering moment on those steep, dust-covered stairs.

"Why do you ask?" James asked simply, his long fingers toying with the stem of his glass, watching her intently.

"He and I have met," she said wryly, "and under the most unusual circumstances possible. Last evening, to be precise. It was why I was absent from the ball for so long."

"Oh?"

The port was warming as she sipped it and recounted the series of events, but omitting the part where she'd removed her gown, for she was sure James would take exception to that in a protective male fashion. He listened with a faint hint of amusement in his eyes, especially at the beginning when she explained how Damien Northfield had been cornered by Lady Piedmont. But all humor vanished when she went on about the broken key, the intractable window, and their final decision to go through the cellars.

"At least he was resourceful," he muttered, his glass empty now. "But, I cannot believe you agreed to the passageway. Nothing terrifies you more."

"I had to." She felt a bit better for being able to tell someone what had happened. "I am uninterested in being the one who constantly brings scandal to our family."

He made an impatient gesture with his hand. "That's hardly true. One error in judgment is hardly constant disgrace. You made a single mistake and I still blame Sebring for it anyway. The only reason I was worried last night was for *your* sake, not the Bourne family. I think I can say fairly that we all feel that way."

James hardly knew the whole truth about her elopement, and she wasn't interested in enlightening him either, though the loyalty was touching. She asked quietly, "Surely you will cross paths with Lord Damien. Can you please discreetly thank him for me for his assistance? I must admit in my rush to return to the ball without being noticed, I just hurried away. He was gallant and I was too flustered to be gracious about it."

There, that should do it. Surely the reason she couldn't stop thinking about Damien Northfield was that she'd dashed off without acknowledging his assistance.

Wasn't it?

"I'll tell him," James said quietly, but his gaze was speculative.

Damien might have returned from war, but he didn't go home.

Duty was one matter, but he declined to stay at the ducal mansion in Mayfair. After all those years of quietly pursuing the French in his own way, frequently behind enemy lines, sometimes hundreds of miles into occupied territory, catching very little sleep, always on his guard, Damien found it disconcerting to be in such a busy household. There were not only servants around every corner, but now that his younger brother, Robert, his lovely wife, Rebecca, and their twin daughters also had a suite in the family wing, the sounds of children laughing and playing were pleasant, but distractingly different than his normal life.

Perhaps he should refer to it as his *former* life.

A part of him wondered if he would ever quite acclimate to civilian existence.

"You took your time."

He registered the voice with unerring recognition and

couldn't help but break into a grin after the first startled moment. "My apologies," he said in a moderate tone that conveyed no emotion. "I didn't know you were coming tonight. You worked quickly."

"Bloody right it was quick. Isn't that what you paid me for?" The familiar silhouette of Alfred Sharpe, a friend from the war, took shape in the shadows. "You know you've a bloody easy house to break into here with the windows and all?"

"Well, houses in London generally do have windows," Damien murmured. He'd thought the same, but then again, there was no need to be on his guard. Still, old habits took time to fade. "I don't keep much money on the premises, and if anyone is that determined, they are welcome to the strongbox. Let's hope they haven't stolen all the whiskey. Would you like a glass?"

"Am I breathing, sir?"

"Seems to me you are." Damien gestured down the hallway, stifling a laugh. "My study is the third door down."

"I know," Alfred informed him. "I've already sampled the whiskey. Damned fine stuff."

He had anticipated just that answer, so he was amused, not annoyed. Damien knew better than to keep important documents in such an obvious location, so the notion of someone prowling his study didn't alarm him. He led the way. "Thank you. You can use the same glass, then."

Sharpe made no sound behind him in the dark. No surprise. They'd learned that technique in Spain together and both knew it well. Damien already had seen that his silent movements startled and unnerved the housekeeper he'd hired and needed to remind himself to clunk around a bit more when he got up in the mornings. With his pronounced limp, that should be easy enough.

Stealth did nothing but alarm the servants. He needed to adjust.

His study was a bit impersonal, the furnishings new, only one painting on the paneled walls; he hadn't gotten that far. A miniature of his father, done the year of his unexpected death, sat on top of a glass-paneled bookcase, but aside from those two items, there was nothing personal in the room.

Pouring himself a glass, he handed the bottle over to Sharpe with a wry smile. "Well? What did you learn?"

"This wasn't a challenge." The young man lounged back, his nose poised over the glass as he inhaled sharply and then took a long sip. He was a bit of an enigma as he was obviously well educated but there was a slight Welsh lilt to his voice and he had the dark hair and coloring of a true Celt. One of the other operatives had once told Damien that Alfred claimed to be from a farm near Cardiff. The polished speech belied the latter, but what really mattered to Damien was that Sharpe had been an invaluable asset during their time in Spain. The man was a wizard at obtaining well-guarded objects, and that included information. In London and at loose ends, he worked for various solicitors on a strictly private basis, investigating everything from adultery to murder.

"I didn't think it really would be difficult, but understandably, if I were asking questions about Lady Lillian, my interest might be misconstrued." Damien kept his expression blasé. He wanted information, but he wasn't going to explain why.

Actually, why the devil *was* he so interested anyway? He wasn't sure of the answer to that introspective question, but what he'd just said was absolutely true. The *ton* was notoriously observant and any gentleman from a prominent family asking pointed questions about a marriageable young lady was bound to end up in the gossip sheets.

Sharpe went on. "Not too much to tell, sir. The lady eloped with Lord Sebring, but she must have changed her mind—maybe he wasn't all he could be between the sheets, milord, you know what I mean—and he returned her to London, but not until they'd spent the night together at a cozy inn up near Northampton."

Damien rather doubted an innocent young lady like Lillian Bourne would have the slightest idea whether or not her lover had acquitted himself well, so that seemed like an unlikely reason for the marriage to fall through, and besides, she must have known her reputation would be in tatters should she change her mind. "Why wasn't Sebring compelled to marry her?"

"No one knows, at least not those I talked to. Lady Lillian's father never challenged the bastard. Curious, that. You aristocrats like to kill each other over lesser slights than letting your daughter be tupped and then not made respectable after the fact. That's why I think it might be her as refused Sebring, rather than the other way around."

It *was* unusual, Damien had to admit. Her father had been an earl, and the English peerage was infamous for not taking insults lightly, not to mention the lingering taint on his daughter's reputation. "Interesting," he agreed, leaning back thoughtfully, his gaze fixed on the painting above the fireplace.

He'd bought it in a dusty shop in Madrid and brought it back with him. The depiction of a Moorish castle at sunset reminded him of Spain in more than just the dramatic landscape, but also the brooding passion of a people who were never quite conquered despite their tumultuous history. The superimposed turrets against a lurid sky were reminiscent of the bloodstained past.

"It is," Alfred agreed, his gaze speculative, "but not half as interesting as why you sent me sniffing around. If you don't mind me saying so, you are well known for keeping your private entanglements separate from business."

Had it not been for his recent meeting with Charles Peyton, Damien would have acerbically pointed out he no longer had a profession. Maybe that's why he was so intrigued by the daring Lillian . . . because he was at loose ends, with an inheritance from his father generous enough he didn't have to work if he didn't wish to, but not the nature to sit idle.

He said with no inflection, "She isn't an entanglement. We simply met under unusual circumstances and I was curious."

"Memorable, is she?" Sharpe had remarkably already drained his glass and set it aside with a definite click.

All that pale skin, the enticing swell of her breasts under the flimsy chemise, the luminescent blue of her eyes . . . yes, Damien remembered Lily Bourne very well. "What about Lord Sebring? Anything unusual there?"

"Has himself a wife now. According to the parlor maid, a bit of a demanding one, Lady Sebring is, but she has her reasons. His lordship doesn't spend a lot of time at home."

Still pining for the woman who had agreed to run off with him but then refused the actual marriage? Damien had to wonder.

And also wonder why he cared one way or the other. It wasn't like they knew each other beyond that one encounter.

Perhaps *that* was the problem.

Chapter 7

The piece of vellum was in his pocket and James had taken it out twice during the course of the evening and looked at it, a small ironic smile touching his mouth.

It was so very Regina.

Tonight.

Nothing more. Just that one word, and she expected, of course, for him to not only understand but also come running.

He would resent it a little more, but he knew she didn't intend it that way. Her artistic soul resisted formality and she would be confounded if he'd take offense because she'd invited him to join her for the evening in such a succinct manner.

So once he'd delivered his cousins back to the Bourne family residence in Mayfair, he requested to have his horse saddled. It was only a few blocks, but it had started to mist and he wasn't so much reluctant to walk, but reluctant to *wait*.

Entirely different.

It was late, dark because of the drizzle, and he walked up the front steps after giving his mount over to a sleepy stable boy with his collar up around his ears.

This time, with her note, Regina had included a key. A first. A coup.

She invited no one into her life lightly.

James inserted it into the lock, turned it, and went inside, doing his best to not drip all over the polished floor of the foyer. It was no surprise there wasn't a hovering servant, as she didn't believe in them, so he carefully hung up his greatcoat himself. Light-footed, he made his way toward her studio.

As expected, there was a light under the door. He thought about knocking, especially as Regina was such a private person, but instead he thought of the key, turned the knob, and stopped cold in the very act of opening the door.

She'd been waiting for him. Or at least he hoped so, because all she wore was a pair of black silk stockings and ruffled garters. Nothing else. Her gaze was intent on the painting he'd seen in its inception last night. Without looking over she murmured, "Come in."

He would have obeyed at once but he was frozen, caught in the vision of her lissome body so tantalizingly exposed in an erotic display of satiny bottom and bare breasts, her pubic hair a dainty dark patch between her legs, her long hair loose and shining. She bent forward to dab at the canvas and her lush bosom swayed just enough to make him take in an audible breath.

Which she heard. Half of London might have heard it.

Regina slanted him an amused glance. "You didn't know I often paint naked?"

"No." James struggled for a similar degree of sophistication as he stared at the beautiful silhouette of her luscious nude curves. "But at least now I have a new fantasy."

She pointed her brush at him playfully. "I'd love to hear it."

Her outrageous nature was such a contrast to his conventionality. Was it the attraction? That they were so disparate in personality? Maybe it was, but he sensed it was something more than that. Certainly he was drawn to her in a fluttering moth-to-flame attraction, but Regina was not just eccentric—though he had to admit the description fit.

"I'd love to tell you." He closed the door, his gaze predatory. "Or better yet *show* you."

"There's no bed."

"Do we need one?"

She seemed to consider it. "We've always used one before, but I'm ... adventurous." She stretched then, her spectacular breasts showcased as her spine arched. Regina's gray eyes held amusement. "But let's keep it comfortable, shall we?"

He tugged at his cravat and promised darkly, "Whatever my lady pleases."

It wasn't like she didn't know she'd been deliberately provocative ... because actually, she didn't paint in the nude at all. She wore boring, practical smocks to prevent her clothes from being soiled, and she quit as soon as the natural light faded, and usually took her dinner alone.

This was a theatrical performance extraordinaire designed to seduce.

"I like the idea of you pleasing me." Her tone was low and deliberately sultry.

She'd summoned him and he had answered. Regina enjoyed the balance of power as it stood, but wasn't sure how long it would take him to realize it might not be as one-sided as it seemed. James was intelligent, articulate, and polished—much more so than she was—and he would see through her soon enough. For right now, though, she liked being in control. His desire for her gave her the upper hand, and as long as she held him sexually, she was not required to address any other possibilities in their relationship.

"Hopefully you'll enjoy every aspect of it," he said huskily.

She was older. Considerably so. Not quite a decade, but at least seven years. She wasn't fashionable, and he could easily make an advantageous marriage. At the moment he was still heir apparent to an earldom because his cousin's wife had not yet given her husband a son.

Not to mention when it was all said and done, even though her brother was a viscount and openly—even warmly—accepted her as his sister, she was still illegitimate. It had never affected her sense of self-worth, but it had certainly influenced her life.

It was actually quite simple. While she could have James, she wished to keep him. When they tired of each other, she would go back to her emancipated existence.

Why did she have the feeling it would never be the same?

Regina brushed it off. At the moment all she wanted to think about was how she was naked, he was shedding his clothes as rapidly as possible, and in moments he would touch her and . . .

His shirt landed on the paint-stained floor with disre-

gard for possible damage, and his tailored jacket followed. Bare-chested, he sat down in her favorite chair to
remove his boots and she languidly set aside her brush
and moved toward him, the weight of her breasts heavy
now that they had tightened in arousal. James watched
her, tossing aside the second boot, and he leaned back,
the bulge of his erection under the fine material of his
doeskin breeches prominent.

The color of his eyes fascinated her. Azure, like a
summer sky. Clear, beautiful, framed with long lashes a
darker shade than his light hair. She'd thought about
painting him—of course she had—but wasn't quite sure
yet how she wanted to do it. In her experience, a work
was always first a fleeting thought based on an image. It
then danced back to tantalize and tease, not a solid vision but a ghost, until it finally took solid form and she
set a clean piece of canvas on the easel and went to work.

"I intend to enjoy this very much." It was a travesty to
waste a perfectly good brush, so she walked over and
slipped it into a jar of spirits, and then wiped her hands
on a clean cloth. He watched her—she could fairly feel
the singe of his heated gaze, and she took her time before turning around. She was already readying for him,
warm between her legs, anticipation building. "That,"
she informed him, "is my favorite chair."

He immediately started to rise. "And I'm sitting in the
presence of a lady. Pardon me, but it's blasted difficult to
take your boots off standing up."

"I'm not offended. Stay right where you are."

James froze, and then settled back, his lean body
tense. "Whatever you wish."

"Besides, do proper ladies," Regina asked him in a

provocative voice, sauntering over, "welcome gentlemen without wearing a stitch more than silk stockings and garters?"

"I admit I don't care what other ladies do, only you." James reached for her again, but she stopped short, shaking her head, her hair moving sensuously against her bare back. "Wait a moment, Mr. Bourne. We need to discuss the rules first. Shall we?"

His brows shot up. "What rules?"

She liked him like this—needy, wanting her, his body so obviously aroused. Regina lifted a foot and put it on the arm of the chair so he had a very clear, explicit view of her sex and was rewarded when a muscle twitched in his jaw. It was a decadent position, but she intended to have a decadent evening. "*My* rules. This is my studio, sacrosanct, inviolate, and no one is usually allowed in here. As my first guest, you must adhere to the protocol."

"Why?" James looked at her—at her face—his gaze probing.

He wasn't asking why he needed to follow the rules. He was asking why he'd been the only one invited. Deliberately, she acted as if she misunderstood. She wasn't ready to explain, mostly because she hadn't analyzed it yet herself. She leaned forward and whispered, "Because, as I said, this is my domain."

"You'd better clarify, then," he said on a growl, his hand sensuously sliding up her thigh, "since my ability to be biddable is crumbling by the moment."

"Take off my stockings."

"My pleasure."

He was quite proficient at it, she discovered, with an economy of motion that involved a deft twist of his fingers on her garters and the swift descent of silk that was rapidly tugged away. Yet even enormously aroused, he was thoughtful enough to not simply toss the expensive silk on the floor, but dropped them on top of his shirt.

She'd lowered her foot to the floor after he'd stripped off her stockings and she stood there, letting her gaze drift down the muscled contours of his torso to the strained material of his breeches. "You look uncomfortable. Let me help."

"I am at your complete disposal, as always." His voice had taken on a husky timbre.

Her fingers grazed his chest, and then lower, across the taut plane of his stomach, the muscles tightening under her questing touch. She undid the fastenings of his breeches slowly, parting the cloth, and finally allowing his rigid cock free. Regina lightly ran her palm up the hard length of his arousal and he sucked in a breath and closed his eyes.

"You seem very . . . ready, darling."

"What gave me away?" His lashes lifted and there was a hint of irony in his eyes. "There are *some* advantages to being female."

"Many actually." She knelt on the floor in front of his chair between his splayed thighs, the pose supplicant, but both of them knew he was the prisoner with her hands caressing his erection. "Men only fool themselves into believing they have all the power. Think back on your history lessons. The lot of you are ruled by this."

When she circled her finger around the tip of his penis, the crest beaded with semen already, his body quivered in response.

Regina went on, enjoying how much he wanted her,

how his knuckles were white where he gripped the arms of the chair. "Helen of Troy? Cleopatra?" She leaned and blew lightly against his heated skin. "And what about Eve? Would Adam have taken that apple if he hadn't wanted her?"

"I am not sure I can debate Original Sin at this moment." James caught her shoulders. "I need to be inside you."

She wasn't statuesque precisely, but Regina was tall for a woman. However, he was taller, stronger, and when he stood abruptly and lifted her in his arms it was done with ease.

"The drop cloth," she suggested, the idea of making love in her studio somehow an aphrodisiac, and though the hardness of the floor was barely buffered by the thin cloth she'd tossed in front of her easel, she didn't mind at all when he laid her down, tore off his breeches, and covered her.

James was not an impetuous man. She knew that, and his abrupt entry made her gasp in triumph over his loss of control, the stiff shaft of his cock impaling her fully, his breathing ragged as his mouth found hers and he kissed her hard the way he knew she liked it; she wasn't a shrinking virgin and didn't wish to be treated like one. Regina arched into the carnal possession, wrapping her legs around his waist, urging him on with her fingertips at the base of his spine.

"Take my word for it," he apologized hoarsely as he slid backward and then plunged forward with a silken thrust. "I can't help this."

Perfect. She didn't want him to be able to hold at bay his desire for her. "Don't stop," she instructed him on a pant, the erotic pleasure a contrast to the solid wood of the floor at her back.

"Like I could," he said on a gasp, moving between her legs with an urgency that consumed them both. Before long Regina moaned, her climb toward orgasmic release intense, swift, powerful, all-consuming.

There was something about the quiet of her studio, with the tall unadorned windows and the more than familiar scent of oils and solvents that added to the excitement. Regina arched, angling her body so he drove in as deeply as possible, not quite mindless but approaching that threshold, and from the rasp of his breathing in her ear, he was almost there as well.

In another moment it would happen. . . .

It did. As if the world stopped just for her, the tightening of her inner muscles in conjunction with the frantic clutch of her hands on his buttocks, unconscious in the rapture, halting the motion of thrust and acceptance, holding him still as he also went rigid and the fierce pulse of his release was accompanied by the rush of the breath out of his lungs.

Sprawled together, not speaking, they lay there for what might have been a few moments or a lifetime, his weight balanced, his face averted as his respiration slowed. Eventually, he spoke on a small, explosive laugh. "Not that I have a single complaint, but my knees will have bruises tomorrow and I cannot imagine it was comfortable for you. Shall we go upstairs to your bedroom?"

"If you wish." At this point she would grant him whatever he wanted, she was so languid and satisfied. "On one condition."

"Oh?" James rose and peered into her face.

"Stay for breakfast."

Any expression bled away, as if he was doing his best to conceal his reaction to that imperious edict. "Of course."

Very carefully, she ventured, "The servants might talk if you accept."

"They might," he agreed softly, brushing back a tendril of hair from her temple.

"One of those winsome young ladies so heavily in pursuit of the current heir of the Earl of Augustine might hear it."

It was so difficult, always, to admit to any weakness, but there it was. It just . . . was. She wasn't quite so young any longer at thirty-five. She wasn't dimpled and smooth-cheeked and fashionably blond . . . just the opposite. She was an older woman, not all that eligible even with her bloodlines, because while her father had been a viscount, her mother had been—to not put too fine a point on it—essentially a whore in the eyes of society. Never mind that she knew her parents had been sincerely in love and would have wed if it was possible, but it had never happened. Her mother had gone to Paris to pursue her artistic endeavors and it wasn't until she realized she was gravely ill that she had written to her former lover to inform him he was a father. To his credit, he had come to France at once, but by then Regina's mother was gone. Viscount Altea had brought his daughter back to England and given her everything possible, but he hadn't been able to provide respectability.

"So?" James smiled as if none of that mattered. "I am not going to stay heir apparent long, I assure you. Jonathan's lovely wife is already with child, and even if it isn't a boy, I anticipate they will have a large family given their passion for each other. Besides, I am not interested in winsome young ladies." He eased free of her body and stood, nude and beautiful as a statue, offering his hand. "But I am very interested in breakfast with the most beautiful woman in London tomorrow morning."

She extended her hand in acceptance and allowed him to pull her easily to her feet and into his embrace. His hot breath brushed her ear. "We will need some sustenance after tonight, trust me."

Chapter 8

Charles Peyton was known to work in convoluted circles that baffled the rational mind. Yet Damien had no doubt that the cryptic message had something to do with what Sir Charles wanted from him, so he sat and pondered the small drawing that had been delivered by a messenger the evening before.

It was nothing more than a caricature of a foppish gentleman, beads of sweat drawn on his brow, one coin on the table in front of him next to a deck of cards, and the caption: *The sport of fools*.

What the devil did that mean?

With it was a street address but no other information, which made him wonder if he couldn't just ignore it, pretend it had never arrived, and go on about his business. After all, he no longer worked for the Crown.

The only catch was he didn't really have much business to attend to. Oh, yes, his investments to manage his pay for his years in the service of King George and his considerable inheritance from his father, but truthfully, that took up precious little time. Colton had an excellent steward who took care of a great deal of it for him for a small salary. Damien hadn't had the occasion to actually spend much money since his return, other than the purchase of the town house and to acquire a new wardrobe that would befit a fashionable gentleman, and while he wasn't frugal, neither did he favor extravagance, unlike so many of his contemporaries.

Which, in a roundabout way, reminded him of Lady Lillian.

She'd also spent a few years away from London's elite circles—and though she'd been most elegantly dressed the other evening before she had so tantalizingly removed her gown, she was probably just adjusting to the *ton* again. Rather like him. Distant from society, cut off in a different world . . .

"I'm sorry, my lord."

Damien glanced up, startled.

Mrs. Wheaton hovered in the doorway of the breakfast room, an apologetic smile on her face. "It's a bit early, I know, but there's a gentleman to see you."

When Charles came into the room, a saturnine smile on his face, Damien couldn't exactly say he was surprised, but there was an element of theatrics he found amusing in a man who was understated in every other way.

"I see you received my message."

"Is that a message?" He pointed at the piece of paper sitting next to his plate.

Charles just looked bland.

"Sit down." Damien motioned to a chair in resignation. "I received the illustration, yes, and assumed it was from you. May I ask why you didn't just bring it yourself?"

"Because I wanted you to ruminate over what it

might mean for a while and I see it worked, for you are breakfasting and thinking about it. Intrigued?"

"Forgive me, but I no longer have a dozen agents to call upon for information. You will have to enlighten me before I offer help with the matter you mentioned in our last meeting—which I am not convinced I should even give."

Charles took a seat, his thinning hair brushed back neatly, his expression as unreadable as ever. He looked at the toast rack. "May I?"

"Please," Damien responded, pushing the marmalade jar closer to his unexpected guest. Mrs. Wheaton efficiently whisked back in with a plate, napkin, and the necessary cutlery. She hastened to pour a cup of coffee, adjusted the cream pitcher just so, and then discreetly left the room, hurriedly closing the door behind her.

At that moment Damien realized that though the staff might not know anything about what he'd done during the war, they had no illusions that his visitors were not of the ordinary kind.

"Tell me, what do you think of my little drawing?" Charles dropped several lumps of sugar in his cup and stirred as if he were discussing the weather and stopped by for crumpets each morning.

"I think the subject's nose might be a tad too long for physical symmetry. . . . Is there a point to this special delivery and unexpected visit?'

"The artwork could be better. It's a hobby, nothing more. Dabble in it to soothe my nerves," Peyton admitted.

"You don't have any nerves, Charles."

His guest lifted his cup to his mouth, took a measured

sip, and then smiled. He rather resembled a benign shark baring his teeth as he circled, in Damien's opinion. "Excellent coffee."

"I will convey to Mrs. Wheaton your compliments." Damien sat back, aware enough that Charles did everything in his own time. "I'm sure she'll be flattered."

"We have a small problem that I hoped you might clear up for me."

Well, at least it wasn't going to take forever. Damien made an encouraging sound and took a bite of toast.

"It's delicate." Charles decided on the marmalade and scooped some out of the jar, spreading it liberally on his toast. "It occurred to me that since you've made a rare art form of finding information and keeping the good while discarding the bad, all the while being quiet about it, you might be just the man for the task."

It was a bit cloudy outside, just overcast enough to give the sky a tinge of gray, with a whiff of rain in the air. Damien contemplated the leaden horizon through the window. "Most information is neither good nor bad. It just depends on the perspective of the one receiving it."

"So true." Charles took a generous bite of his toast and then meticulously wiped his mouth with his napkin.

Damien had to laugh. "It tends to make me nervous when you agree with me.... What is it you want, Charles?"

"I thought I just made it clear that I want you to seek and find who is causing this ... sticky problem. There could be more than one quarry. I'm inclined to think so. It should be a small task. From the accolades you gained in the war, we both know the assignment will not be much of a feat for you."

"Last I knew, I was no longer in the service of the Crown," Damien said dryly, picking up one last forkful of eggs.

There was a little bacon left and Charles took it, making an appreciative sound in his throat. "A mere detail."

"Perhaps it isn't to me."

"Humph." Charles shot him a glance. "Is that so? Tell me no, and I will leave. After all, this requires discretion of the highest kind, and I have little desire to waste my time."

Damn the man.

Maybe it was the realization that both his brothers were happily married men with families; that most of his adult life had been spent on a cause that was over and done with, and that while he might enjoy the freedom of not looking constantly over his shoulder, he still had the hunger of the hunt.

And Charles, the sly fox, knew it even as he wiped his fingers on a pristine white napkin and refilled his own cup with a flourish.

Damien said abruptly, "What does the address mean?"

"Ah, I thought you would not be able to resist."

"It seems intrigue follows me, but at least you are not a young lady urgently needing a secret passage."

For once Charles was the one who looked perplexed. "I beg your pardon?"

"Never mind. Who would I be looking for, and why is this important to the British government?"

"Did I mention the British government?"

Damien set down his cup with a decided clink. "Damn all, Charles, if you are asking for my help, don't dance around it."

"As I said, it's all very delicate." Charles sighed. "And

you are right, *I* am asking for your help. It's quite personal, but I suppose you will have to know the particulars. Perhaps you could ask if Mrs. Wheaton could bring us some more coffee. Aside from a bit of sordid blackmail, someone is missing, and I fear he might turn up as another suicide. Ask her for more of that delectable jam, as well, will you?"

"How awkward this is." The words fell starkly into the stilted silence.

Damn, Lily thought, hoping her consternation didn't show.

The chance meeting was unfortunate, but it was also bound to happen. Actually, Lily was surprised she hadn't crossed paths with Lady Sebring before now. Certainly they'd taken care to avoid each other at public functions now that Lily had rejoined society, but until this moment, they had never come face-to-face in relative privacy.

The foyer of the fashionable establishment was a reflection of the expensive price of patronizing it, the polished floors inlaid with Italian marble, and there were twin columns on either side of the etched glass doors and flowers in urns on small tables. Not the best place to confront her former fiancé's wife. Everyone in elite society who could afford it passed through there, but for the moment, at least, they were alone.

There was a minute of pure female assessment, and Lily was glad she'd worn her new muslin day gown embroidered with tiny lilac flowers, for it was both flattering and youthful. The other woman's scrutiny was somewhat unnerving, so she returned it in kind.

Arthur's wife was shorter by several inches, more curvaceous, her dark hair looped into an intricate coil. Up close she was not homely by any means, but not prepossessing either, with plain features and narrow eyes, though she was dressed in the height of fashion in green and ivory, a peacock feather in her stylish hat.

Why not? Her husband was a rich man.

Lily fully understood why Arthur had married the woman. His father-in-law wielded power in Parliament, whereas her father—though an earl—had never been very much interested in British politics and had, in fact, married an American. After his first wife's untimely death, he'd done his duty and wed her mother, a proper English lady, but his unconventional first marriage was what people remembered about him.

All of that didn't matter, Lily thought, doing her best to not hold herself stiffly. Though to save her life, she could not muster a conciliatory smile. "Lady Sebring."

"Lady *Lillian*." The distinction was made with chilly emphasis. "I've heard, of course, of your return to the circles of the *ton*, and it must be true, for here you are at London's most prestigious dressmaker."

Heard? Lily was sure Arthur's wife had been given a step-by-step chronicle of her every move. The gossip mill could never resist a tidbit like a jilted fiancée resurfacing after four years of self-imposed exile, but she'd done it because Jonathan had insisted she no longer languish in the countryside, and also for Betsy and Carole. Toss in the Dowager Duchess of Eddington sponsoring her and tongues were wagging. Lily knew it.

"I'm due for a fitting." She tried to not sound too curt, but as she went to step past, Penelope Kerr, Lady Sebring, moved in front of her.

"Stay away from him." The words were hissed with emphasis.

In her life, she couldn't quite remember ever being so startled. Lily froze and then summoned her composure. "From whom?"

"My husband."

"It seems to me we parted ways years ago."

"I know he came to visit you a few months ago."

Since that was perfectly true, she had no idea what to say. Her former fiancé had called unexpectedly one evening and they had talked for the first time since their ill-fated elopement, but the nature of that conversation had been private and she wasn't inclined to share it, nor did she really think she should be forced to defend herself.

She was the one who had been ruined. *Am I not the wronged party?*

"What's this?"

Normally, Lily had to admit the dowager's frosty voice made her grimace, but in this instance, it was welcome. She hadn't realized they were alone no longer. Eugenia Francis had entered the foyer, small but regal, her tone uncompromising. Her height was diminutive, but her presence immense as always. "Oh, I see. Lady Sebring. Delightful to see you, but we have an appointment to keep. Please excuse us."

As a dismissal it was well done, and grudgingly, Arthur's wife stepped aside. Lily had to admit she was a bit shaken from the incident, for while she'd expected awkwardness, the open venom was an unfortunate surprise. She waited as a footman swept open the door for the duchess and then she followed, knowing to her chagrin her cheeks held a certain level of warmth.

"Think nothing of it," the duchess murmured as they entered the shop. "She is below your regard." There was a pronounced sniff. "It was common of her to confront you. It isn't done."

Certainly not in the company of the Dowager Duchess of Eddington.

For the first time Lily felt a flicker of gratitude to her brother for putting her in the path of such a formidable woman. "Yes, ma'am."

"I wouldn't have scheduled this fitting, because your brother has been most generous in his largess when it comes to your wardrobe, but I feel we need something truly stunning for the Wainworth gala next month."

The next several hours were a bit grueling because the duchess had very rigid ideas and was not averse to expressing them, and bolts and bolts of fabric were trundled out, dismissed, and sometimes ordered brought back in until a delicate blue watered silk was selected, the style of the gown debated from the plates offered, and Lily was measured yet again.

It wasn't until they were back in the carriage that the duchess leveled at her an appraising stare and resurrected the forbidden topic. "*Did* Sebring come to see you?"

Oh, wonderful . . . she overheard.

They were in the ducal carriage, which was an impressive vehicle. Lily leaned back against the comfortable squabs and decided to be as honest as possible, though complete disclosure wasn't an option. "Yes," she admitted. "But it was hardly covert. He called at the house in Mayfair. Jonathan was out with Carole and Betsy, so I did receive him alone, but until now, I wasn't aware his wife knew of it."

The dowager folded her hands in her lap, her gaze direct. "May I ask why you chose to see the man who damaged your reputation and offered nothing in return?"

It wasn't the easiest question to answer. A part of her resented the intrusion, but then again, her mother was gone, and the duchess had taken some time and effort to try and support her sisters—and herself—this season. It was probably only because her granddaughter had married Jonathan, but still, she did deserve a reply. Lily cleared her throat and caught the strap as they rounded a corner. "Arthur came to tell me he feared his wife was barren."

That was innocuous enough, since the viscountess had not yet produced a child, which was hardly a secret.

A frown deepened the wrinkles on the forehead of the woman seated across from her. "I . . . see. Well, no, I retract that. I *don't* see. Why confide in you, of all people? Tell me he wasn't lamenting his decision to not marry you because you might make a more fertile broodmare."

There was no help for it. Though it was hardly a humorous discussion, Lily had to stifle a laugh at the blunt analogy from someone who was usually much more refined. "No." She could say that with conviction. "I do not believe he thinks of me in that manner at all."

"Then?"

There seemed no choice but to be as frank as was possible. "We were friends long before he offered to wed me. I think he was at a loss and just needed to tell someone about his wife's failure to conceive. Someone who would listen. A man hardly wishes to confide in his fellow males he might be unable to sire the needed heir."

"You do not seem the most logical sympathetic ear."

With a gloved hand, Lily adjusted her embroidered skirt as she contemplated her answer. Eventually, she said, "We didn't understand each other back during our engagement, he and I. We do now. I do not regret he married someone else."

"Does he?"

That was a tricky question, to be sure. Lily waited a moment, and then said, "I don't know if he regrets marrying his wife, but I do know he doesn't regret not marrying me."

For a minute sharp eyes studied her from across the carriage and then the duchess nodded once. "Fine, then. Lord Sebring is dismissed. Assure me I am correct."

"Absolutely," Lily was able to say.

Chapter 9

Once a spy, apparently always a spy.

She *was* there.

Damien was not even conscious that he'd been scanning the crowd for her, roaming the room as casually as possible, and usually he was quite aware of his every thought and action. It was another warm evening and several sets of French doors to the terrace were open and he found her near one of those, standing in a small group of ladies, two of whom he realized must be her sisters from the family resemblance, the other a dark-haired young woman he didn't recognize, but that wasn't surprising. He'd been in Spain a long time.

Lady Lillian wore a very delicate shade of topaz this evening, the gown emphasizing her graceful form, her glossy hair upswept but with several long curls loosely brushing her ivory shoulders, and as he watched, the woman standing next to her leaned closer and said something that made her laugh. He was close enough that he heard the melodic sound, and he had to admit he was . . . charmed.

By a laugh? That was unique in his experience. Perhaps, he decided, leaning against the wall in feigned non-chalance, he was adjusting to civilian life. What was there to object to after all? Champagne, leisure time, beautiful women . . .

Well, one beautiful woman anyway. He watched as her hand reached up to brush a wayward curl from her cheek in a graceful sweep.

Why *had* he enlisted Sharpe to find out all he could about her?

He wasn't sure.

"What's so fascinating?"

Damien glanced over and saw his younger brother, Robert, saunter up, a small smile on his face. "I thought you were in the country at Rolthven."

"Obviously not." Robert lifted his brows. "I had some business in London. Which of those ladies inspires such concentrated interest?"

He supposed he had been staring quite directly, but he evaded a direct response. "When did you get back into town?"

"This morning. Rebecca and the children are still in the country. And you never answered my question, which is an annoying habit you have, by the way. The luscious brunette on the left is Lillian Bourne, if I am not mistaken. I remember the year she was a debutante. She looks quite lovely this evening, doesn't she?"

It was irritating to be so easily discovered in covert—or not so covert—observation of a subject. Damien contemplated denying it, but this was not a secret mission after all. Trust Robert also to hone in on the beauty of the group. At one time, his younger brother had been infamously known for his interest in the fairer sex. "Yes, she does. We met recently. I must admit I found her not the usual simpering miss."

Robert was immaculately attired, of course. He was always dressed in the latest style, his cravat crisp, white perfection, his evening clothes fashionably tailored, a hint of lace at his cuffs. He murmured, "But then again, she isn't much of a miss any longer, is she? Her bow was at least four seasons ago."

"So I understand."

His brother gazed at him, open speculation in his eyes. "I recognize that tone."

"What tone? As far as I can tell, I have no particular tone."

"Exactly. When your voice has absolutely no inflection— which you do quite well—it always means something."

Damien lifted the corner of his mouth in a cynical twist. "All it means is that I do not wish to discuss the subject at hand. Is Colt here too?"

Robert accepted a glass of champagne from a foot-man with a tray of fluted glasses and shook his head. "Impending fatherhood has him hovering over Brianna like a nursemaid. Why don't you ask her to dance?"

"Brianna? She's married to my brother and breeding. Not to mention she isn't here."

"Deliberate obtuseness doesn't suit you." Robert dangled his glass in long fingers, his gaze fastened on the small group where Lillian stood. "You know full well who I mean. I admit there is some scandal attached to her name, but then again, I have never been one to care much about notoriety myself, which is hardly a secret. Besides, she's . . . interesting. She has a past, and that is precisely the type of trait you would look for in a woman. No one knows what happened between her and Sebring during their ill-fated elopement. Secrets are your specialty."

"Not of that kind."

"But you don't have the others any longer."

A damnable truth. At least there was Charles Peyton and his interesting request, but he could hardly point that out. Damien murmured, "I can't dance, or have you forgotten?"

It was clear Robert had. He looked startled, a chagrined expression creeping across his face. He said slowly, "Actually, yes. I never think of you as—"

"Crippled?" Damien supplied the word ironically.

"Not at all what I was going to say," Robert muttered. "Bloody hell, Dame, I was going to point out that you've always been able to do anything you set your mind to so easily, it just didn't occur to me that a simple dance would be a problem. My apologies. The war didn't leave you unscathed, I know that."

"No need to apologize." Damien hadn't even realized that it bothered him. Dancing hadn't been high on the list of priorities in his life and he had never thought of his injured leg as anything but a nuisance.

Until now. He really could not even offer Lily a simple dance.

He went on. "But I'm afraid a waltz executed with any finesse is beyond my ability. So while your suggestion is intriguing, a dance with the lovely Lillian is out of the question."

"I suppose that is true." Robert studiously sipped champagne and frowned.

"I dislike that expression on your face," Damien observed. "It means you are thinking, and even worse, thinking about the female of our species, and quite frankly, it makes me nervous."

Robert grinned over the rim of his glass. "It *is* one of my favorite subjects of reflection. Ask my wife."

"In the context of *your* life, that contemplation is fine. Leave my private affairs out of it."

"I am not sure I knew you had private affairs, but it is enlightening to hear you do, brother. Perhaps instead of a waltz, you could simply go over and speak with her."

"Are you matchmaking? If so, I don't need your helpful suggestions."

"No?" his brother drawled.

"No." The one word was firm and definite.

"Well, you should form your own plan, then, for the lady appears to have noticed you as well. She is headed in this direction."

Had Damien not been rigidly trained to conceal any reaction unless the situation warranted it, he would have looked. But he merely stayed where he was with one shoulder against the ballroom wall, his demeanor diffident.

"Lord Damien."

He straightened and turned with a polite smile. "Lady Lillian."

She was only a few paces away, the topaz gown flowing around her, just a hint of vulnerability in her eyes. "I . . . I . . . Good evening."

"Good evening," he said neutrally, wondering why the slight falter. "Have you met my brother Robert?"

"Indeed, we have been introduced." Robert bent over

her hand with the smooth charm that had served him so well before his marriage, when he had been one of England's most noted rakehells. "But it has been far too long. May I say you are dazzling this evening, my lady."

"Thank you." The slip in her composure was gone and she spoke with calm dignity.

"If you will excuse me, I believe I asked Aunt Beatrice for the next dance and if I do not show up promptly, I will never hear the end of it." Robert released her hand and smiled.

It was an obvious enough ploy and Damien watched him slip back into the crowd with amusement over the lack of subtlety.

"I did not mean to interrupt."

Damien lifted a brow. "Not at all. I would much rather converse with a beautiful lady than my stodgy brother, trust me."

"Stodgy?" Lillian said incredulously. "Robert Northfield? I rather think most people would disagree with you, my lord."

"You'd be surprised what a respectable marriage and fatherhood will do to a formerly disreputable rogue," he murmured, doing his best to not let his gaze drift down to where her décolletage showed a tantalizing hint of the valley between her breasts. Her gown was not scandalous in the least, but perhaps because she was not an innocent young miss, it was a bit more daring than what most of the unmarried young ladies were wearing and he . . . noticed.

Definitely noticed.

"Is that so?" Her blue eyes held a hint of laughter. "Spoken as the only unmarried brother out of three?"

What else did she know about him? He had to wonder if she'd also been asking questions about her partner
in their little misadventure with the library door. "Let's
just say having the concentrated attention of my entire
family on my unwedded state is a bit of an annoyance.
Fighting the French was an easier proposition."

"You are speaking to the woman who currently holds
the attention of the Dowager Duchess of Eddington,"
Lillian said dryly. "At the end of the evening there will a
summary of how many times I was asked to dance, what
comments were made about my gown, and a recounting
of what events I've been invited to in the next few weeks,
not to mention a reminder that the season will not last
forever."

He liked her candor. *And the shape of her lips, and the
way the length of her lashes throws shadows on her delicate cheekbones, and . . .*

"Thank the heavens for that last bit." Damien hesitated, but his limp was no secret to her after his near fall
on the stairs the other evening as they made their inventive escape, so he said simply, "I cannot ask you to dance,
but maybe a few minutes of fresh air on the terrace?"

It was a starlit night with just a few wayward wispy
clouds and a scythe of a moon, and though maybe she
shouldn't have stepped outside with him, they were in
plain enough view of the crowded ballroom and it was a
relief to escape.

"I wondered if you'd spoken yet with my cousin
James," Lily said in way of explanation for her forward
behavior in approaching him in the first place. She wasn't
vain enough to think the entire ballroom was focused on

her every movement—they certainly weren't, and besides, it was quite crowded—but it probably would be noted she'd come over to talk to him.

Lord Damien shook his head. "No. Why?"

"I asked him to thank you for me for your aid the other evening, should you run into each other."

"Thank me?" He actually looked surprised.

"You did provide an unorthodox but effective rescue." She tried to keep from blushing when she recalled how she'd taken off her gown in front of him, but felt the warm rush of blood into her neck and face anyway.

"There's no need for any gratitude. I believe I was the one who intruded on your privacy, with Lady Piedmont barging in as well, and then locked the door at her departure, the cause and effect bringing on the possible catastrophe. Entirely my fault."

"You are just being gallant."

"Not at all."

He was more handsome than she remembered, or else it had just been the lighting in the library. There was an elegant cast to his features, and his thick hair was deliciously wavy in places, curling against his cravat.

And those dark eyes. So penetrating . . . as if he could look right through her and scrutinize her soul.

What does he see?

The lilt of the music came through the open doors and she listened to the crescendo, enjoying it much more out of the crowd. She said lightly, "The point is there *was* no catastrophe, due to your fast thinking, and I hurried away without expressing my gratitude. I felt decidedly ungracious when I realized it later."

His lashes lowered a little and the intenseness of his

regard made her want to fidget, though she stood by the balustrade and kept the most serene expression possible on her face. "Tell me, did you jilt Sebring, or was it the other way around?"

The personal nature of the question made her stiffen, but then again, she'd told him outright the other evening she couldn't afford social disgrace again, and no doubt he had been curious as to why. He'd hear it sooner or later anyway, but it bothered her more than it usually did to think he'd been told the tawdry story of her failed elopement.

She barely knew him. *Why do I care what he thinks of me*?

Very carefully, Lily said, "That is between the two of us."

"Fair enough." He inclined his head, tall in the filtered light, his lean body shifted just enough to one side so she knew his leg pained him. It was curious, but while she'd been crippled socially, he had been physically, and she had to wonder if that was why she'd experienced a sense of camaraderie with him so quickly.

"The question isn't unreasonable," she said with as little emotion as possible in her voice, "but without explaining in detail, the answer isn't simple."

"Perhaps I phrased it poorly, for what I meant to say was that I find it hard to believe he would change his mind."

There was a strange little flutter in the pit of her stomach. "If that was a compliment, thank you."

"It was indeed."

"That was all four years ago. Arthur is a married man, and I see no reason to dwell on the past."

"A sound attitude." His smile was remote, brief, detached. "I've been trying to decide since my return to England exactly how to do just that, but with very little success so far."

She rested a gloved hand on the balustrade and gazed out over the garden. "I am sure war is not easy to forget. I can't imagine."

"I wouldn't even want you to try to do so."

The temptation was there to ask him about his leg since they were on the subject, but she had just declined to explain to him, and though she doubted he was the type to be sensitive on the subject, maybe his disability did bother him. Men could be the oddest creatures when it came to pride.

She had that same flaw also. It had cost her to rejoin the higher circles of the beau monde with her head held high. Thanks to the duchess, she'd been invited to almost all the notable social affairs, but her welcome was usually lukewarm at best, and it stung each time.

The British aristocracy was not known for its forgiving nature.

Lily opened her mouth to say something innocuous then, a change in subject from the uncomfortable topics of disgrace or war, when he touched her, his hand closing over her wrist, and he tugged her back into the darker recess of the shadowed corner of the terrace, away from the doors, saying softly, "Shhh."

Chapter 10

He hadn't attended this event for the social aspect of the festivities. Yes, once he'd arrived he had found himself eagerly looking around for the woman now standing next to him, but he'd really come for a different purpose.

Edgar Kinkannon.

The man who resided at the address on the drawing Charles had sent him.

How convenient the gentleman in question—who upon inquiry wasn't much of a gentleman at all—had just ventured out onto the terrace. He was alone, but Damien recognized easily that studied nonchalance, the casual air, the assessing and seemingly unconcerned sweep of his gaze. . . .

Not all thieves were spies, but *all* spies were thieves, if one counted information as property, especially when put in valuable documents. It was easy enough to recognize a man on his way to an assignation, having done the same many times himself, and Damien had no desire to be recognized at this point, so he turned to Lillian just enough so his face was averted, and leaned forward to whisper in her ear. "You can return the favor of the other evening by doing as I ask."

He very lightly set his hand at her waist, his posture loverlike, his mouth brushing her slender neck, making her take in a sharp inhale over the liberty, but the pose effectively hiding his identity in their shadowed corner. "Just pretend we are out here to have a moment alone and please watch and see which direction he goes."

The lovely Lillian was a quick study. Under the circumstances she could easily have been outraged, but she instead nodded almost imperceptibly. She smelled delicious, Damien noted, like spring flowers, light and sweet, and her skin was delicately smooth. Unbidden, the image of her supple body clad only in her chemise came to mind, and for a moment he wished Kinkannon would do him a favor and linger, but unfortunately, the man was not so thoughtful. Damien heard the rap of footsteps on the stone steps and then nothing but the light flutter of the leaves on a nearby ornamental tree brushed by the evening breeze.

She said very quietly, "He took the path to the right."

With some reluctance Damien lifted his head, evaluated again just how much he wanted to help Charles on this little matter, but then decided he shouldn't keep her outside any longer anyway for the sake of propriety, and offered his arm. "Thank you. Allow me to escort you back inside."

Her fingers touched his sleeve and she said under her breath, "On the provision you might in the future provide an explanation."

Damien smiled at the touch of asperity in her tone.

Whatever had happened between her and Sebring, she was not a woman to be lightly dismissed. "I certainly should, shouldn't I? I'll call on you, Lady Lillian."

Had he really just said that?

Her startled glance told him he had, but this wasn't the time to linger. Making sure their public entrance back into the ballroom was noted, he politely excused himself in the hearing of others, and made his way through the crowd toward the front entrance.

Then took an abrupt turn in the main hallway.

If he hurried, he might not miss the meeting. It wasn't too difficult to determine the layout of the house, and he found the conservatory, which opened, of course, to the gardens. The glassed room was redolent with the scent of hothouse flowers and damp soil, and not lit, so he had to inch along the rows of plants set up on shelves. There was no way to tell where exactly his quarry had been headed, but if it were up to him, he'd choose the back where a small vegetable garden joined the floral beds, certainly not frequented at this time in the evening, and never by guests.

Unfortunately, he and Mr. Kinkannon did not share the same crafty views on furtive meetings.

The vegetable garden was empty, the starlit landscape of plebian plants undisturbed, and Damien stood there for a moment, weighing his options. He was unconvinced his particular level of professional expertise was suited to the task at hand. It should be simple.

So . . . *think simple.*

That was not his first impulse. Complicated was more his bent. He tended to walk around a problem, expecting to pit his wits against a formidable opponent. The need to circle first was paramount, like sending out a scout to find the perimeter of the enemy lines.

This was a much more straightforward matter.

So where would there be cover but not damp? Privacy but without the inconvenience of soiling his boots in garden dirt?

Kinkannon was in the arbor, he discovered, waiting with an impatience that was evident even in the filtered starlight, his fingers drumming against his thigh. The man was stocky, but not given over to fat, his fair hair brushed back in a fashionable style, and really, had Damien not known Charles's suspicions—and Charles was rarely wrong—he would not have guessed him an amateur blackmailer that fastened upon susceptible victims of society who cringed at the idea of their sins being exposed.

He might also be a murderer.

There was the matter of the missing Niles Hand, the valet of a very prominent man.

Unless, of course, the young man had simply left of his own accord. But according to Charles, all his belongings were in his room, and he'd been a faithful servant whom no one thought would abandon his post without due notice. When the rest of the staff had been questioned, one of the footmen had confessed that Hand had seemed preoccupied and edgy, and mentioned the name Kinkannon in connection with some meeting just a few days before he disappeared.

If Kinkannon was responsible in some way, he'd made a grave error, for it had brought him to the attention of Charles Peyton, and anyone who had something to hide should avoid that possibility at all costs.

"What do you want?"

A figure materialized on the path outside the neatly trimmed trees, his stance unmistakably tense even in the uncertain light. Damien stood back, deep in the shadows, silent and unmoving.

"Lawson, unless you pay me, you will be exposed for the wastrel you are."

The new arrival was a slim young man who clenched his fists at his sides, his face working. "I couldn't pay my debts. How can I possibly pay you?"

"You'll think of a way."

"Damn all, Kinkannon, don't you think if I could I would have by now? Why are you doing this to me?"

"Just helping out a friend."

"By buying my markers and asking for twice as much?"

"Do you think Lord Hanover would let you near his precious daughter if he knew the current debacle you've made of managing your inheritance? You've squandered every farthing and then some. If you are at all fond of Hanover's winsome daughter, and the idea of debtor's prison is unappealing . . . well . . ." Kinkannon spread his hands and shrugged. "I'll give you a week."

In the starlit garden, Lawson's face was bone white. "You're trying to ruin me."

"Pay and I won't."

"I *can't*."

Raw desperation held a singular note that always touched Damien's soul. It did not, however, have the same effect on Kinkannon. He said coldly, "You are an addle-brained fool to find yourself in these circumstances in the first place. You gambled away a decent portion and now your lady love might not be interested after all. That's hardly my affair. All I want is my money."

As Damien watched, the young man turned away, shaking. "I'll . . . I'll get it somehow. The last thing I want is for him to know, but my uncle Charles will help me."

Uncle Charles.

As in . . . Charles?

Damien's attention sharpened. No wonder there was such keen interest in a possible blackmail scheme. Charles had a habit of being cryptic, but the request for this surveillance now made sense. His uncle, Damien hated to tell the young man, evidently already knew.

"There's another choice." Kinkannon's voice was silky smooth. "I gave you the note on our last meeting."

"No. Never."

"You might want to reconsider."

"No!"

"As you wish." Kinkannon shrugged.

"I *can't*."

"I'll expect payment soon, then," Kinkannon said scathingly and turned away.

Damien waited for them both to leave, Henry Lawson stumbling down the path first, and then Kinkannon strolling along later after him, his features set in a mask of self-satisfaction. Charles had wanted complete discretion, and it was no wonder. His own family was involved.

It had taken the efficient Alfred Sharpe all of a day to gather information on their suspect, including the fact that he was going to be at this event. Edgar Kinkannon was a bit older than the rest of the circle of youngbloods he kept company with, and oddly enough, there was little to no information on his background but some vague story of being in the army. It seemed, too, he was getting richer, though his investments were modest.

Recently, one of Henry's friends, the son of a viscount, had committed suicide.

Damien wondered, as he stood there in the darkness, if he didn't know why now. This could be more of a problem than Charles imagined, for he'd already determined Kinkannon didn't act alone.

What was the second choice Henry declined?

At home there was a book by her favorite chair and no doubt her nightdress on the neatly turned down bed. She could order up tea and read by the fire. . . .

But for now Lily had to waltz with Sir George Hardcourt, who seemed to be inescapable after tea the other afternoon.

Damn all.

Part of the trouble was James was right. Sir George was basically a nice man. There was nothing disrespectful in the way he looked at her, or in the way he treated her, and he didn't seem at all reluctant to be obvious about a possible courtship. All of that was thanks to the duchess, she had no doubt, for even with her father's status, she'd seen the way supposed *gentlemen* had looked at her after her botched elopement. Those sly, lecherous glances were both embarrassing and infuriating. The double standard held her accountable for that infamous night at the inn, but Arthur had emerged from the scandal unscathed enough he still made an advantageous marriage.

She'd fallen in love with a man who had effectively fooled her in every way. At least Sir George was everything he seemed. Bluff, a little too earnest maybe, but . . . a good sort.

Nothing at all like the much more mysterious Damien Northfield.

As quickly as the dance ended, she smiled and escaped, fleeing toward where the duchess held court in one corner, surrounded by her entourage, most of them ladies of a similar age. Lily smiled at the sharp look she received as she sat down, doing her best to seem artless and innocent, but . . .

The Dowager Duchess of Eddington wasn't easily fooled. She leaned over once the music started again and asked, "Was it really seemly to go outside with Rolthven's younger brother?"

"He can't dance, so he invited me for a moment on the terrace instead."

"Oh." The duchess looked nonplussed for a moment, which didn't happen often. Of course, she recovered at once. "I suppose he can't. I'd forgotten."

Lily smiled serenely, adjusting her skirts with a languid hand.

"But still, he is an unmarried young man and—"

"And do not worry—he can hardly ravish me. I believe I can run faster, so I felt safe enough should Lord Damien's intentions turn lascivious."

It would have helped if at that moment she hadn't recalled how his warm breath felt feathering across her neck. While she was intensely curious as to why he'd reacted in such a way to the arrival of the man whom he'd asked her to watch leave the terrace, she couldn't quite shake off that one singular moment.

There were times when Lily thought possibly—

though a bit of imagination was required to picture it—
the duchess had a sense of humor. Just perhaps her lips
quirked a little, but then she settled into a stony glare.

"Lord Damien's mobility aside, you cannot afford a
single blemish this season."

The issue wasn't her complexion, but her reputation.
She knew it, and that is why she'd shied away from society for four long years. The only reason she'd complied
with this return to social events was her family. Jonathan
had all but ordered her out of her self-imposed seclusion
and she was willing to do it until Betsy and Carole were
settled. Mildly, Lily pointed out, "He's the younger
brother of an irreproachable duke."

"Perhaps."

"I don't think the bloodlines are disputed."

"I meant"—the duchess looked severely disapproving at the levity of her tone—"that I am not so sure
Rolthven's immaculate reputation outweighs that of his
younger brother. Robert Northfield was a rake of notorious stature before he married. Of the three brothers,
Lord Damien is an enigma to the *ton*, and as such, of
interest."

Lord Damien, as far as Lily could tell, was no doubt an
enigma to everyone, including France's finest intelligence
officers. However, she found herself thinking about how
tantalizing it had been to feel his lips whisper soft on her
throat, tracing a trail down from her ear, and the warm
clasp of his hand at her waist. She revealed almost invol-
untarily, "He mentioned he might call on me."

The music had started again and the duchess seemed
not to hear, her gaze fixed on the swirling melee of dancers before she murmured, "That is interesting."

"I agree," Lily acquiesced, because it was the truth. Damien Northfield could easily sit in a drawing room and sip tea and converse politely, because she guessed he could do almost anything easily, but she doubted it was his entertainment of choice.

Why call on *her*? He was handsome, and he had that inexplicable aura of quiet competence that signals power, and power was somehow very attractive . . . look at the fawning Lady Piedmont.

Yes, if he undertook a seduction, he would find success. No doubt there had been many women in his life and he knew exactly what to do in the bedchamber. . . .

It startled her to realize she was even thinking about such an unladylike subject as Damien Northfield's masculine appeal on a sexual level. Since Arthur, she hadn't so much as experienced even a slight stirring of interest in any man—not that there had been much opportunity to meet any during the four years she exiled herself to the country.

It wouldn't startle anyone else though, she imagined with a stab of cynical reality. All of England had already tried and condemned her as a fallen woman, and if it hadn't been for her prestigious family and the duchess, she would not now be sitting at a ball, and while not immune to the gossip, at least buffered from it.

"Do you object to Lord Damien?" Lily would not have dreamed of asking such a direct question even a few weeks ago, but in truth, even with her formidable presence, the duchess was more approachable than she appeared. Lily suspected she missed her granddaughter very much now that Jonathan had whisked his wife away to the country for the duration of her confinement.

"Sir George is rather a better prospect, my dear." Pale blue eyes regarded her as if assessing her reaction. "The man is interested. I've heard from more than one person he's making it quite public he's a serious suitor."

"Despite my tarnished past. How decent of him."

For the hint of sarcasm, she won a reproving look.

Lily cleared her throat. "He's two decades my senior."

"He's a baronet with a solid fortune." Almost as soon as she finished speaking, the duchess sighed. "But you are young and beautiful and Northfield is quite an attractive young man despite his disability, and much more intriguing, I'm sure, than Sir George. Let's see if he actually calls, shall we?"

If there was a way to retort to that, she would have found it, but she wasn't quite sure either if Lord Damien had been sincere or not, as he certainly had wanted to be rid of her.

"I suppose we shall," Lily murmured.

Chapter 11

He was undeniably jealous.

Of a painting.

It was ridiculous.

Or was it? Art was her passion. How disheartening to be second best.

James ran his fingers through his hair and crossed his feet at the ankles, staring moodily at the window, sprawled in his chair. He hadn't seen Regina in well over a week, and when he'd finally called because he'd heard nothing from her and couldn't wait any longer, she'd been sequestered in her studio and refused to see him.

His first true love affair was not going as he'd imagined it would.

Nursing a glass of brandy, he acknowledged to himself that the rejection stung, and moreover, he couldn't be sure it wasn't the beginning of the end. Regina did not keep her lovers.

"Damn," he muttered and took a drink, and the melancholy call of a night bird drifting through the half-open window reflected his restive frame of mind. It was cool out, the air scented with chimney smoke, but warm by the fire in his personal study. He'd declined to go out, disconcerted by his chaotic emotions when he was usually calm and content with his well-ordered life.

His eclectic lover had that effect on him and . . .

"Sir?"

He turned, unaware anyone else was within hearing, and found his valet in the doorway. While James handled business affairs in the family home in Mayfair and dined there often, he had his own set of modest apartments a few blocks away, privacy and autonomy much preferable to a busy household with all of his cousins in residence. Branson shifted his weight, looking uneasy. "Forgive the interruption, but I'm to give you this."

James eyed the envelope and then glanced at the clock. It wasn't late by *ton* standards. Not even midnight, but still an odd time to receive a note. "Who sent it?"

"There's no return address, I'm afraid, and a servant delivered it and departed."

Did he want to play this game? James recognized the elegant handwriting on the extended envelope and knew he'd play . . . no matter that she set the rules. "Thank you," he said in a clipped tone, and rose to take it, waiting until Branson had discreetly closed the door before he tore open the missive.

We're ready now.

What the devil did that mean? No one else he knew would send a cryptic message like that without an explanation except Regina.

Now. It held an immediacy he responded to on a primitive level, but should he go running there when he'd been turned away before?

Fifteen minutes later the answer was yes when he dismounted his horse in front of her town house, his pride be damned because he couldn't resist her if he tried and the plain facts were he wasn't interested in trying.

She answered the door herself, attired in an interesting ensemble, considering the time, in a blue day gown and paint smock, her fingers stained, and her eyes alight. Loose dark hair brushed her shoulders and hung down her back, and there was a unique freedom in her brilliant smile. "I'm finished."

It was cool enough James had donned his greatcoat, and he slipped it from his shoulders. "Maybe I should come in and we can discuss what the devil you mean."

"Yes." She took the coat, but as he stepped in, she dropped it on the floor and caught his shirt, pulling him close so their mouths were inches apart. "I may show you later. I haven't decided."

They kissed all the way down the hallway, stopping, touching, her slender fingers rumpling his hair, his hands cupping her bottom and bringing her against his arousal so she understood how much he wanted her.

Regina laughed and playfully licked his lower lip as they reached the base of the stairs, her silver eyes glimmering. "I adore it when you are impatient. It isn't like you."

"I like you naked," he said hoarsely and unfastened her smock to toss it aside, so it caught on the banister and hung there in the dim illumination.

Definitely not like him.

"Fair is fair." She adroitly twisted free the knot in his cravat and pulled away his neck cloth, casting it aside. It landed on a nearby table.

"I'm not making love on the stairs," he warned her as she started to unbutton his shirt while standing on the bottom step so they were eye to eye. She liked to be spontaneous and that was well and good, but he was traditional enough to like a soft warm bed and a closed door. Besides her studio floor, they'd used a moving carriage, a chaise in a summerhouse that had been decidedly too small for such vigorous exertion, and a grassy knoll by the river one afternoon where they would have been in plain sight if any boat had happened by. He wasn't an exhibitionist by nature, nor did he like the idea of being interrupted. "I'm not an acrobat. I'll toss you over my shoulder if I have to, but we're going up to your bed."

She yanked his shirt from his breeches and then pressed the palm of her hand against the prominent bulge between his legs. "If you insist upon a bed, then I will come along meekly."

"Meekly?" His brows shot up and he choked out a laugh, the pressure of her hand causing him to harden even more. "You are never meek, my love. Now, since we are in agreement, shall we?"

My love. It was not as if he dropped to his knees and declared himself, but there was a moment where Regina gazed at him, unmoving, her remarkable silver eyes shadowed, and then it passed and she dropped her hand, turning to lift her skirts and hurry up the stairs, throwing a teasing glance over her shoulder when she reached the top.

He still stood there at the bottom, paralyzed by that wistful look before he took off after her, rushing up the steps two at a time.

This chase represented their relationship. The thought struck him even as he gained on her, his shirt hanging open, his body on fire. She was the elusive one, unre-strained, passionate, unconventional, but still aloof in many ways. He was the petitioner, the hot-blooded lover who had to have her despite the fact that it was not a role he usually played.

Were they ill suited?

Or perfect for each other?

At the moment he didn't care. Not when he entered the bedroom to find her shimmying out of her unfas-tened gown. His mouth went dry at the sight of her full breasts, the womanly curve of her hips, the downy thatch between her pale thighs enticing in the firelight from the glowing embers in the hearth.

But it wasn't *just* the potent physical attraction.

He'd been infatuated before ... mildly so, he realized now, as it was never like *this* in any way. The normal path of his life had been turned upside down and had he been asked before he met her, his answer would have been: *impossible. ...*

Jonathan, the current Earl of Augustine and his first cousin, whose mother had been a member of an Ameri-can tribe, would assure him the gods—heathen ones—were invested with a sense of humor and dabbling in the lives of the human beings they benignly watched was one of their pastimes.

Gloriously nude, Regina tossed back her hair in chal-lenge. "And here I thought you were in a hurry."

It brought his attention sharply back into the mo-ment, where, considering the insistence of his swollen cock, was exactly where it should be. The flush of sexual need warmed his skin and he stripped off his shirt, watching with appreciation as Regina turned her back, sensuously lifted her hair so her luscious bottom was exposed, and then exhaled audibly as she walked to the bed.

"Shall I wait for you?"

The delicately phrased question was meant to titillate and it usually worked. He said with a telltale rasp of sexual need in his tone, "Not if you don't wish. I'll join you in a moment."

"That sounds . . . lovely."

As he sat down to try to divest himself of his boots and breeches, she moved to recline on the bed, her dark hair spilling over the white linens, her hands moving to cup her breasts, her eyes drifting closed as she circled a nipple with a stroking fingertip, making it pucker and harden, the dark rose of the areola a contrast to the creamy purity of her skin. Knees bent, she parted her legs enough to give him a tantalizing view of her sex as well.

Her unabashed sexuality never failed to amaze him, and James heard his breath go out in a hiss as one boot landed on the floor. The other followed, and he yanked off his breeches, watching her pleasure herself, and when he stepped to the bed and pulled her hand away, replacing it with his mouth, she gave a soft gasp and her fingers sank into his hair.

Good. She held *him* in a damned thrall, so he should have at least a little retribution.

She always did.

It was his turn. He'd never really turned the tables on her in bed. That had suited him fine—he wanted to be her lover, not her master. This evening, however, it had rankled to be turned away only to be summoned back, like an eager puppy one would shoo away and then pet later, once they had the time.

A logical part of his brain reminded him he didn't understand fully the artistic process and it was possible she *couldn't* be interrupted, but another part of him, vulnerable in a way he hadn't experienced before meeting her, was afraid he would always be second.

Or that she might end their relationship altogether.

He'd have to analyze later the tumultuous emotion produced by contemplating that possibility, but at the moment, he intended she would be very, very glad she'd sent that note to summon him.

There was no question she wasn't good at sharing her life.

After all, she was the outrageous sister of Viscount Altea, who was notorious all on his own, not to mention her questionable birth. To add to her sins, she embraced art as if it wasn't considered a plebian endeavor—a trade—and despite her personal wealth, thanks to her generous father, she in general refuted society.

James knew it all. She'd never hidden that she had little use for conformity.

He didn't seem to care. What's more, from the glitter in his blue eyes, he embraced it.

So did she. Without shame she arched slightly under the seductive suckle of his mouth at her breast, his tongue making little wicked circles around her nipple.

While his mouth seduced her breast, sending tingles of sensation to her belly, between her legs, everywhere, his hands were not idle either, stroking her thighs with leisurely caresses belied by the hot press of his erection at her hip. The sight of his blond head bent over her was as arousing as the erotic ministrations of his tongue and lips, and when he moved slowly to the other breast, taking his time to nuzzle the valley between her cupped flesh, she began to tremble.

Does he know?

Regina wondered if he realized that she'd *never* trembled before him. She'd had only three other lovers and those affairs had been brief, fleeting, meaningless in too many ways, which was why she'd ended them quickly and generally lived her life in self-imposed celibacy.

She'd very much considered not seeing him this evening. The past week she'd found herself distracted even as she attempted to finish her latest work, which never happened to her. Usually the frenzy at the end was the most satisfying part of the creative process, but thoughts of James had crept in and compromised her concentration and she still wasn't done with the painting. Certain that all she had to do was concentrate, she'd turned him away when he called, but it hadn't worked.

She'd abandoned it a few brushstrokes away from completion.

For this. Because she needed to see him. The desire was so strong it had even disrupted her art.

"You taste indescribable," he murmured, the movement of his lips tickling her skin as he moved his mouth to the sensitive underside of her breast. "Like a fine dessert. Complex, yet simple. Sweet and salt. Like undefined paradise."

The bedchamber was only lit by the brazier of the dying fire and the musculature of his lean body was all hollows and sculpted curves as he lay on top of her tasting and licking and . . .

"James." His name left her lips in an involuntary plea, her hips shifting in an unspoken message that he couldn't fail to understand.

But he didn't position himself for penetration; instead he rose up to kiss her, his mouth gentle in contrast to the throbbing need she sensed in him, the fine sheen of sweat on his skin as she rubbed her hands up his back evidence of his arousal. "Tell me about the painting."

Regina blinked, and then stared at him. His eyes were an intense blue, like a summer sky on a hot day, and he stared right back. "What?" she asked, a part of her incredulous, because she knew he wanted her—there was no mistaking it—and she had not invited him over for a discussion about art.

"James—"

He nibbled on her neck. "Tell me."

"Why?"

"Because earlier you sent me away."

"I was working."

"I know. It was too important to stop. Tell me why."

That silenced her because she wasn't sure exactly how to answer. She'd abandoned the work when it was almost born, like failing to push a child from the womb, though she wasn't sure she was qualified to make that analogy. It sounded, however, correct when put in the context of how the final minutes could be when the last touch was given to the canvas, when the artist stood back to behold what he or she had done, and the sense of relief flooded over because it was, after all, completely formed and perfect.

No, not true. Never perfect. If given the chance she would change each creation over and over until eternity, but at the moment she wanted James, and he unmistakably wanted her, and if she could only say the right thing, maybe they would both be rewarded.

"I left him for you."

"Left whom?" James kissed her, a lingering pressure of his mouth, possessive and hard. "Define it for me so I can understand or I swear I won't fuck you."

Shock rippled through her because he didn't swear in front of ladies and he was never *that* crude, or least not in her presence. That wasn't James Bourne in the least, but he held her hips with a firm grip and his eyes had a certain steely gleam.

Desire was a tangible entity in the candlelit room, her unsatisfied body pinned under his larger, rangy form, their eyes locked, the scent of arousal in the air. . . .

He needs this from me.

"I left the painting almost completed and I never do that," Regina told him, her voice barely audible. "I still don't know if William's decision . . . I can't explain why my perception has changed, if you want the truth, for I was sure all along what I wanted from the picture was to portray his dilemma . . . but then I found myself distracted by thinking about you."

James touched her cheek, his fingers just a brush. "Why are you conflicted?"

"Because it is supposed to be a simple story." Her arms twined around his neck and she lifted her pelvis so her stomach pressed his arousal. "But in the end it isn't. I couldn't continue because I can't, as an artist, relate to his conflict."

"You aren't going to finish it?" He sounded genuinely startled.

"I doubt it."

"Why can't you relate?"

"William Tell took a terrible chance, James." She didn't wish it to be, but her voice was hushed.

"Do you believe life-altering decisions are ever simple?" He looked at her, close and real, like the images she created, but he was so . . . alive. She could smell his unique scent, male and spicy, and every detail of his face was clear; the straight line of his nose, the quirky line of one brow that was slightly higher than the other, the sensual curve of his upper lip. She didn't think he was precisely handsome, but good-looking certainly, and his potent attractiveness had much more to do with *who* he was as a man. Thoughtful, fair-minded, responsible . . . all traits she should find dull but somehow didn't, not when balanced with his undeniable intellect, his kindness and sense of duty to his family, his innate passionate nature.

His passion for *her*.

He was too young, she reminded herself, but at the moment all she wanted was to have him, and for him to have her.

"Does it *need* to be life-altering?" she asked, her hand sliding downward between them, circling his rigid cock so he briefly closed his eyes. "Now, I did my best to define it, and you need to keep your part of the bargain by fucking me."

"No." He caught her wrist and pulled her hand away.

"No?" Regina's eyes widened and the sharp bite of disappointment tightened her throat. The firelight cast shadows over his features, making it difficult to read his expression.

"No." He smiled then, but the light in his eyes was still

heated, molten. "Don't mistake me. I am not leaving. I want to make love to you, and that is different." Adjusting his position, he began to slowly enter her, the pressure of the invasion measured and slow and wickedly arousing. She was wet and ready for him, and Regina caught her breath at the exquisite pleasure as he joined their bodies. Her senses were heightened by the unusual surge of emotion, and when he began to move in deliberate thrust and withdrawal, she responded with uncharacteristic restraint instead of fervent wild passion, allowing herself to feel each slide of his sex into hers, tightening her muscles to hold him at the apex, and relaxing to let him glide almost out again.

James didn't close his eyes but held her gaze as he moved, the cadence of their bodies taking on a magical quality that reflected not just the sheer intimacy of the act, but also the union of their mutual desire.

The blending of their souls.

She was hardly a mystic, but as Regina clung to him at the pinnacle, where surreal rapture and the earth met as she surrendered and should be oblivious to anything but the intemperate, carnal joy, she relinquished the battle, not to him, but to herself, by admitting this was different.

Different in every way.

And awash in the blissful aftermath, with his hands tangled in her hair and their damp bodies pressed together, she understood how to finish the painting.

Chapter 12

"It's all rather ironic," Vivian Lacrosse said in her understated way, "because surely inglorious spinsterhood is better than a well-placed marriage with a condescending prig."

Lily laughed. It was genuine and spontaneous and sparked by the appreciation of a like spirit. They'd become friends almost immediately their first season, and while Lily had been popular and pursued until her downfall, and Vivian had not nearly had the same success despite not having a catastrophic scandal, their instant affinity for each other had not changed over the course of the past four years.

In short, they liked each other.

And what was better than a loyal friend?

The path was strewn with some fallen leaves and their skirts brushed them as they walked, their pace a stroll, the afternoon cool but clear. Soon it would be crisp and chimney smoke the order of the day, but at the moment it was simply a lovely day in the park, and it was rather crowded too, with everyone out and about.

"I mean," Vivian went on doggedly, clutching her parasol, "Lord Gregory could not tell a petunia from a weed and I am supposed to consider marrying him? That is perhaps not his fault, and maybe a gentleman doesn't even have to possess that knowledge, but . . . *still*."

"At the risk of committing blasphemy, Viv, not everyone knows their plants." Lily sent her friend a mischievous sidelong glance. "Most of the aristocracy employs gardeners for that purpose. Though, just to impress you, I confess I do know a petunia."

"*You* happen to possess a working intellect." Vivian frowned and then sighed. "But I'm told I'm too particular—mostly by my disapproving mother's standards. My father doesn't pay much attention, which actually I am grateful for, but then again, he is a botanist."

Had she never been subject to family censure, Lily might not have understood so well. She murmured, "Yes, well, I've never been terribly good at pleasing others either. My inclination isn't to disappoint everyone, but then again, I'm not willing to live my life differently just so that society approves of me."

"I'm not sure I know how to *get* them to approve of me." Vivian's voice had grown quieter. "I have suitors, just none I like. I know I am considered odd, but truly, I enjoy my work. I always have had an interest in growing things, and I happen to be quite good at it. I have never understood why plants are considered so unladylike. Every simpering debutante shows off her embroidery, which usually involves roses and daisies and fields of tulips. I can't stitch them, but I can *actually* grow them. Why is that so *outré*?"

A wayward leaf was caught by the breeze and danced across the path and Lily deflected it before it caught in her hair. She stifled a laugh. "I think it is the dirt involved."

"Wet earth is a lovely smell. It reminds me of spring," Vivian said defensively. She looked particularly pretty today in a yellow day gown that complemented her dark hair, though her chignon was a bit careless, with raven tendrils escaping to frame the oval of her face, and a disgruntled expression drew her fine brows together.

"I am not arguing, take my word." Lily thought of her family home in Berkshire with the green fields and meandering river. "I love spring, and yes, it smells like damp soil and growing things."

Vivian smiled in approval. "The stirring of the world coming back to life. There are times when I have wondered if I would not love to live somewhere tropical and exotic like I have read about. Where it is always lush and warm and I understand the variety of plant life is staggering. But I fear I would miss England and its seasons too much."

"Not to mention the pesky insects and snakes and other nasty creatures in those jungle climes," Lily pointed out, "and the abysmal heat, which is quite bad enough here in long skirts and undergarments, but there I imagine would be unbearable."

"I could don native garb, I suppose." Vivian laughed, her green eyes sparkling. "I've heard some of the women go bare-bosomed. Can you imagine?"

"Not really." Lily had read of that too, and considering the merest glimpse of her ankle was forbidden, the idea of it so foreign it was a little intriguing. "That sounds like a bit much. Your complexion is much too lovely."

"And a bit pale for it, I suppose. Those Celtic ancestors did not frolic in the sun often."

"That too." Lily lifted a brow in amusement. "But there wasn't much sun for them to frolic in either."

"So how was your stroll with Lord Damien Northfield the other evening?"

The switch in subject came somewhat unexpectedly, though Lily had assumed from the dowager's reaction that their brief exit from the ballroom had been noticed. However, Vivian paid no attention at all to gossip. Because of that exactly, she didn't dissemble. "He can't dance, so the offer of a breath of fresh air, which I'd prefer anyway, was what he suggested instead of a waltz."

"That is a sensible alternative, I suppose, and you are not some giggling ingenue he has to cart around with a chaperone in tow."

"Thank you." The response was ironic.

Her friend sent her a reproving glance. "You know I didn't mean it in an offensive way. Neither am I, for that matter. I simply was stating that there is a certain freedom in our on-the-shelf status."

"Perhaps." A small bevy of ducks flew past, low and swift, their wings in a silent ballet of synchronized motion. "The season is about over."

"It is. There is no use but to be pragmatic about it." Vivian sighed dramatically, a touch of becoming pink in her cheeks due to the breeze. Dark curls danced against the collar of her walking dress. "I will still be as unmarried as ever, or at least I hope so. Lord Gregory is *not* an option I wish to consider."

"I have Sir George hanging over my head," Lillian pointed out. "Despite his age I think I am supposed to be grateful he is willing to overlook my reputation."

"What nonsense. You are a beauty, Lily."

"So are you."

Vivian made a small face as they strolled along. "I have some mannish habits that make me less than desirable, as we just discussed."

"There is nothing wrong with your hobby."

"Most of the *ton* does not agree with you."

It was hard to argue the point and they *were* both stuck in a similar position. "Still," Vivian said, her skirts brushing the grass. "I am glad I have waited. It is possible I am flattering myself, but I am not an empty-headed foolish girl who wants to have a man to take care of her. Call it absurd romanticism, but I wish to meet a man who will intrigue me. Who will challenge me intellectually, who will find my interests to be similar to his own; who *likes* me. Is that foolish?"

It was rather difficult to not think of Damien Northfield with his enigmatic smile, dark eyes, and air of mystery, not to mention his interesting background. What could be more intriguing than a former spy?

"No," Lily said quietly, the breeze brushing her face. "It isn't foolish at all."

He'd never done it before and it was a bit daunting.

Odd to think, as he'd climbed rocky hills in the pitch darkness, scaled fortress walls, interrogated prisoners, infiltrated enemy lines, and hunted traitors, and yet he'd never formally called on a young lady.

It was a thought-provoking commentary on his life, Damien decided as he alighted from the carriage and limped up the steps. He was very, very good at subterfuge and inept at the simple social act of presenting his card, waiting for the summons to the drawing room, and conversing politely about mundane subjects.

Lucky for him, he didn't think Lady Lillian was interested in mundane either.

But before he called upon a lady for the first time, he needed more information. That was much more comfortable for him, as gathering intelligence was a necessary step before embarking on any mission.

"Is Lord Sebring at home?" Damien asked the sour-faced servant who answered the door. "Damien Northfield calling."

His old friend was there, he discovered, and he was shown into his study moments later, Arthur rising with the familiar affable smile on his face. "Northfield. This is a pleasant surprise. How many years has it been?"

"Too many," Damien replied, because while this wasn't precisely a social visit, he'd been gone from England for what now felt like a lifetime.

Arthur indicated a chair. "It's good to see you. Can I offer a glass of claret?"

Wine was not what he'd come for, but Damien said pleasantly, "Thank you."

His host poured a glass for each of them and Damien glanced around the room. It was welcoming: wood-paneled tall bookcases, several average oil paintings of hounds and horses on the walls, and a cluttered desk that spoke of a man who took care of his business affairs.

Why, then, hadn't he taken care of Lily?

He took the proffered glass and sank into a chair that creaked comfortably under his weight, and studied his friend. Arthur had actually changed very little since their days at university, still good-looking and athletically built, though there were a few lines that hadn't been there before around his mouth, and his blond hair was thinning a little, but essentially the same physically. They were of a like age at thirty-two, so he'd have to have been subject to enough seasons of debutantes to have had his pick of lovely young, willing ladies before he'd settled on Lily and persuaded her into a folly that had destroyed her reputation.

There must have been an attraction there and Damien understood that well enough—he was also attracted to the winsome Miss Bourne—but Arthur had bowed out and let her bear the brunt of a torrid scandal.

Then he had married someone else.

And no one seemed to know why.

But Damien was curious as hell.

Besides his interrogation of Colton, which hadn't been all that enlightening, he'd asked a few discreet questions in other circles and gotten nothing from it. Hence this direct visit.

How to play it is always a bit of a gamble. He was much more used to dealing with those who were gifted in the art of deception and he doubted Arthur belonged in that circle. Damien took a sip, sat back, and said conversationally, "I understand Richard Seasons has opened a stable near Newmarket."

Arthur's well-known affinity for horse racing proved a perfect segue into old familiar conversation, though Damien was well versed enough in human nature that he still sensed a wariness signaling that while they might have been friends at one time, Sebring noted this visit as unusual.

Interesting.

On his second glass—it was Arthur's third, he noticed—of wine, Damien casually brought up the subject he'd really come to discuss. "You've married, I hear."

No imagination or great sleuthing skills were required to see his friend's features smoothed into a stony mask. "Yes," Arthur said shortly, finishing his drink by tossing it back abruptly.

"My felicitations."

"Thank you."

"Three years?" Damien lounged back, much more comfortable in his role as subversive interrogator than social acquaintance, his sprawl in the chair casual but his intense scrutiny anything but. If he was going to glean the information he wanted from this visit, it was now.

"Yes. Three years."

Was there the slightest edge in his host's voice at the affirmation? Maybe so.

"I understand her father is very influential in Parliament."

Lord Sebring leveled a look at him. "Is that why you're here? To talk about my father-in-law?"

He hadn't been as subtle as he thought. Or . . . it was a sore subject. Damien lifted his brows at the acrimony.

Arthur stood abruptly and walked to the window, staring outward. "I'm sorry I was just so abrupt."

Something was off. Damien recognized the signs. The set of Sebring's shoulders was tense, and his hands braced against the sill as he stared out the glass.

Damien murmured, "No offense taken."

Arthur took in an audible breath. "My marriage is a difficult topic to discuss at the moment."

"I see." At this point maybe he should make his excuses and leave, but then again, he had enough experience to sense that wasn't exactly what his friend wanted either.

"No, you don't, unless you are privy to information I've told no one else." There was a mirthless laugh. "My wife and I are estranged."

"That's unfortunate." Damien deliberately kept his voice even and unemotional, which he was quite skilled at doing after years of practice. "Though hardly unusual for our class."

"I suppose not." Arthur's profile was remote, austere. "I was never sure what to expect from marriage anyway, but I didn't think I would experience . . . *this*."

A strange statement indeed. "I'm not sure what you are referring to, but I am certain you are not the first man to feel it." He wanted to bring up Lily Bourne, but his companion's demeanor stopped him.

With a mirthless laugh, Arthur turned, his expression cynical. "I am sure you did things during the war that did not appeal to you, Northfield, did you not?"

"Many." No exaggeration there.

"I hear you were quite a gifted operative for Wellington. Maybe you can help me."

Damien shrugged, but he was suddenly very attuned to the conversation.

Slowly Arthur spoke, "How would you feel if the world—*your* world—found out about them?"

"Them?"

"Every dirty little secret. Those tasks you performed that were perhaps not to your liking but you did them anyway because that is what you had to do."

His now empty claret glass dangling from his fingers, Damien took a moment to answer, wondering exactly what was at stake. He finally said, "I don't think anyone wants their foibles common knowledge."

"I am not talking foibles."

"No?"

"No." Arthur squared his shoulders. "I am talking sin."

He hadn't had this intriguing a conversation since he'd left Spain. Damien nodded at the sideboard. "Pour me another glass of claret and tell me what kind of sin."

Sebring's smile was mirthless and his hand not quite steady as he dispensed more wine. "I am sure you are not interested in my small troubles, Dame."

The nickname wasn't precisely jarring, but it did strike a chord of the old camaraderie. During the war he was "sir" or "Major" and at the very end, "Colonel," but it had been a long time since someone had addressed him with the familiarity of old acquaintance. Damien took the glass and deigned to mention that he had navigated his way through much larger dilemmas with ease, and simply looked bland. "If they are small, they are easily dealt with."

"Since you're here . . ." Arthur trailed off and restlessly ran his hand through his hair. "It's fortuitous really, because I was starting to wonder where to turn, but I've . . . heard things."

"Oh?" Damien kept his expression only mildly interested.

Unverified information, he'd found, was barely worth the time it took to listen to it.

"You did work for my Lord Wellington." It was a tentative statement.

"Indeed."

"In what capacity?"

"Confounding the enemy," Damien clarified, wondering if he should just mention Lily and be done with it.

"Can you," Arthur asked quietly, "confound mine? I have a friend with the War Office. I mentioned your name once and he told me that you were unmatched in gathering information."

That properly caught his attention. "Did he, now?"

"I have someone threatening me."

This wasn't what he'd come for, but then again, it was interesting. "Who?"

"I'm not sure. He wants money to keep quiet about a certain matter. We've never met, but he contacts me through the post."

That sounded familiar. In his probing—and he'd only just started—into Kinkannon's activities, he'd immediately discerned that it was possible the man was bleeding a great deal of society's more wealthy members and making quite a profit from it. Damien had to work at staying noncommittal. "I see."

Lord Sebring went and settled heavily into a chair, his gaze level. He rubbed his forehead. "No, Northfield, you don't. This could ruin me."

Like you ruined Lily?

Not the time to say it. "Maybe you should clarify how."

"You might not want to help me."

"But then again, maybe I would. We're old friends. Why wouldn't I help?"

Besides, you might be able to give me some valuable insights on Lady Lillian.

"I'm not willing to reveal what he is holding over my head, for one." To give Arthur credit, he didn't look away, his gaze steady. "It's personal, and though it isn't a measure of my trust in your ethics, I don't wish to discuss it."

This was his type of challenge, though Damien didn't say so. His mouth quirked up at the corner. "So what you'd like is for me to help you find an unknown person without any knowledge of whom I am looking for or why I should pursue them?"

"Put that way it sounds damned foolish." His lordship's smile was rueful. "I know it, but that changes nothing about my resolve."

It just so happened that Damien wouldn't believe any man who claimed to have no secrets was telling the truth, so the admission was probably a positive. "You do realize I at least need some information."

"I will give you the letters the blackmailer wrote me."

Chapter 13

He didn't call on her as promised.

Well, perhaps she'd been optimistic in the first place, and that surprised her a bit, because Lily had actually thought she was immune to unrealistic expectations. So Lord Damien had been insincere, and she admittedly hadn't expected it of him, but then again, he'd been trying to expediently shrug her off.

There. Yet another reason to not trust deliciously handsome gentlemen with chestnut hair and compelling dark eyes. She'd thought she'd learned that lesson already.

It was fine, she promised herself, and duly smiled through a not-very-satisfying rendition of *The Magic Flute*, and did her best to come up with an original reason for wanting to head home directly after the opera.

The next day he did not call either.

Fine. *Blast him*.

Other gentlemen did, most prominently Sir George, and Lily did her best as the gracious hostess, all the while wanting to be honest with the man and in the interest of fairness inform him his suit would never be accepted. But the duchess arrived each afternoon to preside over the formalities, and truthfully, Lily was not sure how to argue with the formidable dowager.

It wasn't—naturally—until she had donned her oldest—but most comfortable—day dress on a rainy afternoon, and settled in for a long stint of reading, that there was a knock on the door and a maid stood there, holding out a calling card with a slight smile on her face. "You've a visitor, my lady."

"Now?" She'd been ensconced in the library long enough that she wasn't sure what time it might be. Lily squinted at the clock and realized it was long past four. "Oh, I see. Thank you, Molly."

Why did Damien Northfield have to call *now*, when she was rumpled, her chignon half escaping from the pins, and . . .

"Not too surprising to find you here, I suppose." Her unexpected guest strolled in, albeit crookedly with his limp—urbane in dark breeches and a tan jacket, his hair just slightly windblown. "Am I interrupting? I'd much rather join you in the informality of the library than sit in the stuffy drawing room."

Lily fairly scrambled up from the chair where she'd been sitting, no doubt looking as disconcerted as she felt. "No . . . yes, well, no, I suppose not."

"I assume some kind of chaperone will come dashing in at any moment to make sure I am not doing anything wicked to you, but I wondered if we could wrest out of this visit a few moments of privacy. I asked the young woman who took my card if she could take the flowers I brought and put them in the drawing room, and then took advantage and went in search of you myself. Rather an old ploy, I admit."

"Flowers?"

His mouth quirked. "I presume you've heard of the practice of a gentleman bringing a lady flowers?"

Lily wasn't quite sure how to respond, so she merely gestured at a convenient settee and sank back down in her chair. "Please . . . have a seat, my lord."

His smile was a bit devilish. "I could lock the door."

Was there any woman on earth who could resist that gleam of amusement in his eyes? Lily did her best to summon a proper censorious tone. "I think the once was quite enough for us to be locked in together and I doubt this room has a secret escape staircase."

He'd brought her flowers. Not that other gentlemen hadn't done so, but it was different now. Before her debacle with Arthur they had brought them to woo her, and now they brought them as a mere formality. She deeply resented that she was supposed to be grateful Sir George was willing to court her, and she resented even more that a part of her *was* grateful.

With impractical romanticism she wondered what it might be like to fall in love—not with a man who deceived and abandoned her, but with one who might share her interests.

What kind of flowers had the Duke of Rolthven's brother brought her? Not roses. No, Damien Northfield would not choose anything so obvious. If she had been fooled by Arthur, how much more so could the man lounging so negligently on a faded rose-colored settee incongruous to his stark masculinity trick her into believing in his sincere interest?

It frightened her a bit.

Was she willing to take the risk to get an answer? She

wasn't certain. Lily coolly murmured, "Why did you wish to talk to me in private?"

He hesitated a moment, glanced at the door he hadn't locked but had closed, and then said simply, "Are you, per chance, being blackmailed?"

It was about the last question she anticipated, and Lily blinked in the surprise. "I beg your pardon?"

"I promise I have a reason for asking."

She opened her mouth to say . . . she wasn't sure what, but he preempted her reply by lifting his hand and smiling ruefully.

"I vow if you are, your answer will not leave this room."

The rain tapped at the windows, the sound normally soothing, but Lily wasn't sure she was calmed at all. It took her a moment, but she managed to say with credible poise, "Why would anyone blackmail me?"

"My very point."

"Sir, you talk in circles."

At that he laughed, and it lit his face attractively. "I see we are starting to know one another."

"I am not sure I agree." She tried to smooth a wrinkle in her muslin skirt to no avail, and then gave up, squaring her shoulders. "The answer is no. No one has approached me in any way with a fiendish offer of silence for coin, which is just as well, as I have very little money of my own."

"I see."

"I don't," she said with a small frown.

"That's a valid point." He sank a little lower in the chair, long legs outstretched and his face thoughtful. "As a young unmarried woman, you wouldn't have the resources to pay, so what would be the use of it, after all?"

"May I mention I have no earthly idea what we are talking about?"

"You may point out whatever you wish."

There was only one reason anyone could try to extort money from her and it didn't take a giant leap to deduce what it might be. She wasn't exactly a stranger to the fact society remembered her disastrous social stumble. "This must have something to do with Arthur."

His lashes lowered a fraction. It wasn't much, but the reaction told her something. "What makes you think so, Lady Lillian?"

"It couldn't be anything else."

"A virtuous lady. You intrigue me more each time we meet."

Intrigue. She thought maybe he was a bit too familiar with the meaning of that word, but then again, he didn't bore her like most of the foppish gentlemen she knew. In a way—though they were quite different—he reminded her of her older brother. Jonathan was not subtle, nor was he understated, and certainly they looked nothing alike, but it was there in the ironic glimmer of Lord Damien's smile and that same unmistakable dangerous air. With studied control, she let out a breath. Then she said, "Is *this* why you came to see me?"

He liked her in simple moss-green muslin with pink ribbons. The neckline was unfortunately too modest, but he had quite a good imagination. Lily had a lovely, natural grace and it showed in every movement. A lift of her hand to brush back a wayward lock of hair from her ivory cheek. The shift of her slender body on the chair, the turn of her head as she glanced at the rain-streaked window, the sudden shadow across her face . . .

He'd have to address later his instinctive desire to protect her, but for now he needed to answer her question.

"I don't know what happened between you and the viscount, but I suppose I can see how you'd not think of him with kindness," he said, feeling his way because there had been an edge of bewildered anger in her question. "And I never said my question had anything to do with Lord Sebring. You jumped to that conclusion."

"Understandably so."

Actually, he wasn't quite sure of why he was there, in the library of the Earl of Augustine, questioning Lily about another possible scandal, except he had a completely unreasonable curiosity about her past with Sebring. It had crossed his mind that the problem the viscount didn't wish to discuss might be an affair that would not only damage his marriage—or had done so already—but also his political ambitions.

Damien didn't want Lily dragged into another sordid scandal. Charles did not get involved in matters of this sort lightly. If Kinkannon was the problem, he was a true threat.

And Damien was very good at sensing danger. It was also possible he might be jealous. As it was a new emotion, he was inept at recognizing it, but he did know he was unhappy at the idea of Sebring and Lily harboring a secret involvement.

"Are you still seeing him?"

"Who?"

This was ridiculous. He felt like a fool. But then again, his conversation with Arthur hadn't rung true. At all.

Maybe she wasn't being blackmailed, but maybe she was the *source* of the blackmail.

"Your former lover."

"How dare you!"

He'd truly hurt her. He saw the wounded look in her lovely eyes. "I didn't mean—"

"Yes, you did. You are just as judgmental as everyone else, damn you."

The less-than-ladylike language didn't matter to him, but the sudden luminous threat of tears in her eyes did. "Lily."

"Perhaps you should leave, my lord." She stood there in delectable disarray, her hair escaping in small tendrils that framed her face, but just as she opened her mouth to speak, the doors parted and the dowager duchess swept in. "Lord Damien," that lady said with crisp intonation, offering her hand. "I was informed you were calling. Can we offer some refreshment? Claret, brandy or tea?"

Considering the circumstances and time of day, he opted for the tea, but with some brandy to fortify it, and though he could tell the duchess longed to whisk them off to the formal drawing room, he informed her blandly that he found the library just as suitable.

As far as he could tell Lily participated only as much in the conversation as required of her out of politesse. When he rose to leave, he bent over her proffered hand and murmured, "Violets."

Her eyes reminded him of the sky just when it began to darken on a summer day. Indigo with an iridescent quality. A slight frown wrinkled her brow. "My lord?"

"I brought violets exactly the color of your eyes."

Damien then released her slender fingers, wondered just what the hell to make of this visit, and took his leave.

Chapter 14

"**Y**ou must send it to the Royal Academy, of course." Regina smiled indulgently at her younger brother's authoritative tone. "You think I should send every painting to the Academy."

Luke Daudet, Viscount Altea, stood in her studio, casual in a white shirt open at the neck, no cravat, wearing dark breeches, his polished Hessians the only nod to fashion. He gazed at the canvas, his brows slightly lifted. "This one more than the others . . . it's particularly brilliant."

"Thank you." His praise was exhilarating, but the elation in her life wasn't limited to his appreciation and she distrusted it.

Happiness was serenity. It was sunshine when she needed illumination. It was a blank canvas and inspiration. It was driven need and sleepless pacing as the dawn began to lighten the sooty rooflines of the city. . . .

It *wasn't* romance. At least not before now.

"Why not present it?" Luke was still staring at the painting. "The execution is flawless. I admit some of your work confounds a Philistine like myself, but this . . . this I think I understand. I don't know why, but it speaks to me."

Love is why, she wanted to say. Of course it spoke to him. He adored his wife and though their romance had been tumultuous, it had ended in the kind of marriage only depicted in fables.

"It's for private viewing only."

He eyed one of the old, stained chairs with a dubious look, but then shrugged and settled into it. "You always keep your best pieces to yourself, but I have never comprehended why. Usually you are this inspired only when you are distraught over some matter. Talk to me."

He was referring to, of course, her painting of Pompeii after the explosion of Vesuvius, the ash cloud still obscuring the sun, a project she'd undertaken after their father had died. It had depicted catastrophic loss, and she'd labored over it for months, avoiding her grief, but the symbolic catharsis had in the end proved healing.

She shrugged. "About what?"

"Whatever has you currently in such a state of flux that you were compelled to portray so beautifully a once-in-a-lifetime decision on canvas. This is about you, isn't it?"

Her smile was ironic in the shaded confines of the room, the weather still inclement after several days of rain. Regina dropped into the opposite chair and contemplated the tips of her slippers—even she wore shoes when it was dreary outside—then sighed. "I have a lover."

That startled him, his fine features registering surprise. He was the antithesis of her in coloring with dark blond hair and bronzed skin, but they had the same gray eyes and certainly her unfashionable height was a family trait. "I . . . see." Her brother paused, examining the painting again from where he sat. In the end, he said neutrally, "While I am not used to you giving me details of your personal life, may I ask if the painting has something to do with this affair?"

She shook her head. Had she been in command of her feelings, they would not be having this unexpected conversation. "I don't particularly want to discuss it."

Predictably, Luke ignored her. "You are beautiful and talented and a grown woman who is completely autonomous. Why wouldn't you have a lover? Do I know him?"

"The man in the painting? Don't tell me you don't recognize William Tell."

"Don't be deliberately evasive, Regina. If you don't want to tell me, that is fine. You know I won't intrude, but I admit to being curious."

It was true she usually didn't choose her lovers from the beau monde, but then again Luke probably didn't realize she'd hadn't had all that many. It was her choice to keep her private life very separate from her family, but Luke was special in that he was her only brother and he was also one of the least judgmental people she'd ever met.

"Yes." She inclined her head a fraction and grudgingly admitted, "I'd guess the two of you know each other."

"Oh?" With an inquiring lift of his brows he casually crossed one leg over the other, resting his ankle on his knee. "One of *us*, then."

She blew out a short breath. "Us?"

"Insufferable aristocrats. I believe I've heard you use the phrase more than once. Unless you've developed a penchant for one of the footmen, in which case, by the way, I still wish you all due happiness."

"No objection to a footman as a brother-in-law?" She arched a brow.

"Not unless he isn't a good footman," her brother answered with equanimity. "One must have standards, correct?"

A laugh bubbled up in her throat. "I suppose that is a valid point."

"Are you really considering marriage?"

Insufferable aristocrats. She had blithely said that about the upper classes, she realized. James did qualify as one of their class, and the mention of marriage didn't help. At a loss for a moment, she struggled to find an appropriate response. Always she'd subscribed to the ideal that each man and each woman should never be judged by the circumstances of their birth, and she still did, but her relationship with James had nothing at all to do with social standing but everything to do with an undeniable passion, and perhaps something a great deal more. Luke simply waited until she sighed and acquiesced. "No, he isn't a footman. That might be simpler, but he is who he is, and I am who I am, and it is all deuced complicated."

"That explains exactly nothing."

"It's James Bourne."

It was liberating, actually, to say the name out loud. What's more, it was always gratifying to confound Luke, even if it was only visible on his face for a fleeting moment. Her brother said slowly, "Yes, I do know him. Good sort, actually. At the moment heir to an earldom, so definitely not a footman."

It wasn't like she hadn't spent hours and hours trying to decipher this complicated relationship, not to mention the painting. "And let's not forget far younger than I am."

"I wasn't thinking of that at all." Luke frowned. "Though I suppose he is. I was more thinking that he has a reputation as a respectable fellow, whereas you—"

"Are not respectable at all," she finished for him, not sure if she should be amused or burst into tears.

Truly, she never cried. What the devil was wrong with her? Her throat was tight and hot.

"I never meant that," Luke said succinctly, running long fingers through his hair in a careless movement. "Regina, I just pointed out you are beautiful and talented and charming."

"Charming?" she asked, recovering a little with only a slight hiccup in her voice, wondering where the bout of emotion had come from in the first place. "When have I ever been charming?"

Luke grinned. "I concede that wasn't the right adjective. You are far too independent and opinionated to be charming. Beautiful and talented. Can we leave it there? Bourne would be stupid to not be interested. It's just that he doesn't seem like the kind of man you'd choose when you've refused so many others."

"Doesn't he?' She sat back, careless deliberately, both pleased at her brother's understanding of the painting and yet disconcerted he'd seen through her so easily. "Tell me why."

If there was one person's opinion she valued it was Luke's, so why not ask? She wasn't about to confide in anyone else, even James. If there ever was going to be a declaration of love—and she wasn't sure she was even capable of such a commitment, no matter her feelings—it was going to be a long and well-contemplated decision.

In short, dissuade me.

James was her lover, but maybe he was simply enjoying the physical communion and the emotional connection was her imagination. She'd never had it before. How could she know?

"Bourne?" Her brother shrugged, but his eyes were steady. "I'm hardly his closest friend, but he strikes me as steady and unruffled, a gentleman who can move about in society, a canny man of business, or so I've heard, but hardly one with a living that would tempt an heiress."

Rather like James had described himself. Regina wasn't quite positive how nonchalant she could seem, but she said flippantly, "Even if she's an eclectic artist considerably his senior?"

"Considerably? I think that's an exaggeration."

"Is it?" Her smile was wry.

"Please, Regina, what does your age matter? I'm older than Madeline."

"Not at all the same. Please admit it. I'm five and thirty, and as such, so far past spinster that I've been dismissed as unmarriageable. There's no such word to describe a bachelor. Spinster means you are unwanted, bachelor means you are unmarried by choice. It's damned unfair."

Luke inclined his head. At least he was *that* intelligent for he didn't suffer fools—but of course, neither did he, so at least they were in accord there. "I see your point."

Suddenly she didn't want to sit any longer. Regina rose and walked across to stare at the painting. Her folk hero stood there with his drooping bow, his tortured expression not unfamiliar. Their dilemma was not the same . . . hers wasn't life or death.

Or was it? There was the potential death of her existence as she knew it—as she celebrated and cherished it.

And there was life . . .

"I think for the first time in my life I don't know what I want." Saying it out loud was like stripping her soul bare.

"I think that is significant just in itself, don't you?"

"If I knew what to think," she said haltingly, "I wouldn't be involving you in my personal affairs for the first time I can remember."

Luke considered her, half his face shadowed by the light coming in the unadorned windows. When he spoke his voice was quiet. "Are you in love?"

"How would I know?" She reached out and brushed her fingers across the canvas—very lightly; it was dried, but she didn't want to dislodge a single bit of paint. "I'm confounded. Conflicted. I have no idea how he feels and that's entirely my fault. I insist on a detached approach to any personal discussions. I always have. I assume that sounds familiar, brother mine."

"It does," he agreed, his fleeting smile brief. "But what we think we control and what actually happens rarely coincide. I learned during the war that all the careful planning in the world cannot control the outcome of a battle."

She should have made Tell's eyes dark instead of crystalline blue. Regina tried to study her work with an objective eye, but then gave up. There was no objectivity in art, and there was none in love either.

"I loved Madeline long before I admitted it to myself." Luke was never one to equivocate. "I recognize the signs of denial. In retrospect, I wonder why I waited to accept my feelings. It isn't nearly as frightening as it seems, Regina."

Her smile was brittle. "I hope you are correct, because I'm petrified. Tell me, how did Madeline begin to suspect she was pregnant?"

James calculated that if he gauged the timing to the second correctly, then maybe—perhaps—he'd catch Lily alone. It wasn't that he minded being the only male in residence. After all, he understood Jonathan's reasons for keeping his wife in the country so she had a serene pregnancy without the bustle of the city, and besides, James took care of most of the estate affairs. It made Jonathan's presence in London unnecessary unless there was something pressing.

But the duchess made James want to duck into the corner like an admonished schoolboy. Such determined matchmaking made him uneasy, not to mention that she had not-so-subtly taken over the management of the household. She often took all three of his cousins to the dressmaker or milliner or other shops females favored, supervised elaborate teas, and arranged dinner parties, so she was in residence most of the time.

Regina had summed it up nicely when she'd advised him to avoid the "regal old bat."

It was so very like her irreverent sense of humor he had to laugh at the memory even as he raised his hand to rap on Lily's door.

His cousin answered in her evening gown, but her long hair was still loose, her hairbrush in her hand. "Oh."

"I see you are dressing to go out."

She made a small moue. "The duchess—"

"Insists," he concluded for her. "Can I have a short word first?"

She nodded. "Of course."

He kept his voice low, for her maid was moving around in the background and it wasn't like he'd ask to come into her bedroom. They were cousins and he had nothing but brotherly affection for Lily, but proprieties were proprieties. "Can you step out here for a moment? I just have a quick question."

Obligingly she stepped outside into the hallway and eased the door closed, obviously understanding his wish to not be overheard. "What is it?"

There was no really subtle way to ask for this advice without revealing something he had kept closely to himself, but then again, Lily was trustworthy, so he said simply, "I wish to buy a gift for someone very special to me. A token, as it were, of my affection. In some ways, she reminds me of you. I thought you might have a suggestion."

The way Lily's eyes widened, he knew he'd surprised her. But then again, he was hardly forthcoming about what he did in private, and despite the incident with Sebring, she was still a sheltered, unmarried young woman. One night might have ruined her reputation, but it didn't make her worldly.

No, he didn't need advice on how to get Regina into bed; he needed direction on how to win her in a different way.

"Who is she?"

His smile was crooked. "Someday I might tell you, but for now, no. I just need to outdo myself, for trust me, this is not a lady who will be dazzled with flowers and sweets."

She leaned back against the closed door, and Lily's face creased into a frown. "I . . . I don't know. What does she like? What are her interests? Does she have any pursuits that she excels at?"

"The answers are in sequential order: art, art, and art." His voice was drier than he intended, but then again, he was telling the exact truth. "She is complex in many ways but not so difficult to decipher in others. One of her more endearing qualities is a single-minded obsession with her work." He forestalled further questions by saying gently, "You are not contemporaries so I doubt you know her. Now, then, any ideas?"

Lily was silent, her gaze speculative, then she murmured, "This seems important to you."

"It is." His smile was brief and humorless. How did a man even begin to court a woman like Regina, who was so self-sufficient and content with her life? Thoroughly bedding her was a satisfactory start—most satisfactory— but he was thinking more and more in terms of permanence, yet afraid to broach the subject. Instead he had decided to embark on a campaign to win her emotionally, not just in a physical sense. "I'm in love with her."

Lily stared at him with open consternation. "How could none of us know you were courting someone?"

Courting was not particularly the way to describe his relationship with Regina Daudet, but he intended for that to change. "I can be discreet."

"I could swear the duchess knows *everything*," Lily objected on a mutter. Her gown this evening was pale yellow silk, which suited her, emphasizing the richness of her hair. "She would have mentioned it, considering our familial relationship, if she'd heard the slightest whisper."

"Apparently she *doesn't* know everything and I am

just as glad to not be the object of her scrutiny. Lily, any notion of what I should do?"

She crossed her arms over her chest and smiled then, her face lighting in a natural way he hadn't seen in a long time. "I'm very happy for you."

That was premature. This experience could end up being a lesson in misery unless he could persuade Regina to disregard what she saw as barriers between them, the main problems being her blasted independence and the difference in their ages. He didn't care about the potential ramifications of society's censure over their unorthodox romance. He cared about *her*. "Thank you, but reserve the congratulations until the lady is won. The gift?"

His cousin frowned and pressed her lips together, obviously thinking. "I don't know much about art," she said slowly, "but if that is her passion, I do think that is the direction you should go."

"I'd thought of that already," James said with a sigh, "but how does one give a very talented artist a painting? I know what pleases me in an aesthetic sense, but quite frankly, her work is far above anything I could afford to purchase for her."

"It hardly has to be a painting. What about a piece of sculpture or a small statue?" She brightened. "I know someone who bought a piece recently from a shop that specializes in antiquities; the owner was an archeologist of some renown at one time. It's lovely and very old. Greek, I think, or Roman, and though it is a bit chipped and faded, one can tell it was beautifully made."

Actually, that was a sound idea. Perhaps even a brilliant one. Regina already had an eclectic collection of artifacts, including the menacing mask in her bedroom. James leaned over and kissed Lily's cheek. "I knew you were the right person to ask. Do you know the address of this establishment?"

"Er . . . no, I'm afraid not, but I can ask for you."

He knew his cousin quite well and her tone spoke volumes. He groaned theatrically. "Let me guess, the duchess is the 'someone' you know that purchased this intriguing piece. Tell me, how are you going to explain your sudden interest in ancient statuary?"

"I will leave your name out of it, rest assured." Lily's smile was mischievous. "Unless you wish for her to accompany you and help select the gift? She'd like nothing more than to assist with you winning your lady love."

"I'm going to respectfully decline." He grinned. "She needs to be free to focus her considerable talents on you."

"Thanks," Lily murmured gloomily. "Sir George is no doubt going to be in my pocket all evening."

"What about Northfield?" He'd heard, of course, that the man had called and even brought flowers. Apparently the interlude in the library had made an impression on the duke's brother.

Lily blushed. It was slight, just a small pink tinting her face, but James noticed. Yet she shook her head. "I don't think his interest is serious in any way."

He disagreed from a purely male perspective. Lily might not be fashionably blond, or even conventionally beautiful, but she was very attractive nonetheless, and he'd escorted her to enough events that he knew men admired his pretty young cousin, though some of them were no doubt intimidated by her intellect. It was a damned shame Sebring had wrought such havoc on her life.

Gently, he said, "If you don't want George, don't settle for him, Lil. On the other side of the coin, if you *do* want Northfield, you should consider giving him an indication you would not be averse to his suit."

To his surprise, she immediately shook her head and said quietly, "No. I have no intention of repeating a disastrous mistake."

Chapter 15

Being evasive was quite easy. It was carrying it off with aplomb that sometimes was the challenge.

Damien brushed a stray bit of cookie from his knee, not caring quite so much for the spot on his tailored breeches as for the sudden attention directed his way. "Lady Lillian?" he said as if he'd never heard of her.

Or hadn't thought about her quite a bit lately, especially when he considered their last less-than-satisfying conversation.

All in all, he'd rather have that than nothing.

"Lillian Bourne," Brianna, his older brother's wife, said pointedly.

Frederick, his nephew, who had deposited the offending crumb, ran back into the room in a whirlwind of small arms and legs, a clumsy spaniel puppy, a footman, and a nanny following in an apologetic rush, snatched yet another cookie off the tray, and Damien had to suppress a laugh at the exhibition of three-year-old exuberance as they made just as ebullient an exit. The future duke had quite a lot of energy.

"He's a trial." Brianna sighed, watching her son and his entourage. "I've told them to just make sure Freddie doesn't break too many valuable objects, including himself. This room survived his latest visit, but it doesn't always go so well."

"Colton agreed to a dog?"

"Colton doesn't know. If he doesn't notice it, that is his fault. Now, then, can we get back to the fair Lady Lillian?"

Lillian *was* fair, actually. A true English beauty with flawless skin and those blue eyes . . . not to mention what intrigued him even more was her utter lack of coquetry. He was well beyond the superficial rituals that spelled a budding romance in the *haut ton*. So was she apparently, for despite that she was at least a decade younger than him and leagues less proficient in intrigue and deception, she had nonetheless a guarded soul.

There was more to her affair with Sebring than met the eye, but he still hadn't discovered just what had happened.

"I confess I am not sure just what you're asking."

Brianna said with audible censure, "Come, Damien, do not pretend like you did not call on her last week. I read the gossip sheets."

"Do you?"

"Most everyone does. Now, then, tell me about her."

Truth was, he was extremely fond of his older brother's wife. Brianna not only possessed beauty and poise, but she was remarkably free-spirited. He watched her lean forward and pour him another cup of tea, her movements graceful, but her gaze, when she offered the steaming beverage, was openly curious.

"What it is you want to know?"

"You could start with what it is that makes her so exceptional you'd notice her."

He accepted the delicate porcelain cup and saucer and wondered where the devil Colton might be. A fellow male might save him from this interrogation. "Aren't gentlemen supposed to call upon pretty young ladies?" he asked blandly. "I admit I am out of touch with how it is all done."

"Hmm." His sister-in-law narrowed her eyes, seated on a Queen Anne–style settee, her normally slender figure draped in a less fitted gown in deference to her pregnancy. Brianna was a dazzling beauty, but her looks had never influenced her candid personality. Damien was always amused at how she balanced his normally reserved brother. Their marriage was a lesson in how opposites did, indeed, attract. She lifted her cup, took a genteel sip, and then said bluntly, "You always get that look when you are hiding something."

"What look?" He took two lumps of sugar, stirred the steaming tea with a silver spoon, and lifted his brows.

"Well, there isn't one." Her tone held a humorous edge. "That's the entire point. You go absolutely expressionless, as if you have no idea what I'm referring to when I know full well you do."

"Do I?"

"Ah, parry a question with a question. Is that how it works? I shall have to take notes in case I ever wish to keep a deep, dark secret."

He really couldn't help but laugh. "I think you already have, or so I've heard. It seems to me you purchased a scandalous book written by an infamous courtesan and then proceeded to turn your husband's world upside down while beguiling him with her advice."

The distraction worked, as she indignantly set her cup

and saucer down on the polished table and her cheeks turned a definite pink. "I cannot believe he told you that."

"Actually, he was rather enthusiastic about your ingenuity, and the result of your clever plan is evidence that it worked beautifully. He's never been so content. Colton is happy and I, for one, thank you for it, even if the idea was more than a little outrageous for a supposedly refined duchess."

"Damien!"

The way she said his name made him smile. "There is absolutely nothing wrong with your daring approach. My older brother is not an easy man to understand, and yet you are doing an admirable job of turning him into a real human being."

She sat up very straight and then cleared her throat, still blushing. "Thank you. I am still irritated with him that he told you about *Lady Rothburg's Advice*, but then again, I suppose you are rather close."

It was odd, but he hadn't ever thought of his relationship with Colton in that way. Were they close? He supposed so, as they were just a year apart in age and their father had died young, leaving Colt a duke and Damien a ducal heir, the responsibility cumbersome. He'd responded by attending to his assignments in Spain, playing the spy, and leaving his older brother to shoulder all the duties alone.

After a moment, Damien said, "I suppose we are."

Brianna laughed. "While you do not seem similar on the surface, you and Colton remind me of each other very much. He is also very reluctant to share his feelings."

"I'm not—" He stopped, arrested by the womanly knowledge of her smile. Then inclined his head. "Your point is made."

"I think you should take the scandal surrounding Lady Lillian with all the due weight of the pettiness of the *ton* behind it."

"Your advice is invaluable, though I admit in this case not necessary."

Brianna gazed at him, her eyes direct and curious. "Why not? Are you not interested?"

"Interested?"

"In Lillian Bourne." She paused. "I don't mean to insult you, but I thought you'd be above common gossip."

That was lovely. His own family was not only monitoring his personal life, but also passing judgment. He could live without it, but that said, it was impossible to really explain what he was feeling. Even *he* didn't understand his motives. . . . Maybe he was just caught in the web of the instinctive curiosity he felt over Sebring. Maybe it was Lily's underlying vulnerability, and maybe it was just *him*.

And his infernal habit of looking for intrigue, even where maybe none existed.

"I don't know if I am interested or not." That was the truth. He was attracted to Lily, but it was possible it was primarily because she wasn't an insipid debutante but had a bit of a past.

Bland had never held much of an appeal for him.

"Good." Brianna selected an éclair from the tray.

"How can that possibly be good?" He was admittedly mystified.

"Because that means you have given it some thought,

and if you have given it thought, you are *definitely* interested, which is exactly what I hoped to hear."

"That makes no sense."

"Give it time."

He couldn't help but be fascinated as his sister-in-law ate the pastry in an amazingly swift time even though it was sizable.

"I can't help it," she informed him, inelegantly licking her fingers, her eyes alight with laughter as she noticed his expression. "I am growing a child. It seems to make me inordinately hungry."

A deep voice spoke. "I can attest to that."

Both of then turned to look at the doorway, Damien noting his brother had a slight, uncharacteristically indulgent smile on his face. Colton leaned against the doorjamb, his attire as impeccable as ever but his pose relaxed.

He went on in a dry tone. "I have gone barefoot in my dressing gown to the kitchen in the middle of the night to pilfer the oddest items from the pantry, including pickled eggs, day-old scones, cured ham, and in the midst of the latest robbery I tripped over one extremely disgruntled cat that I do not remember giving the cook permission to allow to live here in the first place."

"She adores that cat," Brianna said without apology. "And all the surrounding countryside envies you her cooking skills, so just apologize to Lord Phineas when you encounter him next on your prowls."

"It's my house," Colton said ineffectually, straightening. Then he muttered, "Is *that* really the blasted creature's name?"

"It suits him, don't you think?"

Colton gave a sound that could have been a very undignified snort. "My impression is hardly that he is of aristocratic descent. The feline was rather mangy, or it could be I was simply distracted by the claws in my ankle."

"Careful, darling, lest Cook hear of you disparaging her pet." Brianna rose in a graceful swirl of silken skirts. "Now, if you excuse me, I believe Damien came to see you anyway and I am unreasonably sleepy all at once."

Colton kissed his wife before she left the room, nothing passionate—just a brush of his lips on her brow, but his hands lingered at her waist before he smiled and stepped back.

And briefly, Damien wondered what it would be like to touch the woman who had conceived your child, to share that knowing look between you, to anticipate the arrival of the babe that was part of you both. . . .

That had never occurred to him before.

To say he was startled was an understatement.

"I'm pleased, of course, you chose to come to Rolthven." Colton chose Brianna's seat, his tall body taking up much more of the settee. He eyed the tea trolley. "I see my wife has devoured all the éclairs. Why am I not surprised? How long will you be staying?"

Damien wasn't sure how to answer such a casual question. He'd left London on a restive whim, but that was not new since his return to England. "I was restless," he admitted, setting his teacup aside and rubbing his jaw.

"I am sure the crowded streets of London are a far cry from what you had become accustomed to, so Rolthven would be a pleasant compromise. This is your home."

"Actually, it is *your* home."

Colton's brows shot up. "Last I knew you also spent your boyhood here; otherwise someone who looks remarkably like you bedeviled me when we were children."

Perhaps that was the problem. That his new lodgings in London were without the stamp of his past; that he was displaced in a family where both his brothers were settled and married. Yet the idea of moving into his apartments at either the ducal mansion in London or here in the country did not hold much appeal. Especially when someone like Charles or Alfred Sharpe might decide to drop in uninvited . . .

His devious lifestyle did not lend itself well to a family environment. Neutrally, he said with a small grin, "I believe that might have been me, and I take exception to being accused of bedeviling *you*."

"I took exception to being exasperated at every turn by my younger brother, so we are even, then." Colton chose a scone studded with currants, setting it on a small plate. He poured tea for himself with remarkable equanimity in a man used to hovering servants. "Is the restlessness due to a specific cause?"

"I'm not sure." Damien knew that as indifferent as he was to gossip, Colton had to remember his inquiries about Lily and obviously Brianna had heard some gossip.

It was like the eve of a battle, when a man knew something was going to happen, but not what it was going to be.

He repeated quietly, "I'm not sure."

Chapter 16

It happened in the foyer of the opera house, right after the season's last performance of *Don Giovanni*. The evening had turned, the wind rising, and the guests were anxious to leave, footmen scrambling to make sure the queue of carriages stayed organized, ladies clutching their cloaks as the rain began to spatter down.

"Lily." The insistent hand on her arm made her glance up, and she took in a swift breath as she registered the familiar voice of her former fiancé, his blond hair as impeccable as ever, his chiseled features set at the moment. "Can I have a brief word?"

"Here?" she asked in disbelief, because really, even with the milling crowd anxious to escape the autumn cloudburst, it was hardly a private venue. Not to mention his wife was in attendance. She'd noticed the unfriendly Lady Sebring earlier, resplendent in the famous family pearls, her haughty gaze sweeping over the company and her smile reserved for only the dearest of her friends.

Which Lily was decidedly not.

The air smelled like perfume, stale champagne, and rain. Arthur Kerr said tightly, "Just for a moment. Please."

"What will your wife think?" Even as she caustically

asked the question she allowed him to tug her across the lobby of the theater, the red carpeting thick underfoot, the hum of voices loud as they wound their way through the groups of people. Thankfully the duchess had been at the forefront of the press of departing patrons. Lily had still been waiting for her cloak.

"It might not matter what Penelope thinks." Drawing her into a relatively sheltered spot by the now deserted drinks table, he turned, his stare penetrating. "Lily, have you told anyone?"

She was admittedly confused by his agitated demeanor. Normally he stayed scrupulously away from her in any kind of public place. "What?"

"About *me*."

Had he not been so pale, so resolute, she might have pretended to not know what he meant, but, once she'd struggled past their initial rift four years ago, the bitterness had eased into a more enlightened acceptance. With complete honesty she was able to say, "No one except my brother Jonathan, and he would never repeat it. He understandably wanted to know why our father would allow you to ruin my reputation and not demand either a marriage or satisfaction."

Arthur briefly looked away, his posture tense. "I suppose that is a reasonable question to have, isn't it?"

This evening he wore superbly tailored dark evening clothes with a silver embroidered waistcoat. The hint of melancholy in his expression emphasized his extraordinary good looks. Lily murmured, "Trust me, Jonathan gave me his word and he would never break it. I've told no one else."

"I didn't think it was you," he murmured, loosening

the grip on her arm as if he suddenly realized how tightly he was holding her. "Take my word, I *knew* you wouldn't, but ... something has happened, and I had to ask."

... are you being blackmailed? ...

Damien's question had puzzled her because she had no real secrets. But Arthur certainly did, and it was easy to come to the conclusion that one might have something to do with the other.

"Arthur ..." she started to say, but was interrupted.

Rudely interrupted.

"What is *this*?" The tone of the voice jarring into their conversation was so full of venom, Lily actually stepped back. Arthur dropped her hand as if she were something poisonous, his features blanching.

"Nothing," he informed his wife woodenly as she swept up, the diaphanous skirts of her fashionable ivory gown brushing the floor, her face livid with outrage. Behind her the crowd was a blur, but no doubt they were watching. Inwardly, Lily had to cringe.

If she could have sprouted wings and flown off, she would have.

"Nothing? You just dragged off this ... this ..." Penelope Kerr sputtered, no doubt searching for the most insulting word possible.

"Careful." To his credit, Arthur's voice held a steely tone. "Do not insult Lady Lillian. She doesn't deserve it."

"*She* doesn't deserve it? You'd humiliate me like this in front of all of London?" The question was shrill and much too loud, and heads turned, some of the conversations around them stilling. His wife's face held twin blotches of mottled red on her cheeks.

Lily fought the urge to turn and run, as that would

just add fuel to the fire. If she had nothing else, she hoped she still possessed her dignity. *This is absolutely the last thing I need....*

"Humiliate you, no. Never on purpose, and I hardly think all of London is here." Arthur's voice was reasonable, his demeanor settling into contrived calm. "Come, my dear, I think if anyone is going to humiliate you, it is yourself. You've had too much champagne. Shall we go wait for our carriage?"

Lily received such a lethal look of hatred from the current Lady Sebring she said a prayer of thankfulness that this was a public venue, even if the scene was mortifying. If ever she could have been stabbed through the heart with a single glance, it would have happened at that moment.

Penelope Kerr shook off her husband's hand and hissed out, "No. I'm not finished."

Lily went pale. She was sure the blood drained from her face as she braced herself for the upcoming open warfare. Lady Sebring had the avenging look of a woman who didn't care for a possible scandal, and perhaps, in her shoes, Lily wouldn't either.

"Here you are."

The smoothness of the male voice made her glance up in surprise as Lily felt a warm hand cup her elbow. Damien Northfield smiled down at her with affable good nature even though she was sure he was neither affable nor particularly easygoing. His elegant clothing suited him, and his dark eyes held a telltale glint of amusement and sympathy.

So the spy was not quite as impervious as he seemed.

Lily recovered enough to murmur, "I thought you were bringing the carriage around, my lord."

"Deuced slow in this weather." Damien nodded toward Arthur, his fingers curling possessively around her arm. "Sebring. Hope you enjoyed the performance."

It was with some satisfaction that did not speak well for her character that Lily noticed the man she had once imagined she'd marry flinch and look away. Arthur straightened and said in a level tone, "I did indeed. Please excuse us."

His victories were usually personal, certainly uncelebrated and unremarked except at the highest levels of British military intelligence.

But, as Damien deliberately tucked Lily's hand into the crook of his arm and escorted her toward the doors of the theater, he found he was enjoying his role as knight errant. What he didn't enjoy was the slight tremble of Lily's fingers on his sleeve.

"That was expeditious," she said so low he could barely hear it. "Thank you."

"Let Sebring deal with his wife." Damien smiled at an acquaintance with a nod, a small part of him wondering if he'd lost his mind. He hadn't thought it over; he'd just seen the pending confrontation, noted Lily's tension and distress in her stiff posture, and a primitive protective reflex had surfaced. "And no thanks are needed."

"She hates me." The woman at his side walked with her skirts brushing his boots, her profile remote. "It's so odd. I don't think I've ever been hated before, and she has no cause."

He doubted the issue was quite that simple. "Her husband wanted to marry you."

Lily flashed him a look. She was striking this evening in pale green with matching ribbons woven through her shining hair, her ivory shoulders bare. "Her husband *declined* to marry me."

Damien said nothing, because there were too many people around, not to mention the Dowager Duchess of Eddington leveling a look his way that might melt a lesser man into a puddle of fear.

So instead of responding he relinquished Lily to her chaperone's care and gallantly bowed. "Your Grace."

"Well handled, my lord." The older woman spoke with cool inflection. "You have my gratitude, and I am sure Lady Lillian feels the same. Who would want to dredge up a long-past incident solely for the benefit of a public scene? Very *outré* if you ask me."

It was neatly done and the disparaging sniff entirely for the avid listeners, making Lady Sebring sound like a shrewish wife—which from what Damien had witnessed he wasn't sure she didn't deserve. A few of the women nearby twittered behind their gloved hands.

And God bless the British aristocracy, Damien thought in amusement, for being able to always outface any embarrassment, even if it involved an angry wife confronting her husband's former love in the lobby of the King's Opera House.

But the question remained that if Sebring had known his wife might react in such a way, why had he risked it? What was so urgent?

The blackmail was the obvious answer, which meant it involved Lily.

He'd suspected that all along, but it still puzzled him.

"It's always lovely to see you, Lord Damien," Lily said formally, her tone just a bit stiff. At that moment the ducal carriage was called and he simply smiled and inclined his head as they ducked into the rain, watching the departure with thoughtful contemplation as a footman assisted both women into the elegant equipage under the dripping awning.

Lily had been at first relieved to see him, but it had faded almost immediately, replaced by a certain cold dismissal that he felt he didn't deserve and certainly did not understand.

But he would understand it, he thought with cynical conviction, because that was what he excelled at, what drove him, what gave him a name for dealing with secrets. He sought out the truth and it didn't matter to him if it was ugly—often it was—or shameful, or even dangerous. As a weapon, truth was invaluable.

More and more he was convinced Lily might know something that would help him, and the note he'd gotten earlier in the day from Charles was like fire to dry tinder.

Young men ruined, suspicious suicides, a missing servant . . . any progress?

In a word, no.

It was time to do something devious.

There was a moment when she didn't understand what was happening, when the gloved hand over her mouth translated to a bad dream, her foggy mind not quite registering the circumstances. Lily blinked, tried to roll over, was unable to move, and then as more awareness seeped through her senses, panic kicked in and she screamed.

It did not go far. A muffled sound was the best she could do, and though she twisted, whoever had crept into her bedroom held her easily in place and proceeded to deftly secure her wrists somehow with one hand, while keeping his other over her mouth.

"I won't hurt you." The words were low and accented with a Welsh brogue. "But someone does need to speak with you, miss. Quiet now, or the whole house will come running. I can be gone in the blink of an eye. Think of the scandal if you claim there was a strange man in your bedchamber. Can't afford that, can ye? What if they decided you invited me? I give you my word that you'll come to no harm."

Of all the threats he could have used, that one was the most effective, though the word of a strange man didn't hold much weight.

This does not happen in Mayfair, her mind protested when he hefted her over his shoulder, her nightdress rumpled above her knees and her bottom definitely up in the air, her abductor's grip like steel. Unspeaking, he carried her toward the door and out into the hall, the house dark and quiet. That moment of indecision had been fateful, as if she'd wanted to scream right now, a squeak would probably be all she could manage, her ability to breathe compromised by his shoulder pressing into her diaphragm.

Her mind whirled, her captor's reassurance hardly enough to keep her fear at bay, but sure enough he held her securely as he began to negotiate the stairs, his grip firm but gentle, and he did manage it all without even breathing hard, taking her out through the servants' entrance, the narrow hallways unfamiliar, especially in the dark.

A closed carriage waited. The door creaked open and she was deposited on the seat in a flurry of loose hair and disheveled nightdress, before her captor muttered something, slammed the door, and then they lurched away.

She didn't know him. Heart pounding and the interior too dark to really make out his features, she shrank back and tried to stifle a whimper of fear because she refused to give her abductor the satisfaction.

"Oh, aye," he said softly, his voice a whisper in the gloom of the carriage, "I can see his interest in ye, I can."

Had she been able to ask what the devil he meant by that cryptic statement she would have, but it was difficult to put a coherent thought together.

So instead Lily attempted to give her best glare even though she doubted he could really see anything except for the rigid set of her shoulders and maybe the pale gleam of her face. Then she realized she actually could do something and kicked out, her toe colliding with his knee hard enough to make him jerk and utter a curse. It hurt her as well, but if nothing else, there was one small measure of satisfaction in his oath and his hand coming to rub the affronted spot.

"Was it really necessary to tie my hands?" she sputtered out, almost more furious than afraid.

"Aye, it was, for I was warned you have a bit of spirit. Beware, my lady, or I'll tie your pretty ankles together as well," her abductor muttered, shifting his body so he was out of reach. "I like 'em wild, but not violent, if you get my meaning."

She didn't get his meaning at all, but at least he didn't seem to be vicious himself—had she thought about it more perhaps she would not have kicked a man who held her helpless in a carriage. Not to mention she shivered now in her nightdress, some from the chill of the evening, and some from fright.

Then he did something entirely unexpected. He slid off his cloak and cautiously leaned forward to drape it around her. "Sorry. Should have thought of the cold. I was just tryin' to get in and out as quietly as possible."

To say she was bewildered at that moment was putting it too mildly, and when they reached their destination a short time later, she was no more enlightened, especially when she was hauled out of the carriage like so much baggage, the cloak pulled over her face so she couldn't see anything at all, though she had the impression her captor climbed a set of steps, and even had the audacity to smack her lightly on the bottom when she squirmed. "Quiet, miss."

Then they were inside somewhere, the pounding of her heart making it difficult to hear anything else, until there was a creak of a door opening. She caught a hint of tobacco that reminded her of her father's study, felt the warmth of the room with gratitude, still slung over her captor's brawny shoulder and carried down what was no doubt a hallway, for his steps echoed on the polished floor. Finally she was deposited on something soft and comfortable.

The cloak was pulled from over her head and in the dim glow of banked embers in a marble fireplace a young man executed a cheeky bow, his eyes gleaming. He was deceptively slender, especially as he had carried her so easily, and had jet-black hair. "My apologies for my method of delivery."

Lily sat up and did her best to shake her hair out of

eyes, her frantic gaze sweeping across the room. It was some sort of sitting room, not particularly illuminated except for the dying fire, and she was on a brocade chair, her bare feet resting on a patterned rug.

"I believe all I said was could you persuade the lady to accompany you so we could meet privately. I am not denying she's here, so you completed the task effectively, but we are no longer fighting a war, Alfred. Remind me to be more specific next time."

The voice was familiar with its cool, slightly cynical overtones, and a wave of relief replaced her fear, followed almost immediately by bewildered outrage. It was dark enough she hadn't noticed the figure that stood in the shadows until he stepped forward. Casual in an open-necked white shirt, dark breeches, and boots, his face lit to saturnine angles and hollows by the inadequate light, Damien Northfield smiled briefly.

"You!" she said, but it was impossible to be as scathing as she wished as comprehension of just who had orchestrated the kidnapping flooded through her.

And maybe something else. A glimmer of excitement perhaps?

"Alfred, if you will liberate the lady, I will get her either a glass of wine or a cup of tea, though the latter might not be hot. The housekeeper left some time ago."

"What *is* this?" Lily demanded, finally finding her voice, grateful that the bonds around her wrists were swiftly severed, though the wicked knife the man called Alfred so casually produced gave her pause.

"An opportunity for a conversation I think we need to pursue."

"By abducting me from my home?" It was all so incomprehensible that she wasn't quite sure if she was just dreaming. "Couldn't you call with another bouquet of violets, my lord? Are you mad?"

"You brought her violets?" Northfield's partner in crime looked amused, sheathing the knife back in his boot. "Really? This becomes more interesting by every passing minute, sir."

Sir?

Damien shot him a glance. "I will manage this situation from here."

"Yes, my lord, of course. I suppose I should take that hint and with it my leave." A moment later the door shut without a sound behind Alfred's departing form, his silent exit explaining a great deal about how he'd entered her home and made it to her bedroom undetected. The man moved as light-footedly as a prowling cat.

The real question was, of course, why did she find herself clad in only her nightdress in the middle of the night, detained by no less than the younger brother of the Duke of Rolthven?

Unfortunately, as Lily modestly jerked at the hem to arrange the skirts of her nightdress, she thought she could guess at the answer.

This was about Arthur. She knew it as sure as she knew she sat there in her state of undress, her hair loose and tangled, after being spirited away from her bedroom.

Would that fateful night haunt her forever?

"My lord, I repeat, have you lost your mind?" she demanded.

This gamble was probably as damned foolish as any he'd ever made, and there had been that time back in the infamous Hundred Days when he'd infiltrated French troops and pretended to be an aide to a colonel in the Grenadier guards, bluffed his way through the line with forged papers, and then pilfered battle plans by simply asking for them and then riding away.

It had taken quite a bit of nerve and his French accent was only marginally passable, so he was sure he'd sounded like either a drunkard, or a man with a bad cold, but the ploy had worked, and that was all that mattered.

And yet he wasn't sure he'd been as daunted by that stroll into the enemy camp as he was now with a very flustered, angry—rightfully so—young woman who he had to admit looked absolutely enchanting even if her night rail was a bit virginal for his taste, with lace around the sleeves and hem, and a bow at the prim bodice.

Mild equivocation seemed the best reaction. "Lost my mind? No doubt. And you never answered me, Lady Lillian. Tea or wine?"

She looked quite fetchingly furious, her face flushed and her hair tumbled around her slim shoulders. He waited for her response, lighting a small lamp with efficient movements, not wanting her to feel threatened, but to at least have a sense of vulnerability.

He'd hate himself for that later, but right now he wanted answers. "Tepid tea it is," he remarked, moving toward the cart when she didn't speak.

"I'd prefer wine." Her voice was sulky.

At least it was dark enough he could hide his wry smile. Had he suggested wine, she would have chosen tea, no doubt. There was a small sideboard beyond the tea cart and he moved to splash claret into a goblet, turning around and still wondering how to play this hand.

Or why he'd chosen to play it in the first place. Yes, for the sake of Charles's nephew and for the disappearance of the young valet, and even for Sebring, he wanted to solve this puzzle, but was having Lily brought to him in the middle of the night necessary—or did he simply want to be alone with her?

If the answer was both, he could live with that. His conscience was much more elastic than before the war. If it was just the latter . . . maybe he was more jaded than he thought.

It came down to the fact he was an expert in life-threatening decisions and definitely a novice in life-altering motivations.

He moved toward the chair, very aware of her tension, and even more aware of the state of her undress as he handed her the glass of wine. "I'm sorry for the abduction, but I very much need your help."

That surprised her. He could see it in her eyes, and in the tremble of her fingers as she raised the glass to her mouth. Lily took a sip and then cleared her throat, her eyes still flashing indignant fury. "Nothing could be so urgent you had to resort to such barbaric tactics."

"A man could die. Or I should say *another* man could die."

That stopped her, as he had calculated it would. Shock blanked her features. "You . . . you're being melodramatic," she finally stammered.

"Am I?" He poured himself a glass and took a sip. "How often do the younger brothers of upright peers of the realm abduct young ladies from their beds? It seems like quite a drastic measure to me, but I deemed it necessary. We need to be able to speak frankly and alone, and that is impossible during the normal course of the day. Even if I were to take you for another stroll on the terrace—and this discussion will no doubt take more time than we would be allowed—we could be watched and even overheard."

And, he added silently, *I would not get to see you so delectably disheveled and flustered, not to mention so adorably affronted.*

Lily stared at him. "I suppose there is a sort of convoluted logic to that, though may I mention that if anyone found us here alone together, I would be ruined." She stopped and then added on a breath, "For the second time."

"Ah, but no one will find you, and I implicitly trust Alfred to deliver you back to your bed as deftly as he took you from it."

"Hopefully not trussed like a chicken."

He had to laugh at that mutter, though this was not all a laughing matter. "I apologize for that." Any amusement faded. His own wineglass was cupped in his fingers, the liquid inside ruby red in the lamplight. "Lily, are you still having an affair with Sebring?" he asked. It wasn't his business, but then again, Arthur Kerr had asked for his assistance, and damn all if a part of him wasn't interested on a personal level.

Lady Sebring certainly seemed to think they were.

Her lashes fluttered downward and then rose as Lily lifted her chin and looked back at him steadily. "Having an affair? No. But may I inquire as why you wish so urgently to know? Does the answer matter to you personally?"

That was equitable, he supposed, as he'd just asked an

extremely personal question. "I don't think the issue is *my* personal life, but I do have an interest in Lord Sebring's. He and I are old friends. We were at Cambridge together. I would appreciate it if you'd just be honest with me."

"Are you jealous?"

There was an edge to her tone that stopped him, and not just that, but an insidious feeling that there was something he was missing. She didn't look at him like she wanted him to say he *was* jealous.

She wasn't looking at him at all now, but staring into the fire.

What the devil?

He said carefully, "I thought it was long over between the two of you, but obviously his wife has cause to think otherwise." And if so, considering that Arthur did not want to lose the support of his powerful father-in-law, he could be blackmailed over the liaison if he were still seeing Lily.

Touching her, seducing her . . . bloody hell, Damien thought. He hated the idea of it.

"This is what you dragged me from my bed to discuss?" There was a look of disillusionment on her lovely face. "Arthur's possible infidelities? I cannot see how that could be life or death to anyone, my lord, and, it isn't a subject I would know anything about. If you *are* jealous, it is misplaced and you are as blind as his wife."

"Jealous?" he started to deny, but it was more reflexive than anything, because he actually might *be* jealous . . . but then he registered her averted profile.

Hell and blast.

Blind? It struck him then, arresting his arm in the act

of lifting his glass to his mouth, the truth like a brilliant flash of light, the realization his perspective had been skewed all along because of his attraction to Lily, causing the entire situation to shift, focus, become all too clear.

Usually he thought of himself as a worldly man. Certainly he'd seen just about everything during the war, or if he hadn't, he could say he'd seen more than enough.

It was more her expression than anything. Not wounded precisely; if he had to guess, four years had taken some of the sting away from her split with Arthur, but definitely guarded, distrustful even, and there was an air of innocence shattered.

He understood in crystal clarity the botched elopement, her refusal to discuss it, her air of wariness in general when it came to men....

At the moment he wasn't sure if he wanted to still help his old friend, or slam his fist into Sebring's jaw.

A log in the fireplace snapped, breaking the moment.

Chapter 17

"Lily."

His voice was quiet. Soft. The tone of it was even, but then again she doubted Lord Damien North-field was ever not in control. She really didn't wish to look at him, because truly, he was so very normal and unruffled and blasted unaffected under any circumstances, and besides, she was afraid—quite afraid—of what he was going to say next.

Against her will she glanced up, not willing to meet his gaze, but not able to quite resist either.

He stood by the fireplace, his figure limed by the glow and his face in shadow. "I didn't realize."

It was much too ambiguous a statement to respond to, but she had the sinking feeling he *did* realize now because he was staring at her, his mouth a tight line. She knew she shouldn't feel foolish and humiliated, but yet it was still there.

"Neither did I," she admitted, her voice low. That was, of course, the very heart of the matter. She certainly had never expected that soul-wrenching revelation from Arthur on the night of their elopement. Even now, with four years of contemplation behind her, she didn't truly understand.

"It must have been a shock to discover his inclinations."

"I had no idea that men ... well, that ..." She trailed off, not certain how to proceed.

"Take my word, I very much like women, and so I don't understand either. I can't get out of my mind how you looked in just your shift. It's been keeping me awake at night."

That rendered her speechless, and it was her turn to stare, her pulse quickening.

He audibly blew out a breath. "I've not heard a breath of rumor of it, so Arthur must be very discreet. Men talk. Gossip is not just limited to the female population." The words were slow and measured. "Even back at Cambridge there wasn't any indication that I ever observed, but then again, I wasn't looking for it either."

In the four years since Arthur had told her, she hadn't broken his confidence except to Jonathan, and that had been more to protect the viscount from her brother's possible vengeance than to reveal his secret. How much of a betrayal was it that she had told Damien Northfield the truth?

A large one probably, but on the other hand, it seemed he had known already.

"He told me he didn't accept it himself," she said in a whisper.

"I take it you discovered his preference for men the night you eloped."

Put so starkly, it brought home the memory of that unwelcome journey with vivid clarity.

She could recall the windy evening, the jostle of the ride, and in retrospect, the strained expression on Arthur's face. When they stopped for the evening, his hesitation as he secured two rooms for them was a sign, though that they hadn't shared a room was a detail that society tended to ignore.

"Not in the way you think." She crossed her arms over her chest and lowered her lashes a fraction, the moment etched indelibly in her psyche, not sure why she wanted to make it clear to him, but it was important to her suddenly that he know what happened in truth. Slowly, she explained. "He never tried to seduce me, or even as much kiss me, but I thought he was merely being a gentleman. When he persuaded me to forgo the long engagement, I thought"—she felt the scalding heat rush up her neck into her face at the intimate nature of the revelation—"I thought he simply didn't want to wait for me any longer. He'd already asked my father for my hand and been accepted, so I suppose this makes me hopelessly naive, but I interpreted it as a romantic gesture."

Damien tactfully said nothing, for which she was grateful.

"And then he told me. He came to the door of my room and knocked, and when I answered, he was so pale I thought he might be ill. He came in and knelt at my feet and begged my forgiveness but said he couldn't, after all, go through with the marriage because, in fact, he loved me, but not in the way I loved him. And he never would because of his ... preference. Our friendship meant enough to him that he couldn't use it to trick me into an untenable arrangement in which I would be cheated of the husband I deserved."

"A pity he hadn't thought of that before he persuaded

you to go off to Scotland." Damien's voice held an icy edge.

She brushed the skirt of her nightdress with one hand in a restless movement, remembering her former fiancé's tortured confession. "I think he had convinced himself he could provide me with friendship and security and a privileged life and I might count that enough, but the immediacy of the moment tormented his conscience. He gave me a choice. We could go through with the marriage, or he could take me back to London." She took a moment and a deep breath. "I chose the latter. I knew what it meant, but I was willing to endure it."

"I am not surprised, and that, my lady, is a compliment."

"Thank you." Lily stilled her hand. "This might sound ridiculous, but I still very much admire him for telling me the truth rather than forcing both of us into a life of unhappiness."

"Yet he still married."

"He needs an heir. And besides, she didn't love him. She coveted his title. There was no deception in their betrothal."

"You still defend him." One brow lifted in an ironic arch. "May I point out, from what I witnessed at the opera, it seems to me that Lady Sebring might be possessive of not just his title. How can you know her feelings aren't engaged?"

Lily had come this far, so she might as well tell the rest. "She's distraught because she hasn't yet conceived a child. The doctors say she might be barren. I doubt it is me she resents, but him."

"Sebring made a devil's bargain then, and someone out

there knows his secret. He's being blackmailed, but he refused to tell me why. Now I see why he was reluctant."

Just as she suspected. Arthur's grim demeanor when he drew her aside at the opera certainly bore out that something unusual was happening in his life. "Is he in danger?"

"Thank you for telling me the truth. Working in the dark is not impossible, but a little light always helps."

The evasive answer wasn't exactly reassuring.

"What are you going to do to help him?"

"I think I need to ferret out the source of the blackmailer's information, don't you? Your father must have known. Otherwise he would have challenged the man who so damaged your reputation with his ill-conceived rush to try to get you to the altar."

"I didn't tell him. It was far too embarrassing, yet somehow he understood." Her smile was tremulous. "I suppose I am not good at lying."

Damien paused and then said neutrally, "Not a bad trait."

She still remembered with unwelcome clarity that interview after she returned home disgraced and heartbroken. "He guessed from what I didn't say, just as you did now. My brother knows though, because I *had* to explain."

"He wouldn't—"

"No. Never."

Her lack of hesitation and vehemence must have been convincing, for Damien nodded, his face thoughtful. "I suppose I'll have to look elsewhere, then."

"Why?"

"As I don't think you are the source that provided the information to our villain."

Lily shook her head, her laugh short. "You do not play at misunderstanding very well, my lord. I meant, why would you help Arthur when you claim he is nothing more than an old acquaintance?"

"I don't just claim it, Lily." He straightened and took a predatory step toward her. "My reasons for looking into this are not easy to explain at the moment, but in case you have any doubt about *my* sexual preferences, I would be more than happy to demonstrate for you."

Well, he needed to distract her, and she was certainly distracting *him* with the folds of her nightdress draped across her provocative curves and her hair loose and catching glints from the firelight.

Even as Damien moved, a part of him wondered if he'd planned this all along. . . .

Maybe Sebring hadn't wanted her, but *he* did.

He definitely did.

Lily gazed up at him as he stopped in front of her, soft lips parted, her tumbled hair cascading down her back. When he reached down and took her hand to tug her to her feet, she didn't resist, rising, her breasts lifting with a swift indrawn breath. "You have no need to prove anything to me. I—"

"What if I wish to prove it to you?" His thumb brushed her lower lip as he interrupted. Her mouth was soft, smooth, and warm, and he lowered his head, wondering what he was doing. Kissing her was ill advised, but then again, so was kidnapping her.

Who would think return to civilian life would significantly affect his instinct for self-preservation?

"What if I *really* wish to prove it?" he whispered just

before he settled his mouth against hers gently. She didn't pull away but went very still and her lips trembled just a fraction beneath his, her uncertainty palpable.

Her first kiss? She'd just told him that Sebring hadn't touched her . . .

Damned if Damien wasn't grateful, for he was now granted this privilege.

His hand went to her waist, his lips gently possessing hers, seeking, tasting, letting her get used to the tactile sensation of their mouths together, slowly bringing her closer to his body with the pressure of his palm as it slid to the small of her back. At first she stiffened, but he was gratified to sense her feminine yielding, the sway of her body toward him, the slight clutch of her hands on his upper arms.

This really wasn't fair to her, he reminded himself, deepening the kiss, his body stirring into arousal—the intoxication of sexual contact clouding judgment that was obviously already impaired by hot-blooded desire. Lily was not experienced with seduction. Quite the opposite was true. She'd been educated sexually that night four years ago when Sebring had persuaded her to run off with him, but not at all in a romantic way. Instead, she'd been given a lesson in the vagaries of the human existence, and unfortunately, the revelation had been ruinous to her future.

He respected her dignity, her decimated prospects for a good marriage evidently a fair price in her mind to pay for a personal reconciliation between her self-worth and her aspirations.

In short, he already knew she wouldn't sacrifice happiness for pride.

How much would he offer? He didn't know. In a different way, this was as new to him as it was to her. What he did know was that he'd been captivated from that first moment when he'd caught the elusive scent of her in the library.

He'd watched both his brothers fall in love with their wives. They had been much less aware of it than he had been at the time—Colton had already been married— and it had amused Damien no end to watch them struggle to understand what exactly was happening. At this moment, with the intoxicating Lady Lillian in his arms, tentatively beginning to kiss him back with shy enthusiasm, he had to wonder what someone else might see in this particular moment.

"Tell me," he murmured as he broke the kiss, his lips feathering across her cheek, "do you believe in my sincere interest, my lady, or shall I further prove it?"

She didn't answer at once, her lips parted, her quick breathing lifting her breasts against his chest. Lush lashes finally fluttered upward. "I . . . I don't know what you mean."

He wasn't quite sure of it himself. By now he was fully hard, and he really could not remember wanting a woman so badly in his life. Maybe he'd been too long without the intimacy of a tender kiss, a light touch, that singular feminine sigh of pleasure in his ear. . . .

Caution was bred into him as the son of a duke. Embroiling himself in a liaison that might involve an unpleasant backlash in the form of an irate husband, or worse yet a father, was ill advised. As he'd never favored paying for erotic entertainment like so many of his class, he chose his bed partners with care and always made sure they were experienced and unfettered. After Waterloo he'd been too ill for a long time to even contemplate vigorous sexual activity.

Besides, he'd found in maturity, the lighthearted affairs of his youth were not as appealing as they once were. He'd had offers from ladies besides the persistent Lady Piedmont since his return to England, but none had tempted him for one reason or another.

Until now.

And what the devil do *I mean?* he wondered, his aching cock taking issue with his hesitation in responding to her wavering, uncertain question. Moreover, he could not only feel every perfect curve of her body through the thin fabric of her nightdress, but the rapid beating of her heart.

What Sebring hadn't done, he wanted to do very badly, but there was the sticky point that Damien would never compromise her and not play the honorable gentleman.

Marriage. It had always been an abstract concept. Something respectable members of society did, not men who had fought cunning and deceit and brutality on an equal level. Maybe it was that since the war he'd seen his brothers with their wives and families with a different view than that of the cynical bachelor who still had his freedom.

In the lengthening silence Lily must have sensed the measure of his indecision, for she suddenly tried to escape the circle of his arms. "You've learned what you wished to know. Can you arrange to have your accomplice return me, please?"

"Lily." His hold tightened as he looked at her averted face. "Don't turn away."

"Where else am I supposed to turn?" Her palms flattened on his chest and her response was barely audible. "Unless you mean to offer me something honest, I am not interested."

"Define honest." He leaned in and nibbled on her earlobe.

"Damien." She shivered, and some of her resistance departed. Her body was fragile in his embrace. "Don't do this to me."

He could, of course. Already he knew he could. If he lifted her now and climbed the stairs to his bedroom, he was certain he could persuade her to allow him to do whatever he wished to her all-too-tempting body, but that would be a hollow victory at best. Capitalizing on her vulnerability had never been his intention.

Smiling faintly, he said, "I'd like to do quite a lot of things to you, Lady Lily. Will the duchess think I am suitable enough to be a formal suitor?"

He'd shocked her yet again. Her face froze, and it took several moments before she composed herself. "She'd swoon with joy and receive accolades from all her highbrow friends for the coup, but perhaps you should ask what *I* would think."

A valid point, but Damien already knew what she thought. The tips of her breasts were tight under the thin material of her gown, and there was a certain vulnerable dreaminess in her eyes despite her dry tone.

In his life he'd never tried to make a woman fall in love with him.

He'd never *wanted* a woman to fall in love with him.

Life had been dull since his return from Spain until he met Lily in the library that evening, so perhaps it was time for a new challenge. Seduction—he might have success, but she was remarkably independent and intelligent—yes, seduction would be pleasurable, but he needed more.

All of her.

Damien's smile was slow as he touched her cheek and looked into her eyes. He liked the azure color—it reminded him of youthful summers and the cloudless sky. "What would you think," he asked, his voice holding a rasp of huskiness, "if I told you my intentions were ultimately honorable, Lady Lillian, but tonight distinctly *dishonorable*?"

"Ultimately?" Her gaze was confused, but yet defiant. "I don't—"

"You have my word." He swept her up in his arms. "But for now, we're alone and I've every intention of taking advantage of it."

Chapter 18

"I can walk."

The uneven gait as he carried her was a contrast to the easy clasp of his arms, the pronounced limp a reminder that this was a man with a complicated past. Damien stopped her protest with a look, his dark eyes veiled. "You weigh next to nothing and I am not a complete cripple."

I can walk. It was an indication she'd go with him willingly. Had she just said yes?

A tickle of panic stirred in her belly, but the sensation warred with another one—that of wayward anticipation.

That kiss. It wasn't as if just because Arthur had disillusioned her in almost every way possible she had abandoned her innate desire for a hero who would sweep her off her feet—to the contrary, the fantasy lingered and perhaps her bitter experience had even enhanced her romanticized imaginings of what it would be like to desire and be desired.

And Damien wanted her. She'd sensed it in the way his mouth had moved against hers, careful but yet hot and demanding, and then, of course, the shockingly hardened state of his body, easily felt through the material of his tight breeches and her thin nightdress.

"I didn't say you were a cripple, just that I am perfectly capable of walking up myself."

His mouth curved into a slight, mesmerizing smile. "I thought all females wanted secretly to be whisked away against their will by a wicked seducer."

"How would you know?" she asked tartly.

A low masculine laugh was her only answer.

The hallway was dark, but she had the impression of bare polished paneling and the scent of beeswax and lemon. In an abstract way she wondered what it would look like if anyone saw them, and then realized she'd put her arm around his neck. Not an unwilling seduction, that was for certain.

For four long years she'd been the recipient of sly glances and nasty whispers, and it had galled her to know that no doubt many of those who judged her were much more culpable when it came to inappropriate behavior than she'd ever dreamed of.

Until now.

Even the night of their elopement, Lily had never thought she would lie with Arthur until their vows had been said, and it had been a relief when he'd secured separate rooms.

When she'd understood why, the virginal uncertainty had turned into stunned incredulity, but as Damien gained the top of the stairs and shouldered his way through a half-opened door, she knew—*knew*—this evening would not turn out as that one might have, even if Arthur had desired her madly.

The starry-eyed notions she'd had as a debutante of

Arthur sweeping her into his arms were nothing like the stark reality of Damien carrying her to his bed, depositing her on the softness of the mattress, and bracing a hand on either side of her supine body and leaning close, so his breath whispered across her lips. His voice was husky. "I want to make love to you. I realize that other than one bouquet of violets, I have not given you a proper courtship, but in case you have not noticed, life is full of ironies. What we lack in formal calls and genteel dances and poetry, we gain back in secret staircases and blackmailed lovers and midnight abductions."

Lily touched his neck, the tensile strength of the muscles there betraying his tension. "I've enjoyed the latter much more than I ever liked the former, my lord."

"You see? The perfect woman for me."

Am I?

She wanted him to kiss her again and there was a flush to her skin that had nothing to do with the temperature of the room. Even in her thin nightdress she was too warm, and when he straightened and began to unbutton his shirt, she watched in open fascination.

She—the supposedly fallen—should already know all this. The quicksilver motion of a man's fingers as he slipped each fastening free, the way he watched her with heavy-lidded eyes, the slightly rumpled silk of his hair. But she didn't, she never had, and at two and twenty, she was tired of worrying that a Sir George might be her only option. That a twice-widowed man willing to overlook her soiled status would be the best she could do, while other supposedly fine ladies indulged in affairs and took lovers but whispered about her behind their gloved hands.

She was no longer that wide-eyed innocent who had not been canny enough to avoid scandal.

This evening she was making a choice.

What did he say? Oh, yes, the perfect woman for him . . . Does he really think so?

"No one is perfect, least of all me."

He had a way of smiling that wasn't a smile at all. More a shift of his facial muscles, like the sun rising as it slowly spread in a hint of light, so that you knew he was amused but his expression never truly showed it. "What more could a retired spy ask for than a lady of daring and wit, one who lurks in libraries and does not mind being abducted in the dead of night?"

She might have answered except he shrugged out of his shirt and it slipped down to the floor. There was no lamp lit and the only illumination was the glint of the stars and a full moon that shone through the window with the draperies still open, the muscular planes of his chest defined in silver light.

In this moment, she should think of a clever response, but it didn't come. Her gaze was fastened on his half-naked body and her heart fluttered at a rate that made her catch her breath.

Deep in her brain she protested the method in which she'd come to be there, and a traitorous part of her also celebrated.

"Do you want me to send you home?" He sat down and tugged at a boot. "It isn't too late."

It was much, much too late and she had a feeling he knew it full well. "No."

The second boot went flying. "I was rather hoping

you'd say that. We can discuss the future when I call to-morrow, but for now, I think I'll join you."

When he did so, the bed dipping under his weight, she took in a sharp breath. "I hope I am allowed to be nervous."

Damien kissed her lightly, then more deeply after a brief retreat, his mouth insistent and firm and his tongue sweeping against hers, before he lifted his head. "Let me put you at ease."

In the next moments she learned that meant a gentle gathering into his arms and a slow, calculated assault on her senses. Taste—his was like brandy and warm male, the tactile sensation of the slow guide of his fingertips along her bared arm, the scent of his skin, the exhale of his breath, the intense look in his eyes when he raised his head and their gazes locked . . .

"I want to touch you." It was a request for permission, but already his fingers tugged at the ribbon on her bodice. "I haven't bedded a virgin before. . . . If I make you uncomfortable, tell me."

"Everything about you makes me uncomfortable," she confessed, watching the way the moonlight gilded his features, "but not as you'd think. I'm *aware* of you."

"I hope so"—his smile was a fleeting ghost as he parted the material of her nightdress—"for I certainly intend for you to be."

The cool waft of air over the exposed tip of her breast as he pulled the fabric aside was both enlightening and embarrassing, the idea of nudity not completely an unknown—she was widely read—but in reality a bit more immediate than she'd ever imagined.

"Damien," she gasped in protest even as he lowered

his head and lightly licked her nipple. The intimate caress caused the muscles in her stomach to tighten and her head to fall back.

His hand touched her breast, slowly cupping it. His long fingers gently moved against her tingling skin as he did sinful things to the other nipple, lathing it so the wet heat of his mouth made her shudder, grazing the sides of her mounded flesh with his lips, nuzzling the valley between them . . .

Then, as if he knew exactly what she wanted, he switched sides, administering to the aching tip of her other breast as she uttered an inarticulate sound of pleasure and clutched his shoulders.

She was barely aware of how he inched her nightdress lower and lower until it slid free of her arms, and then in a deft movement, he lifted her and stripped it off completely. His fingertips touched the plane of her stomach, making her quiver as his gaze examined her naked body. "As I said before . . . perfection."

Neither voluptuous nor petite, she'd always thought she was rather ordinary. Medium in height, not full-bosomed but with enough curves to be feminine, her hair unfashionably brunette, but with a hint of gold in the brown strands; her eyes being her best asset in her opinion. In short, pretty enough to draw notice but hardly a dazzling beauty, yet at this moment, from the glitter of desire in his dark eyes, she believed he was sincere.

Actually, from the moment they'd met she'd trusted him, because otherwise she would never have dared that dark, narrow staircase nor would she be there now, naked in his bed, a flush on her skin and a curious warmth between her legs.

His finger trailed lower to brush the triangle of hair at the apex of her thighs, the touch light but shocking. Lily went very still, half closing her eyes, her breathing shallow; shy but not nearly as much as she imagined she would be at a moment like this. Though, she had to admit, if it had been anyone else regarding her with that heavy-lidded stare, she would be horribly uncomfortable.

This was ... different. It was beyond anything she'd imagined, and even in her inexperience, she knew it was just beginning.

She *trusted* him.

Allowances had to be made for the simple fact Lily had no idea what she was doing to him. Damien was also somewhat out of his element, in that he didn't seduce young maidens, even supposedly fallen ones.

What he really wanted was to tear off his breeches so they could be skin to skin, but her innocence was a deterrent, and besides, his disfigured leg made him self-conscious.

There were ghosts, it seemed, in both their pasts that were determined to rise and cause conflict at this poignant moment. He regarded her flushed face, the glory of her nude body, the sultry frame of her outspread hair, and knew he was both blessed and cursed.

Cursed he was used to, but blessed was going to take an adjustment. He stood, his fingers going to the fastenings on his breeches, and he undid them swiftly, grateful to be free of the confining cloth. He didn't wish to make her apprehensive, but then again, she didn't seem to be as startled as he expected. As he shoved down the garment and moved toward the bed, her gaze held his, though her lips trembled a fraction as he lowered himself on top of her. He knew she could feel the press of his erection hot and hard against her inner thigh, but there were some parts of this evening he could control and some that were beyond him. His arousal was part of the latter category.

"I won't do anything you don't expect," he promised, kissing her after the soft words. Nose to nose, his body tense over her softer one, he did his best to ignore the urgency of his need. Then he smiled, qualifying his words. "Depending, of course, on what that is. Lily, please help me with this."

"I am supposed to help with my own seduction?" A trembling laugh lingered behind the question.

"Yes." Damien trailed his lips down the curve of her throat. "Absolutely. What could be better? Tell me what you want."

"How could I possibly know?"

Her breath was coming even quicker now, the rise of her luscious breasts against his chest so arousing he had to stop himself and fight for control. He tickled the hollow beneath her ear with his mouth. "Does this feel good?"

"Yes." She arched.

That was too honest to be coy. It was one of her most alluring attributes and she had many. He shifted to settle over her body even more, his hand sliding across her thigh, stroking the satin skin. "And this?"

When his fingers found the warm heat between her legs she shut her eyes, but to his gratification, she didn't resist, though she tensed. "Damien."

Her cleft was exquisitely warm and soft, and though already damp, she was not quite wet enough for penetration. Propped next to her in the bed on one elbow so he could see her expression in the moonlight, he began to stroke her to readiness with a slow, calculated rotation of his hand. Female arousal was not a deep dark secret, though he knew most men would do better to pay more attention to a touch in just the right place, whispered words in their partner's ear, to feather their lips along the arch of her throat. . . .

Lily at first lay very still, her thighs only marginally parted, her eyes half-shut and her beautiful breasts quivering with each sharply indrawn breath. The moonlight silvered the highlights in her silken hair, those shimmering strands spilling in disarray over his sheets.

The compliment he'd given her wasn't simply a lover's words as a prelude to passion, but the truth. The reference wasn't just to physical perfection, as that didn't actually exist, but to his personal preferences. It was odd, but he'd never considered what he found attractive in a woman. Naturally, he was like any other man and found a certain symmetry of features and body pleasing, but with Lily it was something else, something intrinsic in the way she moved, smiled, or as at the moment, exhibited both an endearing courage and the greatest trust a woman could give a man.

Damien wanted this first time to be all it could be for her. He was, in fact, determined it would be. Whether or not it had been intentional, she'd been despicably cheated by Arthur Kerr.

If she were going to fall from grace this evening, Damien was determined she would count it worth it.

"Oh." The soft sigh drifted out and her hips shifted, her slender thighs parting a telltale distance more as her sex softened, his fingers growing wet as he continued to arouse her untutored body. Damien leaned down to press his mouth to where her pulse fluttered in the hollow of her throat. "That's it," he whispered in encouragement. "Let it come."

Her heavy lashes fluttered, but her concentration had obviously shifted to the bombardment of new sensations, for a moment later she moaned, arching her back, and as he continued to stroke and fondle, she finally gasped and began to shudder.

Her climax almost caused him to embarrass himself, the combination of long abstinence and her allure already threatening his self-control so he had to actually fight ejaculation as a primal response to her pleasure. When she finally lay panting and dazed in the aftermath, Damien took a moment and inhaled deeply, his throbbing cock calling for intemperate action when his brain advised restraint.

Smoothing his hand upward over her still quivering belly, he subtly moved his weight so he was positioned between her open legs. It was with some measure of difficulty, because his entire concentration was on his need to be inside her, that he reminded himself this was a lifealtering moment for them both.

"I want you," he said with more vehemence than he intended, his voice low. "I need you. But not unless you tell me yes, Lily."

"Yes. Yes. Yes." Her eyes shimmered in the faint light and her hands smoothed down his back. "Damien, *yes*."

He began to enter her then, the penetration slow, deliciously so, the tightness and heat of her vaginal passage tantalizing and rapturous. He didn't pause at her maidenhead but pushed through it swiftly, catching her cry of surprise in his mouth as he kissed her with soothing tenderness, finally completely within her.

And when he began to move in the age-old carnal rhythm of thrust and withdrawal, at first very slowly, to let her adjust to it, but then with more urgency, his need grew until he couldn't contain it and a groan erupted from his lungs as he pushed in deeply, releasing his seed in a brilliance of pleasure that shook him, body and soul.

They were both damp, breathless, and Damien held her close as he rolled to his side, his damaged leg aching but the pain negligible considering his personal contentment.

He wasn't particularly gifted at sentimental declarations. Most of his skills were in the areas of subterfuge and deception, but considering what had just happened between them was a milestone in a woman's life, he wanted—needed—to say the right words.

"I think I'll have you kidnapped more often," he murmured teasingly.

"Hmm. I am in favor of that plan, my lord." Her hand moved over his bare chest, and she rested against him, lax and deliciously female, her hair tumbled over her pale shoulders.

He brushed a strand away from her cheek and peered down at her. "Tell me how you feel."

"Enlightened."

About me. Us. This. Yet he hesitated to ask, for he really wasn't sure he had the right. Yes, he was now her lover—her first lover—but as he'd acknowledged earlier, he'd never given her a proper courtship, just a proper bedding.

Quite the opposite of Arthur Kerr, who had courted her with deliberate charm and intent, but then declined to follow through with it.

He looked into her eyes. "I'm enlightened, too."

Chapter 19

The figurine sat on the polished floor and Regina studied it from her repose, in this case on a chaise that her father had brought back at her insistence from her mother's apartments in Paris. Even as a child she'd been discerning in her tastes, and the piece had been given to her mother by a gentleman who might or might not have been her lover. Perhaps it did come from one of Marie Antoinette's follies, or perhaps not, but either way it was elegantly carved and beautifully made. She'd had it re-covered in dark blue damask a few years ago and it was one of her favorite pieces of furniture for both sentimental and aesthetic reasons.

One hand propping up her head, Regina studied the statue and thought about the symbolic aspect of the gift.

Does he know?

It couldn't be. She hadn't changed yet, not that she could tell, except maybe her breasts were already slightly larger and definitely more sensitive, but she hadn't seen James in well over a week. She hadn't been ready.

Not that she was sure she was ready now, but she'd indulged herself and held this moment at bay because for the first time in her life she didn't know what she wanted.

"It's supposed to be Rhea, a Greek goddess of fertility." The voice that spoke from the doorway was negligent, almost deceptively casual. "Or so I was told. I cannot pretend to any level of expertise on the subject."

It was a measure of their relationship that now he came straight up to her rooms instead of waiting formally downstairs, and he hadn't asked to be announced first either. James Bourne was inherently polite by nature, so this was progress indeed.

Regina straightened a little, but stayed in her seat, adjusting herself against the plush back in a languid movement. Her heart had begun to pound. It was ridiculous, of course. She was thirty-five, not some chit just out of the schoolroom. "It *is* Rhea," she commented as he strolled into the room, watching him strip off his gloves. "Note the ring of pottery around her head. . . . That's a turret crown, but the tips have been broken off over the years. And those aren't dogs flanking her, but lions, though the chipping makes it hard to tell. It's quite an ancient work. Wherever did you get it?"

"I don't know if that matters so much as whether or not you like it." James looked at the battered statuary dubiously, his blue eyes holding a hint of amusement. "I confess it looked like something one might toss in the rubbish, but the proprietor of the shop assured me it was worth far more than I paid for it, and very old."

"And you thought I might like it."

"Don't you?" His gaze swept to her, his good-looking face uncertain. His blond hair was slightly ruffled by the windy evening, which made him more handsome than ever in her opinion. She liked a little disorder.

He frowned. "It was merely a guess, and I suppose, in retrospect, maybe not a suitable gift—"

"On the contrary," she interrupted with a tight smile. "I adore it. Though it is unsettling you know me so well. Care for a brandy?"

Such an unoriginal ploy, but she'd heard her stepmother use it on her father so many times when she wished to distract him that it came naturally. James was dressed tonight in a formal ensemble of dark evening clothes that told her he'd been out, or maybe was headed to a society event, because a glance at the clock told her it was not that late even though she was tired.

This pregnancy was playing havoc with her usual nocturnal schedule.

Yes, she'd come to the conclusion that she definitely carried his child, confirmed by a discreet physician Luke had recommended who could be trusted to never reveal her identity. In a kindly manner the older gentleman had suggested after his examination that he knew someone to help her place the child with a family far away when the time came.

Never.

The vehemence of her reaction, the intensity of the emotional reflex, was not what she expected, but still it struck deep. Give away her child? Give away James's child? Absolutely not.

That was one part of her dilemma that wasn't a dilemma at all. Like her mother, she might find herself with child out of wedlock, but as she adjusted to the idea, she found she couldn't contemplate giving up her babe.

No. That was wrong. *Their* baby.

For so long she'd been so strictly independent that the

idea of having to share this responsibility chafed, but then again, she knew he deserved the truth. Her father had been denied that, and he'd made it clear that had he been told, he would have played a role in her life much earlier. As it was, he'd been a loving and dedicated parent, but her mother's secrecy had cost them both precious years together.

Her past kept her from giving the baby away—not that she'd ever considered it—and also precluded not telling her lover she was going to bear his child.

Damn.

It might be an unladylike word, but then again, she had never concerned herself too much with being a lady in the first place. Her current predicament of unwed and pregnant certainly bore that out.

James gave her a level look, still in the doorway. "Am I staying? If the answer is yes, I would like a brandy. However, as you've declined to see me for the past week, I was beginning to wonder if I had upset you in some manner, though you have my word as a gentleman I cannot recall what I might have done."

"You are staying."

His brows rose minutely. "I am? That is gratifying to hear."

"You are ever a gentleman, James. That is part of why I have avoided you." She rose then, maybe a bit too swiftly, for she had to take in a deep breath to quell a rush of light-headedness, and swayed.

"Regina." He was there instantly, moving across the room with long, athletic strides, catching her in his arms. "Have you been ill? Why didn't you just tell me?"

It was ridiculous, for she—who had never wanted to

be coddled and cared for by any man—actually savored his embrace and support for a moment, resting her cheek against the superfine material of his elegant coat, briefly closing her eyes. Luckily, these moments passed quickly and the dizziness abated as fast as it had come.

The room was so normal, with the scattering of mismatched chairs, the beautiful Moorish table Luke had sent her from Spain for her birthday one year, and like every other room in the town house, an abstract collection of art on the walls. In this case, landscapes, not of the bucolic English countryside but instead her interpretations of what she'd read of exotic places such as India and the African continent. She enjoyed working that way, with nothing but an image in her mind and a canvas, paintbrush, and a palette of brilliant colors. . . .

But she hadn't painted in days. That had not happened in her adult life.

"I'm not ill." She straightened, doing her best to look coolly composed, idly adjusting the bodice on her gown, a simple pale pink muslin much suitable for earlier in the day. She'd fallen asleep after luncheon and not bothered to change. "But thank you for your concern."

"My concern?" James let her go, but it was reluctantly, and she could see the tension in the set of his broad shoulders and the shadows in his blue eyes. His tone held a bitter, mocking note unlike him. "Fine, we should address my *concern*, Regina."

She crossed over to the decanter, picking up a glass. The mere thought of any beverage but weak tea at this point made her nauseous, so she poured a glass only for him. "Please, go ahead."

"I love you."

In the act of turning to extend him the snifter, she froze.

James exhaled raggedly and ran a lean hand through his hair, his tall body tense. His jaw was set. "Yes, I love you. This past week has been hell. If you wish to end it between us, I suppose I was a fool for expecting anything else, but damn you, I *love* you."

The crystal glass all but slipped from her fingers and she only consciously kept hold of it by tightening her grip enough she was surprised the bowl didn't shatter in her hand.

The nuances of the moment were both clear and yet obscured. The rawness in his voice balanced by her fear of hearing those exact words, her resistance tempered by his evident sincerity, the tick of the clock on the mantel in the resulting silence as they looked at each other symbolically loud and yet absurdly normal.

"Say something." He moved to gently remove the glass from her now shaking hand. "I didn't mean to upset you. I just . . . well, I had to say it, I suppose."

Regina stood there, her hands now dropped to her sides, and watched him take a convulsive swallow of the golden liquor, her emotions in turmoil. It wasn't like she'd never heard impassioned declarations before, but James had been different from the beginning and with the coming babe . . .

Wasn't she in turmoil enough?

The truth for a truth. That was fair enough.

"I'm going to have a child." Her legs were weak, but she straightened her spine and took in a deep breath, meeting his gaze. Her smile was tremulous. "There. I've said something."

*   *   *

He was speechless.

Elated.

Frightened.

Bewildered, James discovered in the next moment, by how he should respond to the revelation of impending fatherhood. Especially because though Regina was looking at him with calm poise, in truth her normally flawless complexion held a singular, unnatural pallor in contrast to the richness of her hair. She was a vision in her soft pink gown, but he had wondered why she was still so informally attired despite the hour, though it wasn't like Regina conformed to any kind of normal schedule.

A child . . .

They had never been cautious because she'd told him it wasn't necessary. That first night, as they'd kissed, touched, and breathlessly made love, she'd said there was no need to worry about a possible conception.

He took a deep breath, trying to assimilate this revelation, to reconcile the tumult of his emotions. "I was under the impression you couldn't have children."

"So was I." Her expression was neutral. "The physician I consulted assures me that this happens. It isn't necessarily the female who is barren, and I haven't had all that many lovers. After my first love affair did not produce a child, I assumed I couldn't have one. Don't laugh at my ignorance, please."

The last thing he would do was laugh at her, especially with the shimmer of tears in her eyes. She cleared her throat and added quietly, "I've always thought I wasn't fertile, but it appears that isn't true."

Normally he would feel elation at the admission he

wasn't just one of many men in her life, but at the moment he was still trying to assimilate the staggering news.

"You needn't feel trapped."

James came out of his initial shock, his eyes narrowing slightly at the flat sound of her voice. "What?"

"Trapped. I'm not asking for anything. I've money enough to—"

"Regina, my love, be quiet and try to not ruin this moment for me," he interrupted, restive, crossing the rug to the window but not really seeing the silken draperies or the view even though he jerked aside the curtain. "You're sure? I am going to be a father?"

"Yes."

He turned, and this time his gaze burned into hers. "I should have phrased it differently. *We* are going to have a baby?"

With very uncharacteristic acquiescence she nodded, her gray eyes huge in the dim light. Her hands folded in front of her belly. "Yes."

He'd come tonight half expecting to be turned away again . . . and now this. His voice ragged, he said finally, "I take it then the child will come in the late spring. Will you stay in London?"

"Does it matter?"

"Of course." His tone was clipped, more so than he intended. That he had no control over what she chose filled him with a sense of frustrating helplessness. "The child matters, you matter, that I love you matters. At least to me." As much as he wanted to reach for her, gather her close and laugh or weep with joy, perhaps even both, he understood from her rigid stance it would not be welcome at this moment. So he composed himself and took in a breath, letting it out with measured control. "I'm trying right now to imagine your position on this. What you're thinking, how you could be feeling."

"Odd that." Her smile was fleeting. "Here I am, doing the same for you."

Slowly, he pointed out, "Before I knew about the child, I told you I love you."

She turned away, her profile distant as she walked toward the opposite window. She always moved with a certain fluid grace and he found it even more mesmerizing now, his perception of her changed, heightened, as if the fertility of her body lent her a new air of feminine mystery.

She stopped and turned. As usual, her hair was only carelessly caught up, the dark curling strands achieving a riotous beauty despite the lack of a sleek, perfect coiffure. Very softly, she said, "Please understand this, but I'm trying to decide if I *want* you to love me."

Had that admission been a surprise, he might have been offended, but he was cognizant of her defenses. Regina did not like dependence. Fair enough, she didn't need a male to care for her, but he wasn't interested in possession. He just wanted a part in her life.

And in the life of their child.

"At the risk of sounding autocratic, you don't get a choice." His voice was just as quiet. "Neither did I. I fell in love with you. It just happened. I love you whether you wish it or not."

"How easy you make it sound." The statement ended on a choked sound.

To his consternation, he realized she was crying. Regina. His Regina, who was eclectic, and liberated, and had never given another human being a commitment in her life. The twin trails of tears down her cheeks glistened in the faint light and there was the slightest tremble to her shoulders as she drew a breath.

An icy vise gripped his chest. "You don't want this babe?"

She glared at him at once through her tears, her expression militant. "Of course I do."

The tightness in his heart eased. "Then what's the issue?"

Soft lips compressed and her eyes were a storm gray he'd seen before. "You're going to offer to marry me."

It was impossible to deny. "I *want* to marry you, and now it is even more pressing, as by doing so, I can make our child legitimate."

"I'm not sure."

That stung, but he'd braced himself for it. He knew she was unsure, and while he had no experience at all with pregnant ladies, he'd heard his cousin Jonathan discuss with affectionate exasperation his wife's moodiness and emotional upheavals. So he reminded himself with as much pragmatic logic as possible that their unusual situation would shake even the most stable of relationships, and it was not a reflection of what they felt for each other.

Usually he'd give her time and not press, but in their case, while she might desire to wait to see if she could reconcile her emotions, they didn't really have it. "Tell me why you have doubts," he said simply, knowing it might be a painful exercise, but maybe if she had to articulate her feelings it would be good for them both. He knew his own mind; he had since the moment he'd politely seated her at that fateful dinner a few months ago, taken the next chair, and turned to look at the dark-haired beauty who smiled at him with a sophisticated ease that instantly captivated his attention.

"Why?" Regina sighed, and for the first time since his arrival, relaxed a little. Enough to go sink down on the chaise she'd occupied upon his arrival, crossing her ankles negligently and swiping her wet cheeks with trembling fingers. "Oh Lord, James, where do I start? Our ages?"

As reasonably as possible, he pointed out, settling into a sagging chair that he'd decided was his favorite, the worn velvet immune to the occasional splash of claret if they got into a particularly animated discussion, "Our ages? Not a valid issue, my darling. Try harder."

"How is it not a valid issue?"

At least she hadn't taken exception at the endearment. He gazed at his glass for a moment before he looked at her. "I would never discount your sentiments, but truly, for me, those seven years mean nothing at all. You are a lovely, intelligent, and sensual woman. That is what I see. Every man in London will envy me."

"And every person in London will talk about us as if we are the most scandalous couple to set foot on British soil if you married your much older pregnant mistress."

"I think you exaggerate our potential infamy, and since when do you care what they think?" He grinned, because experience told him that the opinion of society mattered to her not at all. "You never have before."

I am going to win this argument.

Regina—the Regina he knew—sat up a little indignantly, and then she subsided. "What about how I am just a by-blow of the late Viscount Altea, the product of his liaison with a woman who bedded him for money? You are the legitimate son of the brother of an earl."

"What the hell does that matter? Besides, you don't think of your mother that way." James leaned back and crossed his legs at the ankle, lightly swirling the brandy in his glass. "You loved her, and your father loved her from what you've told me. Yes, she was his mistress, but not a whore."

"How is it different?"

That he was startled was not in question. Regina had never before acted anything but unaffected by the circumstances of her birth, her blithe acceptance of it an intrinsic part of her personality. After a moment, he said quietly, "They chose each other. She would not have accepted just anyone with coin in their pocket, nor would he have supported any woman just for her sexual favors. I don't know why he never married her because you've never told me, but I am sure there was a reason. Can you explain why this is an issue now?"

"Because I am in her same position."

James had never thought of Regina as his mistress, nor had he ever contributed to her household. She was more affluent than he was by far. But this was evidently important to her, and just the sheer emotional turmoil that was unlike the woman he knew so well told him to tread lightly. "You mean that you are pregnant and not married to the father of the child you carry? Otherwise, I confess I don't see many similarities to our situation."

"Don't oversimplify this."

"Don't overcomplicate it. I am still unimpressed with your arguments against a swift marriage. Have I mentioned I want a girl?"

"Why?"

"Because there's every chance she'll be a perfect replica of her mother and—"

"That's not what I'm asking."

It wasn't hard to discern that was the truth. As difficult as it was to resist getting up to go take her in his arms, he knew that would be a less than prudent way to deal with their circumstances. "Why do I wish to marry you? Because we will suit each other perfectly. Because I love you. Because you carry my child. Because never, ever have I felt this way before and surely fate had a hand in gifting us with such a blessing."

Regina stared at him, her eyes misty. "You sound as if you are sincere."

"I am." He set aside his glass with a definitive click and stood. "I'm staying the night. And in the morning, I will stay for breakfast again, and if you have no objection, then I will obtain a special license so we can be married at once."

When he bent to kiss her she responded with the passion that had captivated him in the first place, her fingertips tracing his jaw. Then she whispered against his mouth, "Do you really want a daughter?"

Chapter 20

"The blackmail scheme is not run by one person alone. Kinkannon is a part of it, yes, but he isn't behind it."

Charles nodded at a passing magistrate with a neutral expression as they walked along the echoing corridor. "Considering the man in question, that does not surprise me. What else?"

"I am now certain the victims are not committing suicide. I still don't understand the purpose in killing them, but I doubt more and more that they've done away with themselves."

That won Damien a sharp-eyed look. Charles murmured, "Is that so? Perhaps we should select a different venue for this discussion."

To talk about cold-blooded murder? Maybe they should.

In the end they walked down the street to a small public house and without asking, Charles ordered them both a tankard of ale, planted his elbows on the less-than-pristine table, and lifted his brows. "Go on."

"I can't say with any certainty yet who is directing Kinkannon." Damien shifted in his chair, which seemed rather suspect and rickety. "This is what I *have* discovered. The threats are all based on small sins that have been committed, not usually anything catastrophic or criminal. Social embarrassment is the order of the day. Payments are asked for, and it appears some of the blackmail targets die."

"Only some?" Charles nodded at the serving girl who carelessly deposited their drinks, and handed her a few coins. In the late morning, the place was nearly empty.

"Yes. That's the dynamic I don't understand. Including your nephew I know of four victims, but there are more, I'd wager." Damien eyed his drink with dubious enthusiasm. It was going to be warm at best, and he was uncertain of the cleanliness of the glass, but then again, he'd drank out of a muddy puddle in the road in Spain once when he was so thirsty, so surely this couldn't hurt him. He picked up the tankard. "There have been a number of unexpected deaths in the *ton*. The son of the Earl of Haversham most recently. Supposedly he was kicked by his horse. They found him dead in the stall one morning, already stone cold. It's possible that is what happened, but when Sharpe asked a few questions, none of the lads thought it likely. The animal was well trained and the young man had been riding him for years. It came out he'd impregnated one of the scullery maids and was supposedly desperate to hide it from his father, which was probably why he was a target. I find the accident highly unlikely."

The taproom was a bit odiferous, but Charles didn't seem to notice. "Do you, now. Why?"

There were quite a few reasons he'd started to doubt the convenience of the deaths and the connection to

Kinkannon's manipulations to be an accident—most of the facts unearthed by the intrepid Sharpe, but the main one, as far as he was concerned, had to do with conjecture. Not a good way to operate an investigation, but then again, he'd saved himself countless times during the war by listening to his intuition.

Damien said slowly, "There's more. Six months ago Archibald Gorsham, the pride and joy of Lord Finnian, supposedly shot himself with a pistol in the garden behind their country house. He was an arrogant ass by all accounts. A strutting peacock, free with his money, with an eye for women and damn the consequences. Discreet inquiries unearthed a variety of sins, from gambling debts to insinuations of affairs with a married lady or two, and more—all the way back to purchased exams while at Cambridge. He was universally disliked by the servants, and his set of friends are among the worst rakehells in England. I am trying to picture him feeling enough remorse for anything to take his life and am unconvinced. In short, sir, he wasn't the kind. I think our blackmailer miscalculated his target, and when our villain does that and knows he won't collect, he kills them. Gorsham probably laughed in his face."

"An interesting theory, to be sure."

"I've more examples. Over the past year society has lost quite a few members due to accident or other circumstances. Kinkannon is behind the threats, of that there is no doubt because I've heard him myself. But he isn't the maestro behind the symphony, if you'll pardon the poor musical analogy. I know the difference between the puppet and the master."

"Indeed you do."

Damien simply smiled.

"I see." Charles wore his usual understated dress: his coat plain, his waistcoat a drab brown, his neck cloth carelessly tied. Taking a sip of tepid ale, he frowned.

"You know of your nephew's gambling debts." Damien idly watched the barmaid cross the room again. "He hasn't the money to pay any of them. He's in deep, though I would have appreciated you explaining the family connection from the beginning."

"I knew you'd discover it soon enough." A thin film of tobacco smoke drifted toward them and Charles waved it away, his hooded eyes betraying nothing. "He finally asked for a loan three days ago. White-faced and sweating, all but weeping. He didn't tell me the truth, but I had a suspicion anyway. The gambling was never a mystery. I have sources everywhere. What stirred my interest was his change in behavior. As I told you in our initial meeting, the prime minister has every confidence in your abilities, as do I."

"I'm flattered," Damien said dryly.

Charles predictably ignored the comment. "True, this isn't precisely a political problem, but then again, it is affecting the most prominent families in England. Blackmail? Murder? I want it stopped, but done so discreetly that the problem just disappears. As I suspected all along, arresting Kinkannon won't solve this. First of all, I highly doubt that any of his victims would appear before a magistrate to give evidence. Sparing themselves the embarrassment is why they pay in the first place. The point of this all is to keep their various sins in the shadows."

"I can make Kinkannon talk." Damien spoke matter-

of-factly. Not all of his skills learned during the war had
practical applications to his new civilian life in England,
but apparently that dubious one could be used in this
case.

That made Charles grin, which was a rather unsettling
sight, his pale blue eyes taking on an unsettling gleam. "I
have no doubt you can."

"Tell me, what did your nephew say when he asked
for the funds?" Damien drank some ale, decided it
wasn't the worst beverage he'd ever had, and gave
Charles a mild inquiring look. After all, if it hadn't been
for Henry Lawson's dilemma, he doubted he would be
investigating in the first place.

"Just that he needed money urgently. It was quite a
sizable amount. Were I not aware of the blackmailer in
our midst, I would have thought it just from his reckless-
ness with cards and dice, but it seems clear to me he has
been threatened with more than just the public humiliation of not being able to meet his debts."

Damien had come to the same conclusion. "No doubt
our friendly extortionist explained that he could meet
with an untimely accident."

"He's my sister's only child, the damn fool. That said,
I'm not giving money over to a vicious blackguard.
That's why I sent Henry to Scotland. I've a hunting lodge
there. Clara would never forgive me if something happened to him, and the boy can use the time to contemplate his weakness for dice while he freezes his arse off
in solitude, but at least he'll be alive. When you straighten
out this little matter, I'll let him come back to London
and we'll deal with his obligations."

Damien thought of Arthur Kerr and his request. "I

have another victim, one that is a friend of mine. That's how I became convinced that this is widespread. His secret isn't gambling, but something else altogether." He wasn't about to go into Arthur's sexual preferences. "I think the question is, How does our blackmailer find out these tidbits about his potential victims? There has to be a connection between all the victims, but so far it has eluded me."

"When you uncover the answer, let me know." Charles looked at his glass of ale and grimaced, setting it aside. "Drop me a note when this is all resolved."

Drop me a note.

Damien had to chuckle as he finished his ale. Sir Charles had an extraordinary sense of humor.

It was like harboring another deep, dark secret.

But quite the opposite of the one she'd held for four years.

Men, Lily thought irritably, but then in direct contradiction, her lips curled into a smile. What had happened between her and Damien was hardly the same as what had *not* happened between her and Arthur.

Deliciously, wickedly, the opposite.

She'd been delivered back to the house before dawn, and had to admit she found it amusing that Damien's detailed instructions about how to slip back up to her room undetected were so accurate. She'd navigated the journey without incident, though the smell of baking bread told her she was not the only one awake in the house.

It was strange, she thought later, while bathing, the overcast sky outside her windows doing nothing to dampen her effervescent mood, how life could change so quickly. The water was warm on her skin, the slight soreness between her legs a reminder it hadn't all been a dream, and she rested her head back on the edge of the tub, the scent of lilac soap drifting in the air.

Falling in love the first time had nearly ruined her life. Doing it a second time seemed reckless and naive, but then again, Lily decided, she hadn't chosen that path, it had chosen her.

Would Damien really marry her? He wasn't in the habit of openly declaring his feelings, which was a bit confusing, but that had been the intimation. Would she have fallen into his arms anyway? It surprised her to realize that she liked the air of mystery and intrigue, but then again, Arthur had seemed like the most respectable gentleman possible, and so perhaps she was drawn to enigmatic men.

The first time she'd fallen had certainly been a mistake. The second time might be a disaster. . . .

When she rose, dripping, from her bath, she brushed the towel over her body with a new awareness of what it meant to be a woman, and with Damien's promise of a call in mind, selected a day dress in apricot lutestring, paying attention to the way her maid did her hair when normally she dismissed that part of her toilette as inconsequential, just sweeping it up in a simple chignon. Today she made sure it was sleek and stylish.

The night before was both an illusion and a reality, for when she recalled those whispered moments, the moonlit madness of it all, she both believed, and didn't believe at all, it had happened.

Squaring her shoulders she made her way downstairs.

The duchess, she was informed, would be present for luncheon.

Marvelous. Lily had to wonder cynically . . . did she look different? Was there a special glow to newly ruined maidens?

If there was, she thought halfway through the cold soup served as the first course, it must not be evident. Carole asked with a pointed look, "Will you be joining us this evening?"

In a bid for time, nothing else, Lily dipped her spoon in the Serves bowl in front of her and said, "The Britton fete?" The invitation had arrived a few weeks ago and she supposed it was no surprise she'd forgotten about it. "I don't—" she began to say.

"I've already accepted for you, Lillian," the duchess interrupted in her usual crisp tone, seated with all due regality across the wide table. "Everyone of consequence will be there. Sir George has asked me if you would do him the honor of reserving a waltz. Naturally, I told him you would be delighted."

A laugh at the presumption was nothing more than a waste of breath. The Dowager Duchess of Eddington tended to make decisions without the influence of other people's opinions, especially those whom her choices might affect.

It was almost amusing, but not quite. Lily could endure a dance with Sir George—he was not odious, just a bit dull, but with the current tumult in her life, the idea of being polite and attempting witty small talk all evening held even less appeal than ever.

Damien might also attend, though. It seemed likely, as he was no doubt invited to everything. . . .

Whereas she was not. The invitation had been a coup, no doubt, orchestrated by the duchess. It was more than a little humiliating to think that strings had to be pulled to gain her entrance to the most elite events, but it was tempered now by the knowledge that Damien knew the truth. She wasn't the disgraced Lady Lillian, who'd failed to follow through with her ill-fated elopement, any longer, no matter what the rest of London society might think.

He'd set her free in so many ways.

"You are smiling at the idea of dancing with Sir George?" Carole sounded skeptical, her brows lifted, her blue eyes inquiring. Betsy was also studying her as if she hadn't seen her in a long time.

"No." Lily composed her expression to suitable decorum. "Not that he isn't a nice man."

"With a baronetcy," the duchess pointed out, but there was a shrewdness in her eyes that said she wasn't fooled a bit.

Perhaps her newly ruined status *did* show, Lily surmised as she reached for the goblet in front of her in the pretense of taking a drink. "I'm just . . . smiling."

"Humph." The duchess allowed the footman to remove her bowl. "I am *always* suspicious of that particular kind of smile from a young, impressionable woman."

"Not so young," Lily argued wryly, "and I take exception to impressionable."

"That," her exalted sponsor said serenely, "remains to be seen."

Chapter 21

He was the proverbial cat, pondering how to most effectively capture the mouse.

A rather dangerous mouse, because there were holes he didn't know about that the rodent could hide in.

But, Damien thought, he was *always* learning. . . .

Kinkannon was the focus of his meditation, his lack of an aristocratic background compensated by his fortune, though where he'd acquired it might be a point of contention when the truth was revealed.

After all, his infiltration of the ranks of the elite had been sponsored by their sins.

All men had weaknesses. Something that could break them. The only question was finding it. In this case, Damien hoped he had.

He walked through the lobby of the expensive establishment, noting the palate of colors that were surprisingly tasteful, masculine overtones in cobalt blue and deep green offset by the ivory of the rich carpet, the chairs arranged in intimate groups—of two, naturally—the dark chocolate of the upholstery a nod to the patrons' tastes, small tables near every grouping containing decanters and trays of sparkling glasses. A curio cabinet in one corner displayed a collection of decorated snuff boxes and the air held a subtle mix of perfume and tobacco.

Not since before university had he been in a brothel, and Damien stripped off his gloves slowly as he surveyed the interior of the reception room, a young man in beautifully tailored clothing hastening to offer him brandy and claret, both of which he declined before he took a chair and waited.

Madame Cyrene, who if he had to guess was not French at all, arrived in a swirl of amber satin and suggested they speak in her private sitting room. It was early, and so the young ladies were mostly at their leisure, lounging in the sitting area, and he received a few appraising looks as he followed the tall brunette toward a doorway that took them into a hall with carved doors and a hovering footman who whisked one open.

"Have a seat, my lord." Cyrene pointed to a chair and settled herself just opposite, gracefully reaching for the glass of sherry she'd obviously been drinking before his arrival. "I read your note and am intrigued. How is it I can help you?"

She was a celebrity of sorts among the males of the *haut ton*, though he had never availed himself of the services she provided. Word had it she herself never took lovers except on a very exclusive basis and he believed it. She was beautiful in an opulent way with dark, shining hair and only a tasteful application of cosmetics tinting her full lips and high cheekbones.

He said, "I need information on one of your clients."

"No." The refusal was decisive. She shook her head, but her smile was gracious. "I would be out of business very quickly if I disclosed any details about the gentlemen who pay visits here. I am sure you understand."

"What if one of them is using your goodwill and services to obtain leverage against other members?"

Her expression altered, but to give her credit, not very much. Had it not been for his experience in being so attuned to the responses of others, he would not have caught the slight falter in her smile. "In what way? Who is he?"

"Ah." He settled back and looked at her steadily. "You see, you are not the only one reluctant to relinquish confidences. I am understandably uninterested in warning my quarry."

She regarded him steadily, the charming courtesan replaced by a practical woman. "And I am uninterested in alarming my patrons with any hint of indiscreet disclosure. They come here with every confidence that they will not only enjoy themselves but also have full anonymity."

She suited the room, her presence vibrant and sensual, the walls paneled in pale pink satin, her dark beauty striking in the pastel surroundings, but he also knew from a bit of investigation she was a canny businesswoman as well, who had started out as the mistress of an elderly duke. "I am quite *sure* they enjoy themselves," he murmured, "but the anonymity is in question. That is why I am here. I do not want a list of your clients. I just wish to know the habits of one in particular."

"How do I know the information will not be traced back to me?"

"How do I know you won't send him a note the moment I leave this room, telling him I was here? I doubt very much he'll appreciate my inquiries. Much of life, don't you agree, is a leap of faith?"

"It is indeed."

Patience was one of the virtues that didn't come naturally to him, but he'd learned it during the war. He waited until she sighed and lifted a languid hand. "I don't want him here if he is disreputable or using our services for other than what they are. I'll tell you what I can if you'll give me his name. Your word, of course, my lord, no one ever knows we spoke."

"My word. His name is Edgar Kinkannon."

"Kinkannon." There was a derisive note in her voice as she repeated the name.

"I thought you'd recognize it."

"Oh, I do. Why am I not surprised he is the one that brought you here?" Cyrene laughed, but it was short and her lashes lowered over her eyes a fraction. "There are some you sense will be trouble from the beginning. He is a regular, yes. What else do you need to know?"

"Has he a favorite girl?"

"Girls. He has certain tastes. He almost always asks for two."

Damien was jaded enough that he was leagues beyond being surprised, and that was tame compared to the depraved preferences of some of the youngbloods of the *ton*. "The same young ladies?"

"Usually, yes."

"Can I speak with them?"

London's most famous procuress gave him an impudent look, her gaze trailing suggestively down and then back up his body where he lounged in the chair. "I am sure Delilah and Mary would be delighted, my lord, especially if the questioning is done under the most *comfortable* circumstances possible. You are very handsome, and they favor tall men. Shall I get you a room?"

It was his turn to laugh, shaking his head. "I am not here as a customer, and I am sure my intended would take exception to any line of inquiry under those circumstances."

Actually, what a presumption. He hadn't asked Lily to marry him yet; nor had he gotten permission from her older brother to make her his wife.

"You are getting married, my lord? That is not usually an obstacle to the gentlemen who come here. In fact, many come here more often because they are affianced and somewhat . . . shall we say, deprived before the wedding?"

"I am not deprived." The words came before he thought and he gave an inward curse, but the image of Lily, soft and receptive and quivering in his arms had sprung forth, unbidden.

"Oh?" Cyrene's eyebrows rose minutely. "How clever of your betrothed."

His mouth twisted wryly. For a man well known to keep England's secrets at all costs, he was not apparently very successful with his own. "My personal life aside, may I have just a few moments with each of Kinkannon's paramours of choice when they have a free moment?"

"Paramours? Aren't you tactful, my lord. I will see what I can do." She rose gracefully and crossed the room, and a few moments later a maid answered the ring of the bellpull.

*   *   *

When he didn't call in the early afternoon, Lily reminded herself at first that Damien no doubt had a good reason, though by three o'clock, she'd begun to fidget, and by the time he was announced just before four she had lost some of her serene poise. More alarming was how when he entered the drawing room, she had to prevent herself from leaping to her feet and rushing across the room.

How very gauche. How very unsuitable for a woman of her age, practically a spinster. How very . . .

. . . *very much like a woman in love.*

Elegance came to him easily. That she already knew. He adapted well to almost any setting, no doubt the chameleon ability that had made him so valuable during the war. For this formal call he wore a dark blue coat and fawn breeches and his chestnut hair curled against the crispness of his cravat.

She could recall this thick softness of it against her fingers as he moved his mouth persuasively against the aching tip of her breast. . . .

"I'm late," he apologized as he advanced to take her hand, his limp somehow managing to be graceful, though it was no doubt due to her current hopeless, besotted state, the lack of symmetry to his gait uniquely *him*.

"Not at all, my lord," Lily responded politely, hoping her blush over the brush of his mouth on the backs of her fingers was interpreted as maidenly pleasure over the arrival of a favored suitor and not as remembered pleasure of a completely different, carnal kind.

And somehow he knew. It was there in the hint of wicked amusement in his eyes, in the slight quirk of his mouth as he straightened.

This time he'd brought orchids. Perfect hothouse

blooms that emitted a delicate scent and pleased the duchess so much when he presented them that when he asked to take Lily for a short drive through the park, there was only a moment of hesitation before he was graciously granted permission.

Ah, the power of orchids and a very—deliberate, she knew him well enough for that—charming smile.

When they left the town house, her fingers on his sleeve, a cloak over her arm because it was still warm enough she didn't need it, Lily murmured, "How clever of you to bring flowers for Her Grace instead of me."

He slanted a glance at her as he handed her into a curricle with two matched bays that he obviously had driven himself. "They were supposed to be for you, but my plans changed and bribery is a perfectly acceptable medium of doing business. I had an unexpected errand, but I did not wish to break my word to you that I would call. If you can accompany me it allows us to spend time together and for me to take care of a small matter."

Lily had to admit she had no idea what he exactly was referring to, but she was elated enough it didn't matter. For the past four years she'd assured herself that she did not need a male dancing attendance upon her to feel alive, but then again, she'd never felt *this* alive before.

He wished to spend time with her and that was enough.

"What kind of errand?" she asked as he swung into the vehicle and took up the ribbons.

"One that would make the dowager faint into her tea-cup and forbid you to see me ever again." His grin was quicksilver in the slanting afternoon light. "But then again, I've already committed more than one sin in that arena."

Lily lifted her face into the breeze as they took off down the street at an exhilarating clip. "I am not trying to disillusion you, but I think it would take a great deal to make the duchess swoon."

"I have every confidence *this* would." His smile widened and a lock of hair played over his brow, making her want to lean forward and brush it aside, but the street was hardly the place to do it, no matter how swiftly they were moving along.

"More than having me kidnapped from my bed?" She raised a skeptical brow.

"And into mine? Perhaps." He grinned. "Still, you must admit that was a brilliant idea."

That lighthearted yet dangerous tone made her give him a sharp sideways glance, for she could not think of a more scandalous scenario than a seduction, but then again, he was far more worldly.

Life with him would be an *adventure*.

Infinitely so, she discovered a few minutes later when they whipped around a corner and were suddenly on an unfamiliar street, not that she really knew London except the well-traveled main thoroughfares. A half a mile or so farther down, he pulled up next to a carriage on the quiet street, holding the spirited horses easily in check with one hand and nodding at the occupant who had rolled up the window shade.

"Milord." The woman who spoke was blond and pretty, though a slight gap between her front teeth gave her a gamine look. "So lovely to see you again."

"Thank you for meeting me, Delilah."

"My pleasure."

The roguish tone of the response made Lily blink, and

for this time of day, she couldn't help but note Delilah—whoever she might be—wore a rather revealing gown and the reference to a planned meeting was a bit disconcerting.

"Do you happen to have what I want?"

The young woman coughed delicately and Damien handed Lily a small bag he fished out his pocket. "Would you mind, my love?"

My love.

Paralyzed, she sat there for a moment before she realized he wanted her to hand the coins over to the waiting Delilah, who snatched it up and in return passed over a packet wrapped in leather. Lily took it, clasping it in her gloved hand, still a bit bemused by not only this unusual meeting but also the endearment.

And that quickly it was over. Damien briefly clicked the reins and they rattled off. His only nod to the fact it happened at all was to say, "Please be careful with that, if you will. I went to some considerable trouble to get it."

Obediently she tightened her grip on the packet. "Who was that woman?"

"Delilah? I am afraid I am unaware of her surname. It often works that way. Best for both parties that might be involved."

"What works?" Perplexed, she turned and stared at him.

Sinewy fingers controlled the reins with seeming effortless ease as they headed down the street. His handsome profile was impassive. "An exchange of information."

Lily took in a deep breath. "What sort of information?"

"The sort a man might reveal to a prostitute if he is ignorant enough to believe that just because of her vocation she has no intelligence."

"I just spoke with a . . . a—" she stammered.

"A strumpet? Actually, I don't think the two of you exchanged words at all."

He was teasing her, she understood that, both from the tone of his voice and his swift sidelong amused glance. As usual he did everything so smoothly one hardly noticed they were swept along until they realized something unusual had happened. It was a rare talent and no doubt made anyone who possessed it a very valuable . . . well, spy.

But the war was over.

"You were correct," she muttered after a moment. "The duchess might faint."

"And perhaps she should." He laughed, but then sobered. "I hope you aren't offended that I included that small stop in our afternoon drive."

It was odd, but she really wasn't as shocked as she should be. "Not as long as it wasn't the entire point of our outing," Lily said wryly. She realized he was heading for the park, which was just as well, for they would be noted driving together.

"No. Not the main point at all. I wanted to see you."

A facile answer, but she believed him.

"What is this?" she asked then, examining the plain missive but not opening it.

"Power." Damien's dark eyes gleamed. "If you didn't know already, let me tell you, information is the most formidable weapon of all."

Chapter 22

He might live to regret his next actions, but hopefully it would be worth it, and in any case, this was a necessary step, even if it did get him into trouble.

The honorable gesture, James thought wryly as he nudged his horse up the long drive, the manor house in the background stately, the well-kept facade warm in the late-afternoon sun, after committing the very *dishonorable* act of bedding Viscount Altea's sister.

If she heard of it, Regina would no doubt have his head on a platter, but that was a chance he had to take. For her sake, for the sake of their child, and damn all, for his sake too, because this was his *life*.

He dismounted and handed the reins of his horse to a stable lad, hoping since he had sent a note the day before Luke Daudet would be expecting him. His lordship, James was informed by the stoic butler, was with his steward, but Lady Altea had requested he be shown to the terrace to join her until her husband was free.

Moments later he found himself being graciously greeted by Regina's very lovely sister-in-law, a stunning blonde with exotic dark eyes who gracefully offered her hand and dazzled him with her smile. A silver tea service sat on an iron table and there were chairs on a flagstone area overlooking the ornamental gardens. A vining plant with frothy white flowers climbed up the pillars, and it the distance he could see a small gothic folly on the other side of a placid pond, complete with Greek columns and a pointed roof. The scene was bucolic and serene.

"Please have a seat, Mr. Bourne. Luke should be out shortly, but in the meantime may I offer tea, whiskey, or like my husband, do you prefer a combination of both?"

Despite his trepidation over the reception of this visit, he had to laugh at the knowing look in her eyes. "I can tell you are a woman who understands men. It was a rather long ride from London."

"Please have a seat and I will pour, then."

He waited for her to settle back into her chair before he sat down opposite her, watching the always pleasant sight of a female deftly serving tea, and was amused to see her splash a measure of whiskey from a small bottle into his cup, and then consider it and add a little more. When he accepted the delicate porcelain saucer, he said, "Can I come to the conclusion that you feel I might need that extra fortification, Lady Altea?"

Madeline Daudet took a dainty sip before answering, her gaze speculative. "If you are here about Regina, and I assume that is the case, you might want to move the bottle a little closer to your cup."

Since James had no idea what—if anything—Regina had told her family about their relationship, he was not quite sure how to respond. In the end, he'd come to talk to Altea about his intentions toward his sister, so he said with raw emotion, "I'm here because I love her."

"And, being Regina, she is resistant to the idea. Not

of you necessarily, but of letting someone else into her life."

"Very perceptive. I see you know her well." His tone was wry.

"I don't know if I can claim that, but Luke does. They are very close." Lady Altea glanced over at where a small bird hopped along the stones, her expression holding a hint of sympathy. "A word of warning: he'll support Regina in whatever course she chooses. A scandal is incidental in his eyes compared to his affection for her."

It wasn't as if James didn't already have that impression. Regina had been allowed to do as she pleased her whole life, she'd once told him—not smug or otherwise lofty, just matter-of-fact, secure in her place within the hierarchy of the Daudet family and their acceptance.

"I am uninterested in him forcing anything upon her, so that isn't the issue, never fear. I am more looking for advice and insight than an ally. I want her, but only if it will make her happy."

"How lucky she is." His hostess regarded him, her slender fingers curled around the handle of her cup. "May I ask what brought you here now?"

Was that a cautious reference to the coming child? They could dance around the subject, or he could frankly say something about it. He cleared his throat and was about to speak when someone interrupted. "Good afternoon, Bourne. I must apologize for my tardiness. A business matter that couldn't be ignored. I am sure you understand after being steward for your cousin for so long. I see Madeline is playing the hostess with her usual flair. Thank you, my dear."

Luke Daudet was a tall man—they were of a height,

and he was fair in comparison to Regina's rich dark hair, but they had the same signature eyes of that crystal gray color that was so unusual. James stood quickly as Madeline rose. She said, "I think there was a hint of dismissal in your tone, darling, but I am going to forgive you because it is time for my afternoon nap."

"I wouldn't dare ever dismiss you, which you know, my love." Lord Altea's smile was affectionate. "But"—he pulled out his pocket watch theatrically and opened it—"it does seem to be four hours since your last nap, so you must be exhausted."

Her dark blond brows drew together. "Trust me, if *you* could have this child, I would arrange it."

When she left in a swirl of silk and disappeared through the French doors back into the house, Regina's brother sat down, eschewed tea altogether and poured whiskey into his cup, then said dryly, "If it were possible, I think she would."

James looked him in the eye. "And if you could do it for her, wouldn't you?"

Luke sprawled back in his chair and lifted his brows. "The image it brings to mind is a bit disconcerting, but yes, of course. Childbirth is not without its dangers."

"Regina mentioned your wife was breeding."

"And since my sister does not gift casual acquaintances with personal disclosures, I assume the reason she told you is because you aren't a casual acquaintance at all."

"I certainly hope not."

Men didn't need to fence and riposte in the same way females chose to avoid confrontation. Altea, if James had to judge, was neither friendly nor antagonistic.

Luke murmured, "So you are my sister's lover and the father of her child. She must have told you."

"What if she hadn't?" James adopted the same cool tone.

"Regina would never keep the pregnancy a secret." Her brother's conviction was unmistakable in the firmness of his tone. "When her mother did that to our father, it cost her five years of childhood memories of him before he found her. No, she informed you of the coming child, and that, of course, is why you are here."

In the past, they'd known each other on very casual terms as members of the same club and the same circles on a social basis. Not friends, but not strangers either, Luke Daudet having spent years in Spain and only returned from the war within the last two. James liked him, but he didn't really know him.

"Just the other evening, I asked her to marry me. I would have asked her before except I was certain it would make her cut me immediately out of her life."

Short and heartfelt. If Regina's brother didn't believe him, so be it, but he wanted to make his position clear to her family.

"Very astute," Luke said finally, his tall body relaxing a little. "God help me if I have a plethora of daughters. I already have two sisters and a wife. More than enough females for one man. What are your plans?"

"Plans?" James gave a short, mirthless laugh. "If we have plans, I am not privy to them. That is part of the reason I'm here."

"I see."

"Do you?"

"I've known Regina my whole life."

That was a valid point. James stared at the tips of his boots, trying to recall the clever speech he had at the ready before he arrived. "I'm at a loss," he finally admitted. "I'm afraid I'll lose her, lose my child . . . I can't—I won't—coerce her into an arrangement she doesn't want, but I don't want to make the mistake of not doing my best to persuade her."

"I hope that's sincere." Luke gazed at him over the rim of his cup.

James looked back steadily, forcing himself to sit politely when what he truly wanted was to get up and pace. "It is."

After a moment of consideration, the other man nodded.

"I can talk to her." James managed to hold on to his composure. "That isn't why I'm here. I don't need an advocate."

"Clarify and I will do my best to help."

James focused his gaze on the nearby park, the grandly held branches of the trees green, the air fragrant. "I don't know how to proceed. I'm not asking you to intervene on my behalf, but just for some advice. As you said, you've known her longer. She stated frankly I shouldn't feel trapped, and I never would, but I think it might be the other way around." He paused and waited a moment before saying with as much detachment as possible, though it was difficult, as he was anything but distant from the situation, "I know the reasons she lists for not having married. Her freedom, her financial stability, her art . . . but there's something more, isn't there?"

Regina's brother considered him from across the table, the muted sounds of birds in the trees in the background, the breeze moving softly. Eventually he sighed. "Damnation, you don't ask much, do you? She won't thank me if I tell you. It's extremely personal."

"More personal than her carrying my child?"

"You have a valid point, but I don't interfere in her life."

He hadn't come there lightly, and though he couldn't force Altea into any confidences, James could be frank about his position. "I didn't either, before now. She isn't alone in this."

"No, she doesn't seem to be." Luke Daudet fingered his whiskey glass and then said in a neutral voice, "It happened when she was barely seventeen. On a visit to our aunt in Bath, she caught the eye of a French aristocrat named Fortescue. His family had been slaughtered in the Terror and he fled to England. He was waiting to see how high Bonaparte's star would rise, I suppose, before he risked his neck trying to retrieve his estates. He was a royalist, though he was adaptable enough to become a favorite of the empress when he did return to France. Loyalty was not apparently his forte." Luke's smile was brittle. "And while he waited for his country's destiny to be decided, he was inclined to amuse himself with Regina. He was handsome, charming, flatteringly attentive, and she was very young and idealistic."

"He seduced her." James said it flatly, a tiny white-hot flame flickering in his brain that might have been jealousy or anger, or a combination of both.

"Why not?" Luke asked sardonically. "After all, she was just the illegitimate offspring of a Frenchwoman who had become the mistress of an English lord, born into sin and destined for a similar fate as her mother, or so he scornfully told her when he discontinued the affair and left her heartbroken and disillusioned."

"That *bastard*." It surprised even him that he had such a violent reaction. James normally was even-tempered and in control, but he felt a surge of murderous rage. He could only imagine the humiliation and pain. It was no wonder she guarded herself so closely.

"He's dead." Luke reached over and helped himself to more whiskey.

That was satisfying. It was on the tip of his tongue to ask how he might know that, but James managed to not articulate the question, something about the tight line of Luke's jaw telling him more information was not forthcoming. Instead, he moodily contemplated the line of trees beyond the formal gardens. "Thank you for telling me."

"I told you for her sake," Regina's brother said succinctly. "What are you going to do?"

"If I knew," James informed him, "I wouldn't be here, trying to gather information. I suppose now I understand a bit more her wariness, but that was a long time ago."

"You do not get over that first foray into love. Years pass, but the memory does not fade."

The words were said in a pragmatic, even tone, but it wasn't hard to discern Luke spoke with some authority on the subject.

"This is my first experience," James told him simply.

It was true. There had been some memorable moments as he'd grown into adulthood; he'd seduced and been seduced, and the ladies of his acquaintance who had graced his bed had given him pleasure, but all had been transient interludes, designed to please them both but never destined to go any further.

"Regina's was very painful. That was when she threw herself into her painting. I am enough younger I didn't really realize at the time what had happened, but I did notice she'd changed. She was still very much a free spirit, but certainly not a carefree one."

It was easy enough, considering her obsession with her art, to see her seek solace in her work. James could picture her at such a young age. . . . She was beautiful now; no doubt she'd been just as stunning then but in a different way, fresh and inexperienced, yet adventurous enough to allow herself to be seduced.

"I am younger than she is also," James murmured, thinking back over their last conversation. "It bothers her, not me. I don't care. I've told her, seven years . . . it's nothing. Certainly not a rational argument against accepting my proposal."

"She's emotional from the pregnancy," Luke informed him with an ironic lift of his brow. "It is, I'm informed, part of the process."

"*I* wish to be part of the process," James said then, his conviction clear. He did. This was his babe on the way, and Regina was the first woman he'd ever loved. It should be simple and she was making it complicated. He wasn't titled, but he was currently the heir apparent to an earldom, and while he wasn't fabulously wealthy, he wasn't a pauper either by any means.

"Some would call you a fool. She's giving you a chance to walk away from her unexpected pregnancy and the burden of it all."

Lord Altea might taunt him, but escape held no appeal. "No," James responded with quiet intensity. "Never. It isn't a burden and I want our child. I want *her*."

"Good." Luke slid a little lower in his chair in seeming casualness, as if something in him had relaxed, his eyes narrowed against the slanting sun. "Stay for dinner and the night. You'll get back to London after midnight if you leave now."

"Thank you, but I must decline." James rose, not exactly lighthearted, but lighter, his understanding clearer. "I would, but I want to make sure she doesn't think that now that she's told me, I'm avoiding her. I need to see Regina."

"Not a bad strategy."

"Do you think she'll agree to a marriage between us?"

"If you'll excuse the painful honesty, I don't know."

It *was* painful, but then again, he didn't know either.

James had to ask, "Once again, any advice?"

"Treat her as an equal and yet care for her. It is a delicate balance, but she deserves it."

A good point and James didn't disagree. He stopped in the act of the leaving the terrace, turning around. "You're sure Fortescue is dead?" James asked matter-of-factly, for really, France was not that far.

Viscount Altea said with soft, emphatic certainty, "Oh, yes, I'm sure."

Chapter 23

He was in his element. Dark night, shrouded alley, thin moonlight . . . even the smell—though a bit noxious—didn't bother him.

Damien edged forward, his back to the brick wall but not touching the filthy surface, his hand clasped around the hilt of his knife. This was what he did, he thought as he stood there, veiled in shadows.

He hunted.

Would he be willing to relinquish the sport for a tamer existence and a wife and family? *Yes. No. Maybe*, but that was not the issue at hand.

Kinkannon lived out on the fringe of the nobility in a neighborhood that wasn't quite fashionable but certainly close, in a town house that had black shutters on the windows and a neat walkway up to the front. At the moment there were no lights visible behind the curtains.

Yet Damien knew the owner was at home.

A perfect time for a visit.

He skirted the shadowed street and went around to the small back garden. The windows were latched but not securely enough if someone with a modicum of determination and skill wanted entrance. He managed it with ease, opening one of the long windows into what proved to be a breakfast room, and slipped inside.

Often—all too often when in the business of gathering intelligence—he'd found himself wondering why he was pursuing a certain angle of investigation. It was no different now as he crossed the shrouded room and cracked the door. It led into a hallway, shadowed and cool, and he moved into the darkness, quiet as a cat, though he had to admit he was aware of his damned crippled leg. Escape was for the fleet of foot. He needed to make sure he gained—and kept—the upper hand.

Sharpe had gleaned a little information about the blackmail scheme, but to their mutual surprise, not all that much. On the surface, it was straightforward. Young men who got themselves in trouble were the target. Kinkannon approached them with the threats, extorting money. . . .

Just men? Maybe, as Lily had pointed out, that was because young women usually had very little in the way of funds at their disposal.

Damien's instincts told him they were missing a bit of the puzzle.

Confronting Kinkannon was the logical way to resolve this nasty little scheme. The man was a thug in tailored clothing, not a mastermind, and accomplices in schemes of his sort rarely held loyalty very deep. Damien hadn't acted before now because he was still not quite sure what he was looking for. However, considering that Kinkannon had boasted to Cyrene's young ladies that he would soon be a rich man, that presented a certain unsettling clue that the situation needed to be resolved in a timely manner.

Up the stairs—he'd memorized the interior as described to Sharpe by a chambermaid—and he reconnoitered the hall, finding the door he wanted.

Damien tested the handle. Not locked. Noiselessly, Damien opened it enough for him to have a narrow view of the room.

That was more than enough.

Kinkannon was there, and though he couldn't be sure these were Cyrene's girls—Delilah was not one of them—two young ladies, also naked, entwined in the shambles of the bed. At the moment, the two women were engaged with each other and Kinkannon, naked and aroused, watched from a propped position against the pillows, his fingers idly tracing the length of his erection.

There was a distinct haze in the air.

Opium, Damien mused, the habit pervasive enough that Kinkannon could watch and become aroused but not participate, which would account for his desire to have two bedmates instead of one. The smoke in the room bore out the assumption, the odor cloying.

The luxury of the furnishings was telling, Damien decided, his gaze scanning the sumptuous bed hangings and thick carpet, the occupants of the room unlikely to notice the cracked door. Not that he didn't already know this, but it was evident Kinkannon was getting his funds from somewhere other than the modest living he supposedly had inherited from an uncle.

"Touch her." The words were thick, almost lethargic, and the subject of Damien's investigation moved a hand in languid gesture. "Do it."

Obediently, one of the women—brunette and reason-

ably attractive—slid her hand down the belly of the
other girl, touching her intimately between her legs. As
he wasn't particularly enthralled by voyeurism and he
had business to attend to anyway, Damien decided that
waiting for the progression of the evening was not going
to fit into his schedule and he went ahead and shoved the
door open and stepped inside. "Good evening."

The pistol in his hand might have been unnecessary,
but then again, he was fairly certain Kinkannon was a
killer.

One of the prostitutes gasped, and they both scrambled up to their knees. Even Kinkannon seemed startled,
and maybe the opium fog was not as deep as Damien
imagined, for he leaned over and jerked open a drawer
on the side table by the bed.

"Don't," Damien drawled with lethal emphasis, his
weapon loosely held in his gloved hand. "I'd love any
excuse to kill you, trust me."

"Who the devil are you?" Kinkannon reluctantly
dropped his hand, his eyes glassy in the candlelight.

Instead of answering the growled question, Damien
gestured casually with his weapon at the discarded clothing on the floor. "Get dressed, ladies, and make sure he
pays you before you depart."

"Are you daft?" The blonde, thickly built, with a mane
of ungovernable hair she tossed over one shoulder as
she slid off the bed, said, "We make this bleeding bugger
pay in advance."

"Bitch," Kinkannon muttered, his gaze glittering,
jerking the sheet up to his waist, his eyes not precisely
clear but definitely wary.

She didn't respond, nor did the brunette, drawing on

their clothes, and when they slid past him, both of them gave Damien a saucy look, which he returned with an amused smile.

As the door closed, he leaned a shoulder against the wall and murmured, "It seems you aren't a favored client. Now, then, with that mentioned, let's talk about your employer. I assume that is how it works—he hired you to do the unsavory part of your little scheme."

"Get out." His unwilling host snarled the words.

Damien smiled, though it didn't reach his eyes. "Who is he? I've already ascertained how he gets some of his information . . . from you. You patronize brothels, ask about certain men who visit and pay the girls well for the information, and then pass it along to whoever is paying *you*."

It was one matter to sneak up on a quarry when they were wary and aware, but this was not particularly a challenge. Naked, his reflexes affected by the drug, Kinkannon was not an adversary to be taken seriously—at the moment anyway.

The other man said thickly, "I don't know what the blasted hell you're talking about."

"Yes, you do. We'll begin with the blackmail and address the murder later."

"Murder?" The word was said with bluster, but it was hardly convincing.

It was telling that the accusation of blackmail didn't have the same effect. Damien chose a chair across from the bed and sat down, though his pistol was still loosely held in hand. "You haven't noticed the recent rise of suspicious deaths among the elite gentlemen of the *ton*? Word has it a communication from you is the light to the fuse."

"What a lot of nonsense."

The denial was vehement, but Damien noted a sudden sheen of perspiration on the other man's face. "They aren't suicides or accidents, are they?"

"I'm not—"

"Innocent? No, you are not." Damien wasn't interested in the untruthful denials. He'd been in other situations like this one where interrogation was essential because other evidence was just not obtainable. Human beings, in his experience, were the best source anyway. "How lucky is Henry Lawson to still be alive?"

"Don't recognize his name."

"You should, because you attempted to extort money from him. As it happens, I was at the same social event and witnessed firsthand your conversation, Mr. Kinkannon. That established, I am interested in the alternative you offered him to paying back his gambling debt. At the time I thought it was a straightforward transaction, but looking back, your comment that he had another option seemed to upset him more than the demand he repay the notes you now hold."

At first it seemed like Kinkannon was going to deny it, but then he sullenly shrugged. "I was just going to give him more time."

"That," Damien murmured disparagingly, "is not even a good attempt at a convincing lie."

"I . . . I don't even recall what I said to the bloke."

Damien adjusted his position in the chair, his gaze fixed on the man in the bed. "Don't you?"

"No."

Futile denial. It really was like being back in the war, with cryptic exchanges and little to no information except from those adversaries who really understood the stakes, only Kinkannon was not a professional by any means.

"Tell me the truth."

"Why should I?" Kinkannon asked, staring at him with bloodshot eyes.

"It is in your best interest." It wasn't bluster or an idle threat. With lethal sincerity Damien said, "I always get the answers one way or another. It is much easier on you to cooperate now before this meeting becomes ... unpleasant. Now, tell me why you began this in the first place. Who set you on the path? I don't believe for a minute you are alone in this. You aren't clever enough."

"What do you know about me?"

"Edgar Kinkannon, born in Ireland in 1780, the youngest son of an Irish peer who no longer acknowledges your existence, from what I understand. You served in the English army, but hardly with any distinction, not rising above sergeant, and you've been in London for the past year, trading on your father's title for admittance into the social whirl. Word has it you've become a bit more affluent as of late, and we both know why." For emphasis, Damien raised the pistol and cocked it. "Now, who is procuring for you the information you use to torture your victims?"

"If you shoot me, someone will hear."

"And I will fade into the night. I've done it before."

Kinkannon went ghostly pale, his face working. "Can't tell you who it is. The notes come in the post, I swear it. It was he who suggested we do this. ... The first letter came without so much as a seal on it, suggesting the game ... and it sounded easy ... and it is. He gives me the names and I put the pressure on. I get my money whether or not they agree to pay."

That had to be significant, but as of yet, made no sense. A blackmail scheme in which a partner is paid whether or not money is collected? For instance, in the case of Charles's nephew, who had gambled his money away, how could he even be expected to have the funds?

Unless murder was the initial intention.

"And you kill them if they refuse?" Damien asked it matter-of-factly.

"No, no!" Kinkannon's thick body shook and he looked longingly at a pipe set on a small tray. "I've never harmed a one of them."

"I think they might take issue with your definition of harm. So what is the alternative choice to paying for your silence? And do not prevaricate. My benevolence is slipping."

Kinkannon stared at the gun in Damien's hand and shook his head, his voice little more than a slurred whisper. "I don't know. I receive sealed notes to give them the first time we meet, when I get the initial information."

Damien lifted a brow skeptically.

"I've never looked," Kinkannon mumbled, huddled under the sheet. "After the first one died, I didn't even want to know."

It was well after midnight and Regina rolled over, glanced at the face of the clock, still visible in the glow of the dying fire, before she tucked her hand back under her cheek. The silken sheets were warm from her body, her eyelids perversely heavy, and yet she couldn't sleep.

"I'm late."

Startled, she half sat, propping herself on one arm as she watched James, who had shut the door quietly behind him, sit down in a green velvet chair to remove his boots. "How did you get here?"

"My darling, you gave me a key."

It had been a stupid question, but she'd been half dozing for hours and the room was warm, and he was finally there and it disconcerted her how much she needed him. Pulling the sheet up under her chin, she murmured, "I meant it's quite late and if you were out squiring your cousins—"

"I wasn't." James stood up and swiftly unbuttoned his shirt. "I was visiting your brother."

"Luke?"

"Yes. Do you have another?"

His breeches went next, and then he was climbing on the bed and settling in next to her, drawing her close to his lean body, the cool touch of his fingers drawing a path along her hip. He kissed her shoulder. "Now, go back to sleep. I didn't mean to disturb you."

She could confess she hadn't slept well without him.

But, no, she wasn't ready for it.

Nor did she want to destroy this moment by disrupting the gentle caress of his hand or the way he rested his cheek on her outspread hair. Regina shifted then, turning in his arms, so her hand slid to the small of his back and pressed there, bringing their bodies closer together. She kissed him, lightly at first, and then with greater hunger.

"Should we?" he murmured against her lips, though his body had immediately reacted, his cock stiffening between them. "The child . . . is it safe?"

"It's fine." Regina had no idea how to put into words her current whirlwind state of emotions, but she knew she craved that closeness, the connection they'd shared from the moment they'd looked into each other's eyes at that dinner party— not just the rush of sensation but the intimacy of touch, and kiss, and mingled sighs.

"You're sure?" He didn't move, just holding her.

"I'm sure." She'd specifically asked the doctor if they could still make love. He'd expressed caution if she had any unusual symptoms but otherwise indicated it was still safe and mentioned some women were more amorous when breeding.

Somehow she'd always imagined when she fell in love again it would be with someone like Rene Fortescue. Dashing and suave, with a dangerous air and the ability to beguile innocent young maidens.

As flawed as that experience had been, she'd just assumed those character traits were what had attracted her in the first place.

Only James was the antithesis of that sort of man. He wouldn't seek to seduce any maiden, innocent or not, nor would he set out to charm deliberately. Actually, he was rational and calm always, but when they were like this together, she somehow felt he understood her.

He wasn't like her. No, not at all. Quite the opposite. Where she was unpredictable, he was in control; where she faltered; he stood firm; where she dreamed, he made practical decisions based on logic. But at the moment, neither of them was interested in practicality of any kind.

"That is certainly just about the best news you could impart at this moment." James rolled to stretch out on top of her, his mouth tracing the line of her throat in a leisurely trail that was a contrast to the hard, hot length of his erection. "I want you, but then again, I always do."

"Why do you think I went to bed without clothes?" She ruffled his hair, her fingers skimming through the thick strands.

"You always sleep nude." His tongue traced her collarbone.

"Since you." Regina tugged his head up and playfully bit his lower lip. "So much more convenient."

"Now that we've found each other, you mean." He kissed her lightly, his knees gently parting her thighs.

Luckily, his entry made her catch her breath, and it was an excellent excuse to not respond as she arched into the penetration, opening and accepting, pleasure spreading outward and inward in a warm wash of sensation. She pressed him closer, lifting her hips as he began to move, and she let the whispered phrases of love caress her like her lover's hands, the words both tender and evocative.

I love you . . . I love our child already . . . God, Regina, hold me tighter. . . .

In the lassitude of the aftermath of shattering climax, hers more intense than usual—which made her wonder if that was typical, and if so, she was going to enjoy this pregnancy very much—James proposed again.

"Marry me." Propped on one elbow next to her, he lifted her right hand and kissed each finger, one by one, his blue eyes gazing into her hers. "I'll make you happy."

"You don't need to make me happy, James." Supine next to him, she was comfortable, sated, warm, damp, satisfied, and languid. "Why is it men always think a woman's happiness is dependent on them?"

Had she hurt him? For a moment his face went still and his lashes lowered, but then his mouth curved into a rueful smile. "Shall I rephrase? Let me try again. Will you *please* marry me, Lady Regina, and make me the happiest of men?"

"Ah, the selfish approach," she hedged in a teasing tone, not wanting to answer the question, sure, but not sure, the quandary uncomfortable. "Now your happiness is dependent on me?"

She wasn't being fair, and she knew it. Yet thirty-five years of independence in a world where women did not normally govern their lives was difficult to give up, even for someone like James.

"Unintentional," he murmured, watching her . . . maybe even really *seeing* her. "You needn't answer now."

"I'm tired," she said truthfully, "so thank you."

"There's no time limit on the offer." He touched her hair, his features blanched by the moonlight. The fire had long since died down. "But tell me . . . you waited up for my arrival. How did you know?"

Sleep hovered, and she almost didn't catch the question. "Know what?"

"That I would come? Altea invited me to spend the night. It was late. I might have just stayed."

"I knew you would come," she whispered as she surrendered and drifted off in his arms.

Chapter 24

It wasn't all that mysterious of a gift considering reading was her favorite pastime, but the parcel came unsigned, and the card said: *Open when alone.*

No signature either. A rather strange message, but very well, she was by herself in her sitting room at the moment.

Lily turned it over. A plain leather-bound volume, somewhat tattered, embossed in gold letters. The title of the work was *Lady Rothburg's Advice.* She opened it, saw it had been originally printed in 1802, and frowned, not recognizing the author's name.

Her birthday was months away—good heavens, she would be twenty-three—and there was no other occasion she could think of for someone to send her something. Idly she flipped it open to a random page.

A male's naked body is quite different from ours and you must understand the dynamics of his anatomy. Just imagining, or better yet, seeing, a naked female can cause the blood to rush to his lower regions, making his cock swell, readying him for the sexual act. We are much more delicate and complicated, but no finesse is usually needed with a male partner. Bare your breasts first. I promise you it will inflame him.

Shock held her immobile for a moment. What the devil? Why would anyone think she wished to read such a book?

Yet, actually, she did. Lily flipped a few more pages, her face warm but her curiosity piqued.

When taking him in your mouth remember that while the crest of his cock is sensitive, you will always gain his appreciation if you also fondle his ballocks. The dual pleasure of your mouth and the touch of your fingers will unman him, I vow it. Beware of that telling groan, though, I warn you, for his control will be sorely tested.

She jumped when someone knocked on the door, snapping the book shut, her cheeks flushed from the small amount she'd just read. Thanks to the other night with Damien she was not an innocent any longer, but she certainly had never seen words like that written down . . . at least not in such outrageous context.

Who would have sent it?

Whoever was at the door knocked again very briskly and Lily leaned over and picked up a handy cushion, shoving the book underneath. "Come in."

The duchess breezed into the room. "At my invitation, Lord Damien will be joining us for dinner. What will you wear?"

A bit off balance from her unusual delivery, Lily stammered, "I . . . I hadn't given it much thought yet."

"I've sent word to Augustine to expect a visit soon from Rolthven's younger brother.... Ah, it is all progressing nicely." The duchess, to her dismay, sat down on the same settee and took her hand in a rare gesture of warmth, her eyes gleaming with satisfaction.

And her regal bottom was nestled right against the pillow hiding the scandalous book.

Were it not so horrifying it would have been immensely humorous. Lily murmured hastily, "Perhaps you should select my gown, Your Grace. After all, you have worked rather hard to make me acceptable enough to draw the attention of such a fine gentleman that I would hate to make a poor wardrobe choice at this crucial point."

Unfortunately, it was extremely difficult to fool the Dowager Duchess of Eddington. Lily should have not uttered the humble, uncharacteristic speech at all, but a combination of her recent fall from grace in Damien's bed and the outrageous arrival of the book had her decidedly flustered.

The older woman let go of her hand and regarded her with narrowed eyes. "Truth be told, I don't know that I did so much, come to think of it. Dragged you off to a few entertainments that you usually escaped from at some point, introduced you to some men you neither liked nor gave much notice to, and in general bedeviled your life a bit. But Lord Damien was your conquest alone, wasn't he? I don't even recall when you were introduced."

"We met by chance." Lily reminded herself it wasn't a lie, recalling that evening in the library. "Um ... Lady Piedmont introduced us."

Well, that was fairly accurate, if she counted the lady chasing Damien into the library as an acceptable initial form of acquaintance.

Somehow she doubted the duchess would think so.

The next cool statement supported that assumption. "Lady Piedmont is a dubious source for fashionable contacts. I won't say more."

She didn't need to. Lily had seen firsthand why the duchess disapproved, though she could hardly mention it. "She does seem to be a bit sophisticated, Your Grace."

"Is *that* what you wish to call it?" The duchess still looked at her with shrewd pale blue eyes. "Rolthven's brother is not particularly the social kind. But then again, he does have that horrid limp from the war. I suppose he is conscious of it."

"It isn't horrid."

"No?" The duchess smiled smugly as if she'd just had a question answered. "I see."

He'd managed nicely to carry her up the stairs, so Lily wasn't too concerned about his crippled leg. Besides, though Damien recognized the impairment, she doubted that he gave a second thought to what others might think of it.

She *was* concerned—and intensely curious—about the book currently hidden in the settee, but her biggest problem was getting the dowager out of there before she happened to notice she was almost sitting on it.

"I was thinking of the green silk," she said, rising. "Unless you have a better suggestion."

"Green? Not tonight. I am thinking the periwinkle

blue that brings out your eyes. He hasn't made a formal offer yet, child."

True, but he had effectively declared his intentions in the most pleasurable way possible.

Lily was partial to the periwinkle herself and had only mentioned the green as a diversion—and thankfully the duchess never noticed the corner of the book sticking out from under the pillow. Not sure if she should be mortified or amused, when the duchess departed, Lily retrieved it and hid it safely underneath several neatly folded chemises in her armoire.

As intriguing as it was, she'd have to look at it later. For now, the duchess had a valid point. If Damien was going to be their guest this evening, she wanted it to be a memorable occasion.

She wore blue.

Her attire was actually very distracting. Damien remembered very little about the food and wine, but hopefully his preoccupation didn't show.

The dominating duchess did not bother him—his own grandmother was a perfect example of the type, so it wasn't like he didn't have experience—but Lily truly did look dazzling dressed in a gown that had some sort of interesting drapery of lace across the bodice and flattered her in every way—as if she needed adornment.

Not given to poetic tendencies—his life hadn't been conducive to literary pursuits except those of the more deadly kind—he still thought he could compare her eyes to the exact color of a cloudless summer sky.

Maybe he'd dabble in poetry for her sake someday,

though if he composed a sonnet it would undoubtedly be an insult to the English language. For now he simply wanted to solve Charles's mystery and then get on with his own life.

Funny, that. He'd never felt that way about a mission before. Unfortunately, it was proving to be a bit tricky. In a philosophical sense, he preferred war. The motivations were entirely understandable, whereas in this case, he didn't quite grasp why someone was killing young men whose greatest crime might be to gamble too much or have an illicit dalliance they preferred kept quiet.

It was the least romantic topic in the world, but maybe if he talked to Lily it would help, given her involvement with Sebring.

"Jonathan has to come over to sign some papers in the next week. You can speak with him about Lily then."

Jolted out of his abstraction, Damien glanced up at James Bourne, the ladies having excused themselves from the table to allow the two of them to enjoy their port. "Thank you for the information," he said neutrally. "I am willing to travel to Essex, but if it isn't necessary, it would be convenient to stay in London."

"You *are* serious, then?" His companion sat back, idly fingering his glass, his gaze direct. Bourne was tall, blond, blue-eyed, and there was a strong family resemblance. What's more, Lily had mentioned that she and her cousin were friends, not necessarily a typical relationship among the beau monde, related or not. Men and women usually had quite different interests.

Damien raised his brows. "About marrying Lily? Of course."

"I'm a little surprised, I admit, Northfield."

"So am I," Damien admitted with rueful honesty.

"I see." Bourne's regard was steady. "Lily told me about the library and your inventive escape."

Facing a male relative who could very well be entitled to some outrage, Damien was a bit cautious. Civilized dining rooms did not preclude confrontation. His intentions aside, he hadn't been entirely honorable by bedding her before their vows were said.

Not that he would change a single moment of that evening.

"She seemed particularly disinclined to summon help, and inventive—as you put it—appeared to be the best course. Not all libraries are equipped with hidden passages, but as luck would have it, this one was." Damien assumed a bland expression. "I didn't know about the scandal with Sebring at that time."

"Yet when a lovely damsel needed rescue, you gallantly stepped into the breach."

"Is that what she said?"

James shook his head. "Actually, she must trust you a great deal to have attempted it. Lily is hardly a timid female, but I know from childhood experiences that she does not like dark, closed spaces."

"No, she isn't a timid female," Damien rejoined with a hint of wry amusement, remembering the night he'd had her kidnapped. "Is it part of the attraction, do you think?"

"That is possible." James sipped his port, looking thoughtful. The windows were open and a night bird called somewhere, the sound melodic. "She's always been very self-sufficient. Even during the traumatic aftermath of her problems with Arthur Kerr, she didn't go into hysterics or even defend her actions. To this day she still doesn't. I assume the two of you have discussed it."

"We have. And we've established that our relationship is nothing like the one she had with him."

Bourne nodded. "No one thinks so."

It occurred then to Damien that her cousin *knew*. It was in the diffident way he studied his drink, and not so surprising, considering Lily was close to him. The man across the table definitely knew about Arthur's secret. Because of the nature of gossip in general, Damien hadn't really explored the possibility of talking to his aristocratic acquaintances since if he asked pointed questions, Arthur's secret would not be a secret much longer. Oh, he could trust his brothers, but Colton simply was too busy and absorbed in his duties as duke to pay attention to sordid gossip, and Robert was also preoccupied with his wife and family.

For Lily's sake, her cousin would not repeat their conversation. Perhaps James Bourne could help him. After a moment of consideration, Damien asked, "First of all, how do you know about Sebring, and can you think of anyone in your circle of acquaintances who would threaten to expose him?"

"Know about him?" Bourne's brows went up in question.

"His penchant for the same sex." If Lily trusted this man so much, he would too. "How did you discover it? I knew Arthur fairly well when we were at Cambridge and I never suspected."

Bourne looked away as if he suddenly found a Renaissance painting of the Madonna and child on the opposite wall fascinating. But then he admitted reluctantly,

"I found out by accident. I've never told Lily, and please don't reveal to her I have any idea. She went through enough as it stands, though I must admit it was enlightening to realize why her elopement was such a disaster."

There were accidents and then there was intentional misfortune. Mistakes happened, yes, but accidents were few and far between. Leaking a story like this about a titled lord sounded more like malice than anything else.

"You have my word I won't tell her you know."

James nodded briefly, his expression resigned. "A mutual friend told me. Sebring's marriage has been less than perfect from the beginning, which isn't necessarily unique in our circles, but Arthur is particularly unhappy in his. It isn't a secret, though most people do not suspect why he and his wife are at odds."

There was a moment when enlightenment dawned in elusive flashes. As Damien had so little to connect the blackmailer to the murders except Kinkannon, and knew the real villain had undoubtedly been the one to approach Arthur, here was a third party privy to at least one secret.

"What friend?"

James Bourne definitely caught his sharpened interest. "You are extremely curious, Northfield. If this is because of Lily and Sebring's history, that is long over. There's no need to take offense now."

"I'm not. Give me his name and I promise to later explain."

"Thomas Fairfield." James hesitated and then said somberly, "I'm sorry to say he died unexpectedly a few months ago of some sort of stomach ailment."

So he had. He was on the list of the suspicious deaths. Ah, at last a viable link.

Chapter 25

At least there was a reward for the blue dress, for the polite conversation during dinner, for the careful attention to her hair.

The duchess allowed them an unsupervised stroll in the garden.

It was ironic, but Damien wasn't nearly as interested in the romantic aspect as she was. As far as she could tell, he didn't want to kiss her, or finally propose, or do anything remotely romantic.

Lily found her lover wished to simply talk. Not that she minded his interest in her life, but she'd been out of society for a while and the questions he was asking did not actually make a lot of sense to her.

Surely a moonlit evening could be put to better use?

"Arthur Kerr. Thomas Fairfield. The Earl of Haversham's youngest son. Henry Lawson."

More than a little bewildered, Lily walked next to him, wishing Damien would at least endeavor to hold her hand. "Yes?"

His sidelong glance was swift. "You've met all of them?"

In her mind they didn't have much of a connection

otherwise, but that was at least true. "I suppose ... You *know* I know Arthur. I've met the others at one time or another." Her skirts brushed his booted feet, and even though his hands were currently clasped behind his back, there was a palpable excitement from just his closeness. Her relationship with Arthur had not been this way. She'd liked him, yes—thought she'd loved him—but she hadn't felt breathless and unsettled around him, and now that she could tell the difference between deep affection for someone and falling in love, she wondered at why the underlying distance between them hadn't been more obvious to her from the beginning.

Friendship and romantic love were very different. Once a person recognized this, she doubted they would ever make that mistake again.

"Why?" she belatedly remembered to ask, having been absorbed in studying the clean line of Damien's profile.

His smile was faint and enigmatic. "I'm looking for a similarity between them. A common bond. The thread that ties them together."

"Those four? Why?"

"Let's just say I owe an old friend a favor and it seems if I fulfill that obligation, I might be able to help a few others also. Any thoughts? One of the many things about you I admire is your intellect. Maybe this needs a woman's perspective."

As a compliment it was nicely done. Lily smiled, pleased, warmed by his presence and the words, but she still had to shrug. "I don't know what I could possibly tell you."

"Anything." He stopped by a decoratively trimmed

yew, his eyes glimmering in the illumination. "It doesn't matter if you think it is important or not."

What actually mattered was that she wanted him to take her in his arms. The lack of an official proposal was not so much disturbing as disappointing. Bended knee was not as necessary to her as much as hearing the words out loud.

Instead he wanted to talk about certain gentlemen of their acquaintance. "As I said, I only know several of them in passing, and one of them, poor Thomas Fairfield—"

"Died recently, I know." Damien's voice was curiously blank, as if he were thinking of something else. "James told me."

"Does this have something to do with Arthur asking me if someone knew about his . . . secret?" She wasn't sure what to call it.

"I don't know, but it does make me wonder."

Half turned away, she looked at where the moon threw shadows across the path. "Is he the friend you owe a favor?"

"No."

"Then why are you asking *me*?"

"A valid point." His fingers caught her chin, making her turn. "Lily, shall we forget Arthur and his troubles for now? We're alone in the moonlight and you are extraordinarily beautiful this evening and I haven't been able to do more than touch your hand."

It is certainly about time, she thought, catching the gleam of his dark eyes. She also knew that singular slow smile was a prelude to a kiss.

And then he bent his head and his mouth touched

hers, lifted momentarily, and then captured her lips a second time in a kiss that sent the blood rushing through her veins.

It was hardly decorous the way she pressed immediately against him or the fervor in which she accepted his embrace, but she didn't care. If there was one lesson she'd learned from being the victim of vicious rumors for four years, it was that innocence did not prevent personal misery, and she was more than willing to welcome happiness now that it was hers again.

His lips were firm, smooth, infinitely warm.... She felt him groan, and reveled in how he pulled her closer. When he tore his mouth away, his breath was hot in her ear. "I might just kidnap you again this evening. How the devil am I supposed to wait for an engagement and a wedding?"

"As I recall, you didn't." She smiled, appeased, the stilted dinner under the eye of her family and the duchess now worth it.

"A valid point," he said dryly, "which further illustrates my impatience. James didn't seek to cleave out my gizzard this evening, so I suppose that is one male relative that doesn't disapprove, and the duchess seems delighted enough. What about your brother?"

"He will ask what I want." At least Lily could say that with perfect confidence. She and the current Earl of Augustine may not know each other all that well, as Jonathan had grown up in America, but she had learned *that* about him. He was fair almost to a fault and genuinely concerned about her future or he would never have put her into the hands of his wife's formidable grandmother in the first place.

"And what *do* you want?" The question was soft and quiet.

Her throat was a bit tight as she answered. "A man who has a map to every hidden staircase in London. One who can pick a tricky lock in a wine cellar. One who has cohorts who abduct young ladies with ease from their bedchambers."

Long-fingered hands grazed her shoulders, his voice like velvet. "And would you marry such a man?"

"I just might." Lily tilted her head back, looking into his eyes. "Were he to ask."

"Hasn't he? How remiss of the gentleman with those dubious skills." Damien kissed her passionately again, and maybe all young women experienced a similar exhilaration, but certainly her pulse was racing when he finally lifted his head.

"Lily . . . marry me."

"Do I have an option?"

"Always." His hand stilled in the act of smoothing up her back, the heat of his touch viable even through the thin material of her gown and underclothing. "If you want something else."

"It was a jest." She touched his face and whispered, "Yes. I want nothing more than to lurk in libraries together for the rest of our lives, but . . . how will your family feel?"

"Delighted." He brushed his mouth against her temple, and unless it was her imagination, the exhale of his breath was in relief. "So far you have the approval of one sister-in-law, and two brothers."

"Surely they know—"

"I am intelligent enough to choose wisely? Yes, they know."

"I meant about Arthur . . . the elopement."

"Don't be ridiculous. Not a one of them cares about idle gossip." His grin was just a flash of white teeth. "I'm glad we have that settled then, Lady Lillian."

For the first time, she believed it.

It had *all* happened for a reason. The insight was profound and moving. The four years of disgrace, the awful night when Arthur had broken down, told her the truth, and shattered her sheltered world, the retreat to the country to lick her wounds. She'd been waiting, and it was all worth it.

Arthur had been a mistake extraordinaire, but now that she could look back with some measure of distance, she knew why she'd been so dazzled, so susceptible. After all, he was titled, wealthy, charming, with those fair good looks. . . .

Lily froze even as Damien's mouth teased her neck. He sensed it immediately and lifted his head, his gaze quizzical. "What is it? You can't have changed your mind already, my sweet. . . . It has barely been a moment since I asked."

"No . . . no." She disengaged herself and he let her go as she paced to the edge of the path and stared at a bush full of overblown roses, their petals scattered on the path, thinking, before turning around. "You asked if I knew anything that would connect those men and it doesn't matter if it seems important or not, correct?"

Immediately the lover was gone, replaced by the calculating spy. "Yes."

"They all look alike."

"I beg your pardon?"

"Damien, all four of those men look alike to the extent that they are similar in height and coloring. Blond, fair-skinned, and of similar size. I once mistook Fairfield for Arthur from behind."

Half in the shadows, Damien said nothing, his lashes lowered slightly, his expression difficult to read and his brow lightly furrowed. Then he shook his head. "That's interesting, but I can't see how it could be significant."

Neither did she, but the more she thought about it, it was true. "I agree, but rather an odd coincidence, don't you think?"

He entered her bedroom without the formality of a knock, but then again, it was late, the house utterly quiet, and rapping on her door hardly discreet.

Just the beginning of his sins for the evening. Damien intended to be very *indiscreet* indeed.

It wasn't every day a man became engaged. Not officially, of course. He still needed to speak with Jonathan Bourne, but by all accounts Lily was destined to be his wife, and the kiss in the garden had been extremely satisfying, and paradoxically, not satisfying enough.

What was the use of being a spy if one could not slip undetected through enemy lines? It wasn't done as smoothly with his pronounced limp, but apparently it could still be done.

She was asleep, he saw in the slanting moonlight, curled on her side, her hand outstretched. The rich abundance of her hair spilled around her slender shoulders and her breasts moved with each slow exhale.

Perhaps he should just leave, he thought, standing there, wondering why this young woman moved him so much. From that first moment in the library when he'd turned around and seen her sitting on the settee, he hadn't been himself.

Maybe part of the problem was that he didn't know who Damien Northfield was any longer. Not a valuable spy, helping defeat Bonaparte. . . . That part of his life was over. Not the heir to a dukedom—his brother had a son—and that was more than fine with him, as he'd never wanted the title anyway.

So who was he? Or he might ask who he wasn't. A husband? A father? What if Lily already carried his child? It was possible.

The odds were it might be even more possible after this evening.

Quietly he undressed, his movements measured but fluid, stealth a familiar friend. The room held a hint of her fragrance and it tantalized him—a reminder of her warm, smooth skin. That he shouldn't be there was not in question, but that he was certainly brought home some disturbing truths, not the least of which was his lack of patience now that he'd made up his mind.

Lily wouldn't insist on an elaborate wedding. That he knew of her. She was far too sensitive under her composed exterior to want to subject herself to a large society affair where she was the center of attention.

He didn't want that either, so it was fine with him. The sooner they married the better. If he was willing to wait, he wouldn't be there now, sliding back the coverlet and slipping in beside her, running his fingers through the silk of her hair to wake her gently.

"Shhh." He watched her eyelids flutter and then come fully open. "It's me."

"Damien?" Confusion crossed her features for a moment as she obviously registered his presence in her bed. She half sat up, her hair delectably disheveled. "What are you doing? Are you mad?"

It was not the first time she had asked him that, and if he remembered correctly, the last inquiry had turned into an immensely pleasurable interlude.

"I must be," he said with amused equanimity, "to risk the duchess storming in at an inopportune moment to toss me out on my ear. Can we please keep it to low whispers? While I am not afraid of facing a French battalion, I admit she does intimidate me a bit."

"She would also intimidate a French battalion," Lily muttered in a lower tone, looking young in her nightdress, the garment quite similar to the one she'd worn when Sharpe had delivered her on his doorstep.

"Make the risk worth my while, then." Damien heard the huskiness in his voice as she realized he was naked and aroused already, propped on one elbow. He watched the progression of emotion cross her features. Surprise, a certain feminine wariness over having a large predatory male so close, and then, to his gratification, a shy welcoming in the way she visibly relaxed, her gaze straying to where she could see his bare chest.

"James might burst in and kill you," she said as he reached for her but going easily into his embrace, her arms slipping around his neck.

"I'm still more afraid of the dowager," he said, murmuring the words against her lips. "James couldn't freeze me into an icicle with a glare, so at least I would have a fighting chance. Women are, in my experience, more frightening than men."

"Am I?" She touched his hair, her blue eyes wide in the insufficient light.

In answer he kissed her. Not like the kiss earlier in the garden, but with open hunger, shifting her underneath him, his hand sliding up her thigh under the lawn of her nightdress. The first time had been an introduction for them both, an awakening in that he was the instructor and she the innocent pupil, but the level on which they played this game was different now. They were engaged, she was no longer the uncertain virgin, and he wanted her with a need that had sent him to this irresistible rendezvous in the first place.

His brother Colton would be scandalized.

Robert would be amused.

Brianna would be delighted.

No doubt Lily's family would want his blood.

But at the moment, he didn't care. His hand slid up to cup her left breast, his thumb circling the taut nipple through her night rail. It was a small lesson in self-awareness to know he'd envied his brothers their personal happiness without actually realizing it. True emotion for the woman in a man's arms meant a great deal.

Perhaps it even meant *everything*.

He'd never experienced such flagrant desire, his cock throbbing now to the beat of his heart, his skin hot, the feel of her softness and curves enough to make him forget the rest of the world. "Lily," he said on a low groan, "far too much separates us. Let me undress you."

*   *   *

At first she'd thought she was dreaming, the touch of his hands part of a hazy fantasy. But the man easing her nightdress up over her head was very real, the intensity of his mouth capturing hers again once the offending garment was tossed away no illusion, and that male part of him, long and hard, pressed against her thigh, was also unmistakably real.

It hadn't occurred to her that Damien might steal into her bedroom, but the audacity of it should not have been a surprise, not when he'd undoubtedly done much more dangerous things in the war.

What was dangerous was how reckless he made her feel, and how *alive*. That had been missing from her life the past four years, for some small part of her had been extinguished that night with Arthur, and Damien North-field had brought it back, like an uncovered ember, barely smoldering but carefully and expertly fanned back into a flame.

She certainly was on fire now.

His hands roamed everywhere, followed by his mouth. To her breasts, first cupped and caressed and then kissed, her nipples teased to high points by the swirl of his tongue. Lily arched at the delicious sensation, her hands smoothing his back, a small gasp escaping at the heated adhesion of his mouth.

The first lesson in the bedroom should be that while you are the object of his desire, keep in mind you are not an object at all, but a willing participant. Most men with a modicum of intelligence and sensitivity do not wish for a woman to simply lie there and let them use their body. Submission is all well

*and good, but the pleasure for both parties is greatly
enhanced when a woman also caresses her lover.*

Lily had stayed up and started that shocking—but
fascinating—book that had arrived so mysteriously in
the post, and that tidbit of advice swirled into her mind,
though she had to admit it was hard to think at this particular moment.

When he trailed his mouth upward, she managed to
murmur, "I want to touch you."

He teased the hollow of her throat where her pulse
beat madly. "You'll receive no argument from me, my
lady."

And the author of that wicked book, Lady Rothburg,
whoever she might be, was correct, Lily discovered as
she ran her hands along the contours of his chest, marveling at the differences between them, tracing the width
of his shoulders, the muscles of his back. Braced above
her, Damien stayed remarkably still until she daringly
ran her fingertips along his side and then slid her hand
between them to touch him *there*.

His cock—Lady Rothburg very bluntly referred to it
that way—was surprisingly velvet smooth, incredibly hot
and hard, and Damien's reaction the moment she circled
her fingers around his erect sex was gratifying.

"Lily," he said on a low groan.

It appeared the not-so-ladylike Lady R. was correct,
Lily found when he kissed her. It was more fervent than
before, his tongue taking possession, his hands cupping
her hips as he pressed his body against hers.

"I need you ready. God help me, I *need* you." He
eased downward, his hand skimming across her quiver-

ing belly, his fingers tracing her navel, his tongue dipping in, and then lower. . . .

And lower.

The vivid experience of exquisite pleasure when he touched her between her legs that first night filled her with a sense of wicked anticipation, and so she parted willingly at the pressure of his palms. She blushed, still shy, but the room was dark and there was something arousing about doing the forbidden. She didn't fully realize his intention until his hair brushed the sensitive skin of her inner thighs, and a strange sensation curled in her belly at the first touch of his mouth as he parted the folds of her sex. His hands cupped her hips, lifting her slightly into the scandalous kiss.

"Damien!"

"Shhh, love."

In her shock, she had said his name out loud, which was hardly advisable, but at the same moment her bones melted and her pulse quickened. Lily thought it impossible to experience such a delicious pleasure, yet as his mouth moved against her, she let out an involuntary but telling moan.

It was incomprehensible he'd wish to use his mouth in such a way, but her eyes closed and her body shuddered, and Lily had to acknowledge it was not just decadent, but *rapturous*.

This time, since she anticipated the growing tension, the elusive need, the pervasive desire for that pinnacle, it was more intense when it happened, and she might have cried out again, she couldn't be sure, left limp as the erotic wave first surged and engulfed her and finally began to ebb, leaving her limp and trembling.

When he slid upward and into her, there was no pain with the penetration, just the pleasure of the joining. His rigid cock stretched her still-contracting feminine passage, his breath rapid in her ear as he began to thrust and withdraw, the rhythm much more primal than that first time. Lily clung to him, her hips lifting instinctively into each inward glide until he stiffened and went still, exhaling against her neck as he dropped his head and the hot rush of his seed filled her.

Once the feverish need was over, she discovered, there was a special magic in the aftermath. His respiration slowed gradually, and he slightly shifted his weight to keep from crushing her, his mouth curving in a purely masculine smile when he finally lifted himself up and looked at her.

His fingertips touched her cheek. "I think I shall steal behind enemy lines more often."

"I'm hardly your enemy." She barely had the strength to say the words. "But I admit to being entirely vanquished."

"A mutual surrender," he said softly.

She loved the way the shadows highlighted his cheekbones and the tousled thickness of his hair, the way his damp skin felt under her palms and ripple of muscle when he moved. . . .

She loved *him*.

Not with a young girl's first infatuation, as it had been with Arthur, though infatuation was certainly a part of it. Not because of his looks, or his illustrious family, or the coup of making such a fashionable marriage against the odds of her disgrace, but just for the opposite reasons. Because she sensed Damien didn't care about any of that any more than she did. Fortune and social standing didn't seem to matter to him, and though they had hardly experienced an identical journey, it seemed to her that they both understood survival.

"If every battle is so pleasurable, I look forward to the next skirmish," she murmured, artlessly kissing his jaw, his sex still deep inside her, her hands resting on his shoulders. Impulsively she asked, "Why is it, do you think, that a certain man and a woman choose each other when in this world there are so many?"

"You expect me to be philosophical now?" He grinned, looking at once much younger and lighter, his weight balanced on his elbows. "I can honestly say I have no idea."

"There have been other women." It wasn't a question, more a statement, and she really didn't want to hear anything about them, so she quickly went on in a hushed whisper. "Why am I different?"

He didn't answer at once, their joined bodies relaxed. One finger traced the line of her eyebrow, the touch very light. "You are more direct than what I am used to in my recent life, where evasiveness was the order of the day. What can I say? I don't know. I think it was that moment when you turned your back to have your gown unfastened before we went down that dark staircase to escape the library. I don't deny I am attracted to your beauty, but your courage moved me first."

"I don't know that it was courage so much as I was trying to avoid embarrassing my family again." The weight of his body was pleasant and she was more than blissfully exhausted, physical satisfaction like a drug.

Damien murmured, "You never embarrassed them as

far as I can tell, and yes, it *was* courage. The same type of integrity it took to not scream to the world Sebring's secret because you are that kind of person, which is why he told you in the first place. He trusted you, and so do I, and quite frankly, I don't trust easily."

"I know you don't." Her throat was suddenly hot, as if there might be tears threatening, and she truly couldn't think of a single reason to cry except for excessive happiness, and who would cry over that?

"Darling." His fingertip caught the first telltale droplet as it slid down her cheek. "I wasn't trying to upset you—"

"You didn't." She reached up and touched his jaw. "I'm just . . . happy."

For a moment his face was unguarded, vulnerable, the set of his mouth uncertain, and she loved him all the more for that poignant look of confusion on his face. He kissed her then and whispered, "Is that what this is? I think I could get used to happiness."

Chapter 26

His lordship, Damien was informed, was not at home, but as it happened, a carriage with the Sebring crest came to a halt before the Kerr residence just as he turned to depart, and both Arthur and his wife alighted.

One of them seemed genuinely glad to see him—and one decidedly did not.

Lady Sebring obviously remembered him from the night at the opera, for he received a frigid look as Arthur greeted him. The viscountess was not a dazzling beauty, but not unattractive either, though her faint air of disdain did nothing to enhance her rather unremarkable features. She did have lovely dark hair, thick and shining, at this moment drawn up under a fashionable hat, and her day gown suited her curvaceous figure.

"Lord Damien," she said in a cold voice that reflected her feelings perfectly. "How nice of you to call."

Her voice said, of course, she didn't think it was nice at all, and he wondered at once if it was him, or if it was her hatred of Lily.

The latter, at a guess. By now all of London probably knew he was interested in the winsome sister of the Earl of Augustine and openly courting her, so he would think

Lady Sebring, if she was truly jealous, would be grateful he was removing what she might view as competition from the fray.

Unless, of course, she despised Lily enough to begrudge her any happiness at all. A flicker of dislike for the woman went through him.

Lily, in his opinion, was much more the injured party than her successor, and if Arthur's wife was jealous, the malice was not at all aimed in the right direction.

"Come in, Northfield," Arthur said in a slightly too congenial tone. "Penelope has another appointment soon. . . . Perhaps we can simply retire to my study."

As the idea of sitting through an excruciating session with the unfriendly Lady Sebring held no appeal, and she wasn't why he was there anyway, Damien smiled faintly. "I can't stay long."

As she swept past him the viscountess murmured, not quite under her breath, "Good."

"Penelope," her husband said in grim reprimand.

"I meant, good day, then, Lord Damien," she said over her shoulder without slowing her pace, a footman hastening to take her cloak.

"I'm sorry," Arthur told him once they were seated in the private confines of his personal domain, his hand shaking slightly as he dashed brandy into two glasses. "Penelope has always been a bit outspoken, but she isn't usually rude."

Damien wasn't all that interested in his friend's wife. Even though she had been abrasive, he was not unaware aristocratic ladies were sometimes both petulant and spoiled. It could be her rich, influential father made her think she did not have to bow to even common courtesy.

On the other hand, there were true ladies like Lily, no matter how blue their blood, who had admirable attributes like loyalty and integrity. Arthur certainly had benefited from both those traits. Damien murmured, "No need to apologize."

Arthur sat down in the chair behind the desk too heavily, making it creak. "God help me, she's worse lately. It isn't an excuse, but she can't conceive the child she wants so desperately. It wasn't a love match to begin with, but this is tearing at even the basest nod to civility in our marriage."

"I suspect her lack of courtesy has something to do with the rumors of my engagement to Lily."

That was frank enough, as he hoped this would be a candid conversation.

"I would guess you are right." Arthur took a solid swallow of brandy. "Is it true?"

"Yes."

It took a moment, but he said finally, "I'm glad for her. I don't know if it is fair of me, but despite our past I consider her a friend."

That softly spoken sentiment gave *him* a twinge of jealousy, Damien noted with an inner cynicism, and he had no idea why, given Lord Sebring's relationship with Lily was strictly platonic, a truth he knew better than anyone. But he was there for a purpose. "And a loyal one. She didn't tell me, but I believe I know why you are being blackmailed. Can you guess how anyone else would discover it?"

Arthur looked disconcerted, his skin taking on a reddish hue, but then he stared at his glass. "I suppose I invited you into my troubles, so maybe I shouldn't be surprised you'd find out."

"The secrecy cannot be easy." Damien kept his tone nonjudgmental, and truly, he didn't think less of his old friend particularly. The war had taken the edge off his fine sensibilities. To his mind the preference for the same sex was not easy to understand, but then again, Arthur was not the first man—or woman for that matter—to have that bent. "And I am not here to discuss your personal life, except to the extent that surely you must have thought about where your tormentor got his information."

"I don't know." The flush faded and Arthur's fine-boned face went a gray color to match the overcast sky outside.

"Have you had lovers?"

"That's a damned personal question, Northfield."

"I thought you wanted my help." Damien spoke with equanimity and sipped his brandy.

"Fine ... yes, then. There have been a few encounters." Arthur shoved himself to his feet and roughly ran his fingers through his hair. "All were anonymous. ... I belong to a small, discreet club, but we do not use our real names, nor do we reveal our faces."

Damien thought privately that seemed vastly unfulfilling whether you preferred men or women, but kept that sentiment to himself. "How did you find this establishment?"

"I overheard two men discussing it at *our* club. They brought it up as a joke because apparently one of them had been invited there as a guest, not realizing the nature of the entertainment there." Arthur looked weary, his eyes closing briefly. "I admit I was intrigued, and not just because of the sexual aspect. I don't know if you understand what a burden it is to keep such a secret. Most of my life I have felt extraordinarily alone. The idea there were others out there. . . . It was appealing."

Not directly, but Damien thought he could understand. There were times during the war when he was working behind enemy lines, the missions so covert no one really knew where he was. Had he been captured and executed—spies were shown no mercy or respect for their rank—it was possible no one would ever know, his grave unmarked and his family left to wonder forever.

Yes, he understood the loneliness of secrecy. Better than anyone.

"Would you know if some of your acquaintances belonged to this same establishment?" He extracted the list of Kinkannon's victims from his pocket and set it on the desk. "I believe there are others who are—or in some cases *were*—being bled for money by the same party as who approached you. Could the club be the connection?"

Arthur retrieved the list and read it quickly. He said hoarsely, "Good God, two of these men are dead."

"Indeed they are."

The meaning in his voice got through, but Arthur shook his head. "I don't think it could have anything to do with the club. We conceal ourselves, and it is expensive and exclusive, which protects everyone who belongs. I suppose it makes it certain we are all from a certain level of society and therefore have an investment in our anonymity. Besides, I know all the men on that list; none of them are . . . like me."

"You're sure?" Damien lifted a brow. "You have managed to keep it hidden all these years."

"I'm a bit better at recognizing the signs than you are, no doubt." Arthur finished his drink in a convulsive swallow.

As Henry Lawson was being blackmailed not for his sexual preferences but his gambling troubles, that could be true.

Which left Damien as much in the dark as ever.

Damnation.

"But they all are from within our social circle." *Except the missing valet, of course.* Musing out loud, he settled back and remembered his brandy, taking a swallow. "Tell me, when Kinkannon first contacted you, what did he want?"

"Money. Ten thousand pounds, to be exact." Arthur's voice was bitter.

"That's quite a sum. Did you give it to him?"

The other man's mouth curved in a humorless smile. "Wouldn't you, if faced with social ruin, not to mention the destruction of my political hopes? Kinkannon, of course, used my marriage against me as leverage, as apparently everyone understands that it is a complete failure."

"What did you expect?"

"Of my marriage?" Arthur gave a negligent shrug, but his eyes were bleak. "I am really no different than any other gentleman who marries for reasons other than love. I needed a wife, her father's influence could help me, and I have done my best to be a dutiful husband."

Sebring was a *bit* different, Damien would argue, but true enough, not much.

So Kinkannon received his money, two men of the four victimized that he knew of were dead, and there was still an unknown accomplice. "Did he offer you an option besides paying the money?" Damien asked, remembering the night in the garden when he listened to the conversation with Charles's nephew. He was still intensely curious about that exchange. It was part of the key to solving this puzzle.

"No," Arthur said bitterly, "he just asked for money, the blackguard, or he would tell my wife about the club. She already blames me for her childless state. I cannot imagine what she would do if she knew the truth. My life would be ruined."

"I doubt she'd want to publicly humiliate you. After all, you are her husband." But even as Damien said the words, he questioned them himself and he didn't know Lady Sebring well.

Arthur walked over to the window and stared outside. It was breezy and overcast, and a few spits of rain touched the glass. "You have not lived with her for three years. She wanted my title, not my person, which is why I agreed to the marriage. I was never going to hurt her emotionally. I knew that from the moment her father introduced us. What I couldn't do to Lily was not the issue with Penelope. It never mattered to her if I loved her in a romantic sense of the word. I doubt she would care one way or the other if I did."

Damien had to admit, being newly introduced to the concept of a relationship based on deeper feeling, he was not envious of his friend's loveless marriage. "Yet she seems to want to give you an heir."

Arthur turned to face him, a humorless smile on his face. "She wants to *produce* an heir. That's quite different. There is no reasoning with her on the subject, no assurances she heeds that if the title passes on to my cousin I am not unduly upset over it. Quite frankly, I think that it is an all-consuming determination to contribute to an aristocratic lineage that has her so obsessed." His mouth twisted. "And despite what you may be thinking, a child is definitely possible. We have been diligently trying for three years. It might not be my preference, but I am well aware it is my duty."

The defensive statement was unnecessary. Damien wasn't thinking about whether Lord Sebring could perform in the bedroom. Sitting there, his half-empty glass of brandy suspended in his hand, he was more contemplating an unexpected angle to the situation he hadn't thought of before.

Reverse logic might be applicable. It wasn't that the men who had been blackmailed looked all alike . . . it was that they all looked like Lord Sebring.

An interesting premise.

Unfortunately, it made sense. Carefully, he asked, "How obsessed is she?"

Arthur Kerr said with chilling vehemence, "There are times I think she might be mad."

The card in her hand made her stare in consternation, as if looking at the embossed letters might change the identity of the caller. A glance at the clock showed it was not even time for luncheon, and Lily rose and smoothed her skirts in an automatic reaction. "Tell the viscountess I will be right there."

"Yes, milady."

With a swift glance in the mirror, she tucked an errant curl back into place, the uneasiness that tightened her stomach hard to ignore. Why on earth would Arthur's wife ever visit her? Their mutual dislike was hardly a secret.

Her steps measured, Lily went downstairs. Lady Sebring, she discovered, was in the drawing room, staring at the painting above the fireplace, her posture rigid and formal.

"Good morning," Lily said coolly.

Penelope Kerr turned around. She wore a stylish day gown of lilac silk trimmed with ecru lace, as impeccably turned out as ever, but there was a cold glitter in her eyes that belied the persona of a friendly call. "Forgive my imposition, Lady Lillian."

"Not at all." Lily stood just inside the door, her wary gaze on her visitor. "How nice of you to call." The polite words were forced and from her thin smile, Lady Sebring was not unaware of it.

"I am sure you are surprised."

Well, that was undeniable. She had to incline her head. "I admit that, yes, I am a bit startled you'd pay a social call to someone you so openly dislike."

"Have I given that impression?"

Lily's response was brittle. "Yes, you have."

"I see." Without being invited, Lady Sebring took a seat in one of the velvet chairs, her gaze steady as she genteelly arranged her skirts. "You should close the door. I am here to discuss my husband. Do you want the servants to overhear the sordid details?"

"I am not even sure *I* wish to hear them," she muttered.

In response Arthur's wife raised her brows in a haughty mannerism that rankled.

It might be cowardice, but Lily suddenly wished for

the duchess to be present. It was true that the Dowager Duchess of Eddington was presumptuous, autocratic, and occasionally overbearing, but she certainly knew how to handle discomforting social conversations.

Actually, Lily thought in wry amusement, the dowager didn't handle them at all. She simply walked over the problem with her typical disdain. However, it appeared Lily was going to have to deal with this one herself.

She went ahead and closed the door. She hadn't protected Arthur for four years for nothing. And the infernal woman was right, there was hardly any point in stirring up the old scandal now, when her engagement was about to be announced. "What could we possibly have to say to each other?"

"I think I need to make my position clear."

"If this is in regard to your husband, I believe you already have, and more than once. But if you are here to make some sort of point, please go ahead and do so." Lily had to admit she was impatient with it all, with a part of her life that should have been long over. She didn't want to deal with Arthur's petulant wife, and she didn't want to look backward but was instead happy to be able to move forward. To any other visitor she might offer refreshment, but in this case she just wanted it over as quickly as possible.

"I hear you are engaged."

It wasn't really what she expected to hear, and she weighed her response. In the end, she just said simply, "Yes."

"The brother of a duke. How impressive." There was a slight, almost chilling edge of malice in Lady Sebring's voice that truly gave Lily pause.

"I wasn't angling for a certain level of social prominence." At least she could say that in truth. *Unlike you*, she thought, but perhaps that was better left unsaid. It didn't seem to her that Lady Sebring had gained much from her advantageous match.

"I am a bit surprised, I must admit, that Lord Damien is willing to overlook your soiled reputation."

To be courteous in the face of such open insult took some effort, but Lily only said coolly, "It's a love match." It was stretching it a bit to claim that, as Damien had never said he loved her, but she certainly was in love with him, so it was at least partially true. "I do not know if you understand the concept, which makes me pity Arthur very much indeed. Now, if you will excuse me—"

"My husband never bedded you, did he?" Penelope sat there, prim in her expensive gown, the silk gloves she'd removed next to her on the green velvet chair, the picture of elegance except for the venom in her eyes. "Did he even try? Never mind, there's no need to answer. He finds the act of copulation distasteful with women. Did you know that? Yet, oddly enough, I think the wretch believes he loves you still. Poor Arthur, so confused. He loved you but couldn't bring himself to desire you, and so he then gallantly—albeit a bit late in the day—decided you would be better off without him and his depravity."

As much damage as what had happened had done to her life, Lily could never have summoned that amount of dislike for Arthur and it appalled her to realize how his wife really felt about him.

"He offered me the choice." She said the words woodenly.

"And you chose infamy instead of a handsome husband with title and fortune. Rather idealistic of you, wasn't it, Lady Lillian? All of London thought you promiscuous, and the speculation was that once he'd sampled your ... *charms*, as it were ... he'd been disappointed enough to refuse to marry you. It's a pity you didn't discover there are ways around his reluctance."

Lily found there were limits to her civility after all, it seemed. "You and I both know the truth, though, don't we? And while this has been an interesting discussion, I am still not enlightened as to why we are having it."

"What about Lord Damien? Does *he* also know the truth?"

At last she understood the woman's purpose. It was difficult to tell Arthur's wife it was not her business, when indirectly it was, so despite how unpleasant Penelope Kerr had been so far, Lily said neutrally, "He would never reveal it to anyone. If Wellington trusted him to keep England's secrets during the war, I believe you can trust him to keep this one. He and Arthur might not have seen each other for years, but they are old friends. There won't be a scandal over it because of Damien."

"That isn't what I meant."

Confused, Lily just looked at her visitor.

"You are hardly in your first bloom and he is an experienced man. Does he know Arthur never seduced you because Lord Damien is the one who took your virginity?"

The disconcerting visit was getting worse, Lily decided. She said stiffly, "I can't see how my engagement is a source of such interest to you."

"But it is. You see"—Penelope paused delicately—"if

you are to be married, you might become enceinte.... Or could you be carrying a child already?"

She *could* be. Lily knew it was possible, but she was hardly going to admit it.

"Ah. I see. That is a very telling blush."

The observation was alarming, but she wasn't sure why. Maybe it was the way Penelope Kerr was looking at her, as if analyzing her reaction to the bizarre conversation, her head tilted just slightly to the side.

"I am not quite sure what it is you are asking."

"Let me clarify it for you, then." In one smooth motion Arthur's wife rose, moving gracefully across the room. Something gleamed in her hand, but Lily noticed it only in an abstract way, riveted by the look on the other woman's face.

She wasn't sure she'd ever seen pure hatred before. It was there in its most unadulterated form in the gleam in Penelope's eyes, the twist of her mouth, the taut line of her throat. Lily took an involuntary step backward, wondering in that split second if it had been a mistake to close the door, before she realized that when Lady's Sebring's hand flashed up, what she held was a small knife, the glint of the blade startling in the late-morning sunshine coming through the elegant drawing room windows.

Sheer disbelief held her prisoner, her mind rejecting what was happening even as her visitor lunged toward her, dagger in hand.

Lily staggered backward, bumped into a table, hearing the lamp wobble. One arm flew up to deflect the blow, and as a slicing pain shot through her, she realized she hadn't quite succeeded.

Chapter 27

It was hardly a secret that she could make a decision or two that weren't precisely conventional, but as Regina alighted from the hired hack, she wondered if calling in the middle of the day at the residence of the Earl of Augustine was precisely how she should handle this matter. Her arrival would be duly noted by the neighbors in this fashionable neighborhood, and the servants would talk.

How much does that even matter?

Perhaps this was *exactly* how she should deal with her uncooperative emotions. Expedience was much more the order of the day. The package she'd brought was bulky in her hands.

All she knew was that the very august butler informed her at the door that Mr. Bourne was not there at the moment but he would present her card to Lady Lillian, who was receiving visitors at the moment in the drawing room if she wished to see her.

Regina didn't particularly, and she hadn't dressed for a social call, though she'd had the foresight to take off her paint-stained apron in the vehicle and bundle it into a ball. Lady Lillian might not be who she wanted to see, but if James wasn't there—she knew he handled business affairs from the residence frequently—she did need to know when he was going to return.

This could not be put off any longer.

The trouble was, she wasn't sure yet what she was going to say to his proposal. Was it yes, or no? The reservations over a marriage were still prohibitive . . . lack of autonomy, her money would belong at once to her husband under English law, not to mention James would no longer be just a welcome visitor but a permanent fixture in her life.

But he claimed to love her, and she believed him. . . .

She believed him.

Damn all. It would be easier if he *didn't* love her. Then this decision would involve only *her* feelings.

"Deuced complicated," she muttered out loud, making the butler glance up in polite inquiry even as he opened the drawing room door with a flourish.

Instead of introducing her, the man gasped out loud.

The tableau was not exactly what she expected from a proper drawing room in the residence of an earl. No doubt it was the presence of two young women, one of them bent backward over a very superlative library table next to the wall, the other one, dark-haired and attired in a beribboned gown, with what remarkably seemed at first glance a dagger in her hand, which the intended victim was keeping from plunging downward by a hand clamped around her assailant's wrist.

For once, her height might actually be an advantage, Regina decided, one glance at the elderly and aghast butler telling her he was not in any condition to go to the rescue. She swiftly set aside her package with care against the wall and then dashed forward, catching the arm of the attacker firmly enough to twist the knife away. It fell to the soft carpet with a dull thud, and she chided, "That is a Queen Anne piece, superbly crafted and no doubt worth a small fortune. Do not desecrate art in any of its forms with blood or a scratch from that nasty knife. Now, then, which one of you can tell me when James will be back?"

Instincts had always been his forte. As Damien jumped out of the still-moving carriage, the ring of his boots loud on the cobbled street, he hoped this particular premonition was dead wrong.

When he limped up the steps of the town house, he found the front door slightly ajar so he just pushed it open, to an entire retinue of servants whispering in the hallway. He snapped out, "Where's Lady Lillian?"

One of the footmen, whom he recognized from a previous visit, pointed at a doorway. "In there, my lord."

To his relief his worst fears weren't realized. The only occupants of the room were a statuesque brunette, her striking silver eyes gazing at him in open query, and his future wife. Lily leaned against an ornate table, at first glance unharmed, but then he noted several droplets of blood on her bodice and the pallor of her face.

His heart stopped.

"Lily?"

Ashen, she turned, and then an extraordinary thing happened. She whispered his name and moved toward him, at first haltingly, and then in a greater rush, as if he was a destination that provided safety and comfort, and in a moment she was against him, enfolded in his arms, her body trembling in his embrace.

He'd never been anyone's sanctuary before. Yes, he'd saved lives—at a guess many lives over the course of his service to Britain. Under his command had been soldiers and agents of the Crown, and various not-quite-as-savory characters, but never in his memory had he experienced someone clinging to him as if they were adrift in a stormy sea and he was the mast of a sinking ship.

Only this ship had fair skies and a trade wind at its sails. He smoothed his hands down Lily's back, noting the small cut on her slender neck, the wound vivid and open. Still holding her, he fumbled for his handkerchief. "What happened?"

"I am actually not sure," Lily whispered in response.

"I believe I know," the brunette answered, her smile holding a trace of cynical humor. "Some bloodthirsty woman tried to kill Lady Lillian for reasons as of yet unknown to me. I suppose we should have detained her, but quite frankly, I was not expecting an attempted murder when I called. The madwoman ran out of the room."

Damien examined the wound on Lily's neck, gently forcing her away enough so he could get a good look. She'd taken a glancing cut from the knife along her collarbone, and had it been an inch either way . . .

He folded his handkerchief, pressing it against the welling wound. "Maybe my arrival could have been a bit more timely, but I am undeniably here now."

"My wife . . . where is she?" Arthur had followed him in and he wasn't surprised. Lord Sebring had insisted on riding along and was resolute, though obviously shaken, his concerned gaze flicking to Lily's face.

"I'm afraid she left rather abruptly in her carriage," the brunette said in a very forthright way.

Sebring said earnestly, "She harmed you, Lily. I'm sorry. It seems like I am eternally sorry."

Any apologies would have to be addressed later, and Damien wasn't positive he was comfortable yet with their lost romance. He said pragmatically, "Your wife can't have gotten far, but it is possible she will try to flee England. I am sure I can prove her a murderess."

"I'm . . . not dead." Lily stared at him, the scarlet drips on her bodice stark, her blue eyes luminous.

"No, but others are, and I think I have figured out why."

"Others?" Arthur spoke sharply. "You said you were worried about Lily's safety, but you made no mention of anyone else."

"Why would Lily need protection?" A new voice entered the conversation, James Bourne appearing in the doorway. "Would anyone mind informing me of what just transpired? Regina, why are you here?"

The dark-haired woman answered cryptically, "I brought you the painting. But word of warning, I am reluctant to part with it, so we might have to marry after all."

Damien sat, his legs crossed at the ankles, his gaze intent. Despite her protestations it was nothing, a physician had been summoned, and her wound treated and bandaged. Lily wasn't positive it needed doing, and she had outright refused laudanum, her only concession to accept some hot tea.

Her future husband, she noted, was a little pale himself as he'd insisted on accompanying the doctor, and she doubted somehow that pallor was usual in the life of a man who had survived those blood-soaked years battling Bonaparte.

"Would you like for me to ring for your maid?"

"No."

"Are you certain you don't wish to lie down?"

"You are the very one who told me at once it was just a scratch." She looked pointedly at him over the rim of her cup.

"I was trying to be reassuring, and I have certainly seen worse, but what if—"

"I'm fine," she said for about the fifth time, now that the furor had died down, feeling a bit of amusement for his concern. "Stop fussing."

The duchess was going to be quite perturbed at missing all the excitement.

"Fussing?" Damien actually looked chagrined, but his mouth finally twitched into a smile.

"Yes." Another voice chimed in, this time holding a distinct bit of laughter. "Hovering like a mother hen."

Regina Daudet, she noted, had arrived wearing an eclectic ensemble: a vivid yellow silk dress with lace at the sleeves, one of which had been dipped in what appeared to be paint in a brilliant cobalt hue, and there was a suspicious smudge of red on her right wrist. Not to mention the glorious disarray of her coiffure, the jeweled pins stuck in haphazardly, yet somehow managing to make her even more striking.

It had not been an auspicious morning, but Lily *was* happy for her cousin. James, once reassured she was fine, was visibly elated over his engagement. He was there also and said in staunch masculine support of Damien's questions, "His concern is understandable."

"Concern, yes, but I feel confident Lady Lillian is capable of asking for something if she needs it." Regina

Daudet lifted a hand in a graceful gesture. "Now, then, as it appears we will all be family, will someone please tell me what in heaven's name happened earlier? Who was that woman?"

"Lady Sebring," James responded, sprawled in a chair, his handsome face holding a perplexed expression. "Lily, why would there still be a quarrel between you? Your engagement to the viscount was severed years ago."

"Attempted murder is not a quarrel." Damien held her gaze for a moment but then glanced at the others. "Part of my explanation is conjecture, but I think it is valid. This really has never had so much to do with Lily as it has with Penelope Kerr's growing desperation. She wants to not only be the viscountess, but to produce the next heir. I think the obsession went from the normal desire any woman might feel to bear her husband a child, to a form of madness. I have to say that if I had any inkling this would have happened today I would have taken steps to prevent it, but now that it has, I am not all that surprised."

To say she was shaken and off balance was an understatement. He was right, of course. It had been the possibility she might already carry a child that seemed the focus of Penelope's murderous visit. "She asked me some very . . . personal questions." Lily stopped, clutching her cup in both hands. If she had blushed when Arthur's wife had asked, she was no doubt a brilliant shade of red now.

"Let me guess. She wished to know if you might be with child," Damien finished for her, looking remarkably unrepentant for being the culprit in her possible fertile state.

"The devil you say," James muttered, sitting upright.

"Oh, James, surely you jest." Regina interjected the comment briskly. "You can't possibly play the outraged guardian in our current circumstances."

At that, Lily had to shoot her cousin a look of open question, rewarded when his face took on a telltale expression of chagrin. "Just the same," he muttered.

Damien went on. "She's always been intensely jealous of you anyway, my sweet. If you conceived a child where she had failed ... I'm afraid our engagement was too much for her. Arthur said she'd been slowly growing more and more absorbed with their failure. If you became pregnant then he would have made a poor choice. It isn't logical to you or me, but to her, I think it is."

My sweet. The endearment was like being touched. Soft, beguiling—a link between them. She liked *him* also in the drawing room, large, male, and capable. Even though, she had to recall with some humor, in this case it had actually been the resourceful Regina Daudet who had come to her rescue. "I think you could possibly be right. Do you really think she will try to leave England?"

"I don't know." His smile was slightly rueful. "I am afraid my usual enemies are much less demented, not to mention devious. I'd guess the reason she was blackmailing her own husband was to have a cache of funds on hand if she needed it."

"Or just to torture him in general." Lily would never forget the vindictive tone of Arthur's wife's voice. "I am not sure if I am the one she truly hates."

"It's clear he regrets what happened four years ago." Damien's dark eyes were direct. "I can't quite decide whether or not to be jealous. How much did you love him?"

It was a question she supposed needed to be asked

and answered, maybe for them both. "Like a girl," she told him. "I think a woman loves differently."

"Well put," Regina said with surprising vigor, gazing at James. She repeated softly, "Very well put."

"And yet you are leagues ahead of me, for I have never loved a woman before." Damien lounged in his chair in his usual deceptive pose. "Will you teach me?"

"Will you be a willful pupil?" Try as she might to control it and sound lighthearted, her voice still took on a tremulous note.

"I might."

Had he really just admitted he *loved* her?

She dimly heard the sound of the door closing and realized her cousin and Regina had risen and left the room and she hadn't even noticed.

"Oh, devil take it, yes, I'll be extremely taxing, I'm sure." Damien grinned and rose to pull her to her feet. His arms slid around her and his breath brushed her lips. "I'm terribly subversive. I will need a great deal of supervision and training."

"I think I can rise to that challenge, my lord." Suddenly she was breathless, his mouth touching hers, the kiss meltingly tender.

"I know I can," he told her with a wicked wink when he lifted his head.

Had not the Dowager Duchess of Eddington walked in at that moment, perhaps he would have further demonstrated his cooperation.

"What the devil is going on here?"

Damien didn't step away immediately but kissed her again in a most satisfying way and then said with perfect equanimity, "Good morning, Your Grace."

Epilogue

"So she killed them."

"I think so." Damien watched the houses go by, the barge slow on this early-fall day. The leaves had taken on a hint of the brilliant hues of autumn and the scent of chimney smoke was heavy in the air. He glanced at Charles, who sat, a pipe in his hand, on the deck next to him. "By her own husband's admission, Lady Sebring is not rational or reasonable."

"The blackmail was to get them to cooperate."

"And service her?" Damien provided ironically. "Correct. If one thinks about it, there is a certain beautiful logic to the plan. Since her husband was less than enthusiastic in the first place, she looked for gentlemen who resembled him as a substitute. Many of us have some small vices; who knows how many Kinkannon approached unsuccessfully before he found the few who were willing to trade paying the blackmail fee for a few nights in bed with a woman who only wanted from them their virility. Naturally, she didn't want the secret to ever get out, so she killed the ones who agreed afterward."

"That's . . . fantastical."

"It happens in nature all the time, actually. Females often devour their mates once their usefulness is done."

"I suppose that's true, but I hadn't ever imagined the application to human beings."

Damien hadn't either, but the evidence was irrefutable. "The truth often is. I imagine only part of it was a desire for their silence. Maybe more of it was that as she didn't conceive time after time, she sought revenge for her disappointment."

"What an odd resolution to our sticky problem." Charles clamped his pipe in his teeth, the breeze off the river cool. "I admit I expected some sort of plot to destroy the sons of prominent British families, not a murderous viscountess who was so desperate to get with child she coerced them into her bed."

"I overcomplicated it myself," Damien admitted, thinking with a shudder of how close Lily had come to death. It wasn't dramatic to think so, as the demented Lady Sebring had killed before.

"Indeed." Charles seemed to remember his pipe wasn't lit and groped in his pocket. "And our missing young man, the prime minister's valet?"

"She knew him through her father in that they were often guests at Lord Liverpool's home. I don't suppose we will ever know what the young man did to allow her to gain enough leverage to begin this deadly game, but I think it is safe to say he was the first victim. His physical description matches Arthur Kerr's very closely."

"Not much was safe about this case."

"No."

There were gulls, white specks in the distance, bobbing in the current. Charles regarded them with his usual heavy-lidded stare. "So?"

"So?" Damien didn't dissemble. He even smiled. "*So,* it is over, Charles. I solved your infernal little mystery, your nephew is still abysmally poor but alive, and I am a married man. Lily and I had a private ceremony last week at the Bourne estate in Essex and—"

"And I'm sure you will soon be raising a throng of small Northfield progeny." Charles rubbed his chin, having still not lit his pipe. "Congratulations."

A flock of swallows wheeled overhead, vibrant and alive against the deep hue of the fall sky. "I don't trust that tone," Damien pointed out caustically. "Forgive my cynicism."

"Actually," Charles said with an enigmatic smile, "I applaud your wary outlook on life. To give you fair warning, I might put it to good use in the future."

"And there is every chance I'll say no."

"I suppose that's possible."

Two hours later, he quietly let himself into the town house that was now not just an escape from the busy, overwhelming Northfield mansion in Mayfair, but a bit more like a home.

Perhaps it was that subtle hint of violet perfume in the air. This was no longer sterile bachelor quarters. He'd understood that two mornings ago when he walked down the hallway and found that someone had placed a vase of fall flowers on one of the tables.

It did not take any special insight or skills to deduct where his wife might be. Damien quietly walked the length of the hallway and turned, going to the second door on the left. Situated at the back of the house, the library opened to the small back garden, but the day was cool and he doubted the windows would be open.

Tricky things, library windows. They could appear to be stuck when actually they might open quite easily. Eventually, he would tell her the truth. That the secret passage wasn't actually their only option that particular evening, but for now ...

Even at the time he hadn't been sure why he had deceived her. Maybe to gain more time with the most intriguing woman he had ever met? Whatever his motivation, in his opinion, considering how it had all turned out, it had been a stroke of brilliance.

But no more deceptions.

Lily *was* there, reclined against the arm of the settee, her slippered feet propped up, her rich hair caught up carelessly in a loose chignon he longed to take down at once. Absorbed in her book, she didn't notice him at first.

That was fine. It would give him exactly what he wanted.

Then it came. The lift of her lush lashes, the recognition of his presence, and then, best of all, the welcoming warmth of her beautiful smile ...

"You're back," she said breathlessly.

"I must be, or else I am having a very satisfying dream." Damien sat down next to her, running his fingers lightly along the modest neckline of her gown.

"How was Sir Charles?"

"Cryptic." He bent to kiss her, their lips clinging, her muffled laugh turning into a sigh.

And the sigh to a moan.

"It's still light out," she offered as a halfhearted protest when he deftly lifted her skirts and unfastened a garter to peel off a stocking.

"Uhm." He licked her bared inner thigh. It was satin smooth and tasted like heaven.

"Damien, we are in the *library*."

"It is your favorite place in the house, if I recall."

"It is, but . . ."

He plucked the book from her hands, arrested even as he went to set it aside. "What the devil is this?"

"Just a book." She tried to take it back, but he held it up out of her reach and read the gilded lettering on the front in the reflected glow of the lamp.

Lady Rothburg's Advice.

He couldn't help the laugh that rang out. "I don't even have to guess where you got this. It is somewhat of a Northfield family heirloom. Tell me, my love, have you found it enlightening?"

"I'm not quite done with it," Lily shot back, beautiful with a vivid blush on her cheeks. "Someone in your family sent it to me?"

"I'll tell you the story someday." He carefully deposited the book on a low table. "But for now . . . I love you, you are delectably close, and I couldn't possibly wait long enough for us to go upstairs. Was I really gone most of the afternoon? Remind me to never leave you for so long again."

"I love you too." Lily's eyes were luminous.

"I think it happened when I saw you the first time, just in this exact position. Who knew a library could be such a catalyst for romantic encounters?" His hand moved suggestively upward, gratified to find that despite her protest about the time and location, her body was receptive to the suggestion of immediacy.

Lily caught his wrist just as his fingers found paradise. "As much as I enjoy the library, really, Damien . . ."

"I will make you like it twice as much," he said in a wicked promise he had every intention of keeping as he eased the sleeve of her gown off one pale, perfect shoulder.

And he was true to his word.

October, 1816
From the Dowager Duchess of Eddington to her good friend, Mrs. Nigella Beecraft

Dear Gella:

I hope this missive finds you well. I am in fair health, though that stiff hip bothers me now and then and I am not quite as up to the social whirl as I used to be in my youth. . . . Do you remember how popular we were the year of our debut? I have never danced so much in my life. Ah, the time passes so swiftly.

You wished to remain apprised of the conclusion of the season. I must modestly admit to not only successfully marrying off my granddaughter to the Earl of Augustine, but taking no small part in the recent nuptials of Lady Lillian Bourne and Lord Damien Northfield, Rolthven's younger brother. It is a coup indeed, considering the young lady was utterly ruined and a bit of a recluse.

Oddly enough, both appear to be love matches, which leads me to believe that I have a certain knack for guiding young women toward advantageous marriages that needs to be further explored. It is true

*both courtships were a little unorthodox, but that
was the challenge, and I must say it added interest to
my time in London.*

*I've found as of late the intrigue and gossip bores
me, and while I didn't expect it, the notion of love
and romance is actually interesting. Perhaps I am
getting sentimental in my old age. Aristocratic alli-
ances are part of our world, but how much better
would it be to make sure the partners are suited to
each other?*

*As pertinent to the current subject, what do you
know of Miss Vivian Lacrosse and Lady Juliet
Stather? I ask only because I wonder if both of them
might not benefit from my help. Any insights you
can provide would be greatly appreciated. They, of
course, have no idea of my intentions, but I am sure
they will be delighted if I take an interest in their
futures.*

Yours in friendship,
Eugenia

Read on for a preview of the next captivating
Regency romance from Emma Wildes,

RUINED BY MOONLIGHT

Available from Signet Eclipse in September.

The first impression was of jeweled colors: sapphire,
brilliant ruby, golden topaz. . . .

Lady Elena Morrow's eyes fluttered open and she
suppressed a small moan. Her head ached, her mouth
was dry, and she came to the startling conclusion that she
had absolutely no idea where she was.

Stone walls rose all around her and the faint colored
illumination came from several stained-glass windows
set in arched niches high above where she lay on what
appeared to be a bed, though she was on top of the coverlet not under it, and she shivered slightly because she
was clad only in her lacy chemise.

In a surge of panic, she sat up, which proved to be a
mistake, because the room spun and nausea caused her
eyes to close again as she struggled to remember just
how she might have gotten in this strange room. Bracing
herself on the softness of the mattress with one hand, she
pushed the fall of loose hair away from her face and took
a deep breath.

Think. . . .

Her last memory was of the theater. The performance,

the music, the glittering crowd . . . She'd worn a new gown of rose silk. . . . Slowly she opened her eyes to survey her unfamiliar surroundings.

It was at that moment that she realized she wasn't alone.

How she hadn't noticed before was bewildering, but she was hardly clearheaded, and as she glanced over, she wondered for a moment if she were hallucinating.

The man sprawled carelessly on the bed next to her was half-nude, clad only in a pair of doeskin breeches, and it was so shocking, she blinked, her gaze traveling over the muscled contours of his bare shoulders and the flat plane of his stomach, finally shifting back up to his face. He had glossy dark hair, disheveled against the white linen of the pillow, and in profile, his features were clean and masculine: straight nose, high cheekbones, downy ebony brows, a mouth that was parted just slightly in sleep, his tall body relaxed and taking up a good deal of the bed.

The one they shared.

The situation registered and she scrambled to her knees in scandalized horror, more confused than ever.

A strange place and, worse, an unfamiliar man, and what in the name of heaven was going on?

Or *was* he unfamiliar?

Doing her best to stay calm, Elena tried to think, incredulously recognizing the infamously handsome features of Randolph Raine, Lord Andrews. It wasn't as if they actually knew each other—he hadn't even asked to be introduced to her this season, and if he had done so, her mother would have probably fainted dead away—but it was impossible to be part of the beau monde and not have seen him now and then at different events.

At this time, he was the reigning rake of the *ton*, his reputation more wicked than sin itself, his name a by-word for seduction and forbidden pleasure.

What is he doing half-naked in the same bed with me?

The infamous viscount stirred then, as if her horrified gaze had touched his psyche in some way even through his sleep, and he took in a long, sighing breath before moving one arm above his head in a careless arch. Even in repose he looked dangerous, with an almost beautiful cast to his features and all that tousled raven hair. . . .

Yes, that was his nickname, wasn't it? Not that her mother or aunts would even mention him in front of her, but tidbits had still sifted through to her awareness. *The Raven*. She'd seen it in the society papers. A titillating and amusing nickname, but at the moment, all she could think about was his notoriety.

There was no doubt in her mind that he was about to open his eyes. She hadn't the slightest notion of what might have prompted her current fantastical circumstances, but Elena was suddenly cognizant that she wore only a thin semitransparent shift, and upon her first swift perusal of the room, there was nothing to use to cover herself. The bed linens might have been an option, had he not been on top of them, but given his height and solidly muscled body, she doubted she could shift him even one inch to utilize them.

What is this place? she had to wonder with frantic assessment, without even a stray blanket and no other furniture besides the ornate bed, a screen in the corner that she hoped concealed the necessary, and a small table that held a carafe, two glasses, and a lamp.

With a true sense of urgency, she wondered what had

happened to her clothes because the viscount was waking up and . . .

Sure enough his eyes opened, the thick fringe of his lashes lifting. He stared at the stained-glass window for a moment and then with a sweeping glance surveyed the entire room, stopping when he saw her kneeling there next to him. He muttered, "What the devil?"

She'd had exactly the same reaction and a part of her was relieved that he seemed as startled as she was, but another part was more puzzled than ever.

In a swift athletic motion he levered up on one elbow and shook the hair out of his eyes, his tone husky. "What is this? Who are you?"

Considering she was the one clad only in a slip of flimsy silk, the warmth of embarrassment flushing her skin, she responded tartly, "I have not the slightest idea as to what *this* is. How did I get here?"

"How did *you* get here? As I've never seen you before and *here* is a mystery to me, how would I know?" He sat up fully and ran his long fingers through his thick hair. His eyes were dark, his skin a light bronzed tone that reflected the dappled multicolored light from the unusual window high above them. Then his eyes narrowed. "Just a moment. I retract that. I do know who you are. . . . Whitbridge's daughter?"

The evident consternation in his direct stare confused her even more. It was genuine, she would swear, and besides, she didn't remember anything of arriving at this place—and as bizarre as it was, apparently he didn't either.

Elena nodded, her lips trembling. Whatever was happening, there was no doubt that her father was frantic.

How long had she even been here? "Yes, Lord Whitbridge is my father."

Her companion swore. It was under his breath, but telling in intonation, and she caught the sentiment if not the exact words. After looking around the room again, he finally said evenly, "I don't remember anything. I can count on one hand the times in my life I've been so foxed that an entire evening got away from me, and those were a decade ago, not to mention I doubt I'd ever forget bedding *you*. I wasn't drunk, so how in Hades did I get here?"

The young woman in beguiling dishabille, who at the moment had turned a very becoming shade of pink, looked at him as if he were the devil incarnate, complete with cloven hooves and a forked tongue.

Perhaps he was, come to think of it.

Irrefutably, Ran would never have said anything so blunt in front of a young, unmarried—even if very beautiful—woman under normal circumstances, but then again, virginal misses were not his area of expertise. Were he concerned with fine manners and social graciousness at the moment, he would apologize for being so indelicate, but the truth was, they *were* in bed together and he had no idea how either one of them had gotten into this predicament.

Finesse be damned at this point in time.

The earl's golden-haired daughter gazed at him with enormous blue eyes, the pale upper curves of her full breasts gleaming above the lace of her demure chemise, the soft rose of her lips provocative. He'd seen her only in passing before, but up close, her beauty was as dazzling as all the rumors held it. "You . . . you didn't," she stammered, her blush deepening. "We didn't . . . we couldn't have—"

Fucked? Luckily, he didn't say that out loud. Courtesy was not his first priority at the moment but at least he didn't vocalize the crudity.

"Exactly my point," he grimly interrupted, partly because he was still unnaturally groggy and had an appalling headache, and partly to spare her, since it was obvious to him she didn't know exactly what she was referring to in the first place. "But you have to admit certain conclusions could be drawn over our location and state of mutual undress."

What he would have liked to say was that while he might have been known for his largesse in the bedroom, at least it could be said that he remembered his paramours, but he made it a point never to discuss his private affairs with anyone.

Still, that raised the question: Why was he here, in bed with the delectable daughter of an earl, who happened to be a young woman he'd never even met?

As far as he knew, there were no rumors about Whitbridge's finances being suspect, but then again, Ran was a very rich man and his initial reaction to this unusually compromising situation was suspicion. There was a reason he stayed away from the eligible young ladies angling for wealthy, titled husbands. At not quite thirty, he wasn't interested in the restrictions of marriage yet. But if he had to do his duty and acquire a wife in order to sire an heir, at least he wanted it to be his choice.

"If this is a ploy, you will wish you hadn't tried it," he said through his teeth with less civility than he might otherwise have used due to his aching head. "I can't be coerced."

In answer, she just looked at him in evident confusion, as if he'd suddenly lost his mind, which, in light of his current circumstances, he wasn't sure he hadn't. "What?"

"I won't marry you."

In any other situation, her horrified expression might have been amusing, but at the moment, he wasn't in a particularly jocular mood. She stammered, "You surely do not think that I ... I ... That this ... Are you insinuating ... ?"

He lifted a brow.

This time it was anger that tinted her cheeks as she gathered her composure. Scathingly, she informed him, "My lord, your legendary charm seems to be in abeyance. I hope it does not offend your sense of self-worth, but rest assured, you are certainly *not* what I am looking for in a husband."

If she was acting, she was quite good.

He took a moment, unclenched his jaw as he registered her sincerity, and reminded himself that she was lovely enough, he doubted that shopping for a rich husband in such a drastic way was necessary. "It's been done before," he said with less steel in his tone. "A man manipulated into a compromising position and honor-bound then to marry the young lady."

"My understanding is that *honor* is a rather loose term to you."

She was wrong. He only played the game with ladies who were as willing and as unattached as he was, but Ran was well-aware of his reputation. "You don't know me," he said curtly.

"I am starting to wish that was still the case," she shot back, her cheeks flushed.

If she was innocent, he deserved the set-down, and it sounded like she meant it.

The infidelities of his class had left him somewhat jaded. He'd been first seduced by one of his aunt's friends—a countess whose much older husband was not that attentive—and after that enlightening experience, he'd seen enough of the value most of his privileged acquaintances put on their wedding vows to have a jaundiced view of the institution of marriage. It was his conclusion that while some species of animals and birds mated for life, human beings were not sophisticated enough for that sort of loyalty. It was usually a mercenary arrangement, and if he were honest with himself, he'd always thought there should be much more to it.

He swung his legs over the side of the bed and stood abruptly, wondering where in hell the rest of his clothes might be, not to mention his boots. In his experience— and he had to admit he had quite a bit—the usual scene of any seduction had clothing strewn on the floor or any other convenient surface as the participants disrobed in the heat of passion. Not interested in defending his morals, he asked, "Now that we've established neither one of us wants to be here, why *are* we? What do you remember?"

"Attending the theater." She lifted a trembling hand to smooth back her shining hair, the long pale strands gilded by the colored light, her expression disconcerted, but to her credit, at least she wasn't in hysterics like most spoiled young ladies might have been. "I was waiting for my father's carriage. It is unclear to me what happened after that."

His last recollection before waking? Ran wasn't sure. He contemplated it for a moment, rubbing his jaw. "I was leaving my club. I'd met friends there for dinner and a whiskey or two, but as I said, I was hardly inebriated enough for this. My last impression was of stepping out onto the street."

The floor was cool stone like the walls, and from the circular shape of the room, it appeared to be in a tower. When he strode purposefully to the door, he already knew what he would find.

As he suspected, the door was barred on the outside. He tried it, and then set his shoulder to it, but it was solid and didn't move even a fraction. When he turned back around, his delectable companion had gathered the blanket from the bed and covered her partial nudity, her eyes pools of inquiry.

Had their circumstances been different, he might have experienced a twinge of regret, but as it stood, it was just as well.

"Locked," he said unnecessarily.

"Why?"

"My very question." He saw the glasses on the table and was grateful—at the moment, for later he might want something stronger—that the pitcher was full of water. First he poured a glass for her, guessing that if she'd been given the same vile drug that he'd obviously been dosed with, she might also be thirsty. She accepted with a chilly thank-you, and when he'd taken a long, cool drink for himself, he asked neutrally, "Can you think of any reason someone would wish to kidnap you?"

"My father is wealthy."

So was he, so it was a possibility, but in Ran's case, his

funds were not available without his presence to sign the proper documents. So that was an oversight on the part of their abductor. However, now that his throbbing headache was easing a little, the whole thing seemed like perhaps there was more behind it than money. To start with, why take their clothes?

"I suppose it could be we are going to be ransomed," he conceded slowly, wondering what drug they'd been given because he'd drained his glass of water and was still thirsty, and his headache was pronounced enough that he was glad the room was shadowed.

"You don't sound very convinced, my lord. Why else are we here? If they had wished to harm us, they certainly had every opportunity."

He *wasn't* convinced. A young debutante locked in a room with a man who had a reputation for seduction?

When he looked at it that way, the angle reflected an interesting light on the situation.

She was sitting on the edge of the bed now, her slender, shapely form wrapped in the concealing folds of the coverlet, and she regarded him with discomforting directness. "If you will excuse me for saying so, Lord Andrews, you are much more likely to have enemies than I am."

"Perhaps," he agreed with a hint of cynical practicality, "but would they exact vengeance by locking me in with a beautiful young lady?"